The
Catalogue
of Men

DAVID POWNALL

The
Catalogue
of Men

PICADOR

First published 1999 by Picador
an imprint of Macmillan Publishers Ltd
25 Eccleston Place, London SW1W 9NF
Basingstoke and Oxford
Associated companies throughout the world
www.macmillan.co.uk

ISBN 0 330 37440 0

1 3 5 7 9 8 6 4 2

A CIP catalogue record for this book is available from
the British Library.

Typeset by SetSystems Ltd, Saffron Walden, Essex
Printed and bound in Great Britain by
Mackays of Chatham plc, Chatham, Kent

For Dom
altering skylines

FIRST MURDERER: We are men, my liege.

MACBETH: Ay, in the catalogue ye go for men;
As hounds and greyhounds, mongrels, spaniels, curs,
Shoughs, water-rugs and demi-wolves, are clept
All by the name of dogs. The valued file
Distinguishes the swift, the slow, the subtle,
The housekeeper, the hunter, every one
According to the gift which bounteous nature
Hath in him closed; whereby he does receive
Particular addition, from the bill
That writes them all alike: and so of men.

Macbeth, Act III Scene 1
William Shakespeare

CHAPTER ONE

'NEXT TIME YOU want to have someone to stay, try to let me know beforehand,' said old Sir George Villiers, careworn master of Brooksby, squeezing Miguel's forearm quite hard. 'Especially if it's a coxcomb.'

Miguel grimaced apologetically, touching the gold ring in his left ear, back bush of frizzy dark hair shaking as he looked up the staircase. The unwanted guest was descending, costume a blaze of lemon satin embroidered with falling leaves. Miguel noticed how, instead of combing side and back hair forward to cover his frontal baldness, as he himself had recommended, having the same hair loss but not the type of hair to do this, Shakespeare had actually polished his dome with oil.

'I'm very sorry. He arrived unannounced,' Miguel whispered. 'You weren't around. I had to ask your wife if he could have a bed.'

'That's all right,' Sir George grumbled. 'From what she tells me, the fellow's the talk of London. That can only be because of his tailor.'

'This is most kind, sir,' Shakespeare said, arriving at the foot of the stairs and making a bow.

'D'you customarily arrive so soon to see your friends

when they settle in a new place?' Sir George asked. 'We were sure it would take an age for people to find him. After all, to become a tutor hidden away in the depths of Leicestershire might signify a desire not to be found at all.'

'Ah, but I'm more than a friend,' Shakespeare responded, unruffled. 'I must always know where he is and exactly what the dear man is up to.'

'And why, pray, must he be so loaded with these attentions?' Sir George asked tartly.

'The needs of the spirit,' Shakespeare replied, tapping his heart. 'No man helps me unravel life better than my friend here. I cannot be away from him for long before melancholy claims me.' Then, flaring his nostrils, he sniffed like a scenting hound. '*Mon coeur!*' he cried in an outburst of fashionable Frenchiness, bangles clashing at his wrists, 'Oh, don't I smell . . .'

At this point he turned to find the source of the sweet perfume and saw Mary, Sir George's wife at the head of the stairs. She had a faint shade of violet beneath one eye where her favourite son George had punched her that morning during horseplay. The upward curve of her smile was profoundly, sweetly dangerous, a perfect setting for the black eye and blossoms bunched at her swelling breast.

Holding a madonna pose, vibrating slightly, she exemplified a certain kind of English beauty at cracking point.

'I smell . . .' Shakespeare croaked, amazed at how swiftly and easily she had stolen his breath away. 'I smell wed and right roses.'

★

The dinner of 15 July 1602 at Brooksby manor was an occasion for satisfaction for Sir George. At last he had found someone to help bring up his spoilt son. Not that the last few weeks had been easy since Miguel's arrival. But a few well-aimed blows early on, the telling of a fund of stories about his fascinating, adventuresome life, and the Spanish Jew had conquered young George's heart.

Miguel — true name Moses Ignatius Gideon Ur El Laghouat, of noble if mysterious blood descended from Moorish counts in the kingdom of Granada — was the first tutor from a long queue of battered contenders to beat young George at his own rough game and win his approval. Mary, the doting mother, did not like the foreigner's educational methods at first, but Sir George had had enough of her soft indulgence of the boy. This dinner was the first to be attended by Miguel, and the old knight gave him a free hand in choice of conversation. 'It is your day,' Sir George said, giving him the head of the table, 'and I thank God my old friend Sir Nigel Main agreed to let me borrow you for a while so we can bring George to heel. The inconvenience to himself is great in losing the best London secretary he's ever had, not to mention the loud protests of his wife, who holds you highly.'

Up until this night Sir George had liked to rule his own table, exercising his own predilections for stories of the chase and crime in the country. His predecessors had never been scholars, or teachers, or men of the cloth, or even widely-travelled merchants, but sturdy examples of that landed class to whom any kind of intellectual enquiry is a threat because it must argue the injustice of their very existence.

Indeed, the disapproval of these swaggering phantoms so impregnated the woodwork Miguel found himself sheering away from what moved his mind at that moment – which was a wide-ranging examination of the power of love in all its forms enshrined in the person of Mary, the zephyr-blown *rosa mundi*, who sat beside him – and instead he opened the conversation by touching upon the unpopularity of potatoes.

Sir George gently put him right.

'Leave that for the market,' he said. 'We have talked enough about such things in the past. From now on our dinnertime in this house is to be kept for the purposes of civilizing ourselves, and thereby this boy, who's been such a headache.'

'Perhaps Mr Shakespeare would like to start us off with news of the plays in London,' Mary said, the candlelight deepening the blue under her eye to damson and softening what few lines her face carried.

'No plays, please,' Sir George said tersely.

'Then tell them the story of how you were part beheaded in Prague, Miguel,' George chipped in. 'Don't bother with the astronomy, popes and emperors bits. They won't understand all that stuff.'

Sir George raised a tangled eyebrow.

'What is this?' he enquired. 'It must be difficult for anyone to be beheaded in part. This sounds a good subject to kick off with.'

Because he had already told the story once that day, Miguel asked to be allowed to choose another topic – the Natural Order in Politics – which drew a shrill objection from young George who thought this smacked of stars, popes and emperors before it had even started. But he was silenced by his father who sensed Miguel was doing them the honour of taking the whole occasion seriously, and Mary also added her voice, advising her son to listen carefully to what the prolifically gifted Mr Shakespeare would have to say on the subject, being a very famous playwright, fresh from London.

Shakespeare, untypically indifferent to the compliment paid him, so stunned he was – sat silent throughout dinner, hardly touching food or drink, unable to sparkle or shine in the talk, his large, expressive eyes soaking up the sight of Mary who sat opposite. He was not acting, nor had he decided to be silent in order to give his friend a free hand. The poor man was so struck by the woman's mature, quivering beauty he was unable to think straight or frame intelligible sentences.

Meanwhile, fully aware what was going on, Miguel had to hold the floor with the subject he had selected and keep the entertainment going.

Mary had been newly awakened to the excitements of love by the arrival of Miguel at Brooksby only a month ago – a misty land of woods, streams and silent meadows which he had invaded, a cross between conqueror, centaur and swain. She had struggled, but failed, to hate him over the robust treatment he had initially handed out to her beloved child – and the only other option seemed to be the love he charged her with. Now she had to recognize another rainbow of adoration being arched to her from Shakespeare in addition to the ardent beams from Miguel's indigo eye. Although convinced Miguel was her heart's desire, enthralled by the Hispanic strangeness and virile power of the man, the famous London playwright's attention frequently drew her glances. She sat at the table in a daze of trepidity, smiling, making the occasional light comment, surprised at her own wanton thoughts.

Another ally in this process of enchantment was Shakespeare's inarticulateness. When he did try to speak and break through his catatonia, such was his bewilderment with himself – he was a man who had never been smitten by love before, being of a coolish disposition until now – the words came out in an embarrassing jumble, and Mary's womanly feelings were touched by this odd childishness in him.

Young George sighed and squirmed, protesting boredom throughout the rest of the meal once the part-beheading story had been stamped on by Sir George. The boy did make one other suggestion to brighten up the entertainment: asking his tutor to take off his shirt and show everyone the hatching of battle-scars he had collected on the plains of Hungary, in the deserts of the Magreb and other wild places, as well as the marks of the overseer's lash from three years in the Bey of Tunis's galleys – which Miguel refused to do. Not to be dissuaded, George then pushed his suggestion further, telling the company someone had cut off Miguel's foreskin in a fight, and George had seen the evidence the day they went swimming in the nearby river Weake together. Mary snapped out of her emotional reverie and quickly covered the embarrassment so caused by singing 'Sigh no more, ladies, sigh no more, men were deceivers ever', from the London gentleman's pastoral play *Much Ado About Nothing*, which had the author and Miguel enraptured. This mood was broken by the arrival of court officers from Leicester carrying writs of restraint on Sir George's goods and property against payment of debts.

★

The appearance of the bailiffs – men who had, until a year ago, been working for Sir George while he was sheriff – and the way these ruffians entered the manor and sat insolently at the dining table, laughing and leering at the discomforted old knight, shattered the sense of intellectual calm.

'It's your turn now, Villiers, you rogue!' the bailiffs cried. 'See how the wheel comes round! In the past you've done us over.'

This brought Shakespeare out of his trance.

When acting had been the only string to his bow, he had often fallen on hard times. Dealing with debt collectors had become second nature. Within half an hour he had put the right amount of money into the purses of the intruders, told them they were fine fellows and a credit to their calling, pressed bottles of good wine into their hands, promised to deliver twenty guineas on account to the court the following morning, seen them to the door and wished them Godspeed – all done with style, smooth skill and bonhomie.

Miguel had the wit to sit on his hands during this excellent performance, his instinct being to run for his sword.

When all was done, the balance between the two lovers had shifted in Shakespeare's favour.

'One doesn't want to let those fellows mess one around,' he drawled. 'Tomorrow I will send to my bankers for funds that will settle this matter.'

Sir George, who had collapsed into a paralysis of silent shame upon the entrance of the bailiffs and was now unmanned by the disapproving gaze of his wife and son, told his guest he could not accept any more generosity.

'You must not put any more of your money at risk,' he said heavily. 'I cannot guarantee to pay you back.'

'Let us talk about it later, in private,' Shakespeare replied cordially. 'Finance is a tedious subject and, as far as I know, we have not yet finished with the Natural Order in Politics, have we Miguel? Isn't there more to say?'

★

Having obtained the necessary credit to stay as long as he liked at Brooksby, Shakespeare moved into a room adjacent to Miguel's. When Sir George came round late one night Shakespeare was next door arguing with Miguel over a scene in *Measure for Measure* which he reckoned to be unworkable.

'We cannot agree about the purity of Puritans,' he quipped as Sir George lowered his bulk into a chair, a quart bottle of canary clutched to his chest. 'Miguel here thinks that the way I have written a certain character beggars belief.'

'If we are to talk about beggaring belief,' Sir George said morosely, 'I direct your attention to my predicament. In spite of your timely help, in a few weeks I will be within sight of bankruptcy again. The bad harvests, the rising prices, the civil unrest, all conspire against me. Rather than sell my houses and lands, there is only one thing I can do, but it troubles me and I would like to know your views.'

8

Sir George's quandary was simple enough, as explained, 'If I hasten George's presentation at Court, ar. he's picked up, will he be ready for the work?'

Shakespeare and Miguel looked at each other. In all the years they had battled over plays, raking through piles of crazed, contorted Italianate tales and absurd chronicles for potential plots they had not come upon such piquant novelty.

'How does my son take to women?' Sir George asked Miguel. 'Does he like them?'

Miguel stroked his beard. Although George was full of lewdness, boasting and foul oaths, as most eleven-year-old boys are, and did not hesitate to prod and pinch the female servants, there was a frustration, a poignant futility behind this behaviour which the new tutor had marked.

'I don't think he yet likes them how they like to be liked,' he observed delicately.

Sir George grunted and said this was what he had suspected.

'One cannot dictate to Nature,' Shakespeare re-marked, ready to appease Miguel whose feelings on this subject were threaded through all his best writing. 'We will have to wait.'

'That I cannot afford to do,' Sir George declared, putting the flask of canary on the table. 'I thought between the pair of you, with all your cleverness and learning, you might know of something to bring him on. His good looks will have to bail me out.'

Both men confessed that although aphrodisiacs were not unknown to them, they had never heard of an elixir for advancing puberty.

After expressing his disappointment that they could

9

not come up with any ideas, Sir George left, muttering he would have to ask elsewhere.

★

It was during young George's long, strange illness in the late autumn of that year he became so close to Miguel and Shakespeare and substituted them jointly for his father in his heart.

Physicians could not diagnose an ailment that gave the outer symptoms of glowing health: sleekness of skin; thick, shining hair; beaming eyes; while simultaneously causing headaches, spots before the eyes and projectile vomiting. It was only when the boy was on the point of death that the cook admitted Sir George had ordered his son to be fed a mixture of boiled flax-seed jelly, ground raw lamb's fries and wilted nettles in his morning porridge, a country potion used on billy goats, tups, boars and bulls to encourage rampant sexuality.

On the morning after his first good night's sleep for six weeks, at last free from terrible animalistic nightmares as well as the sickness, George sat up with Miguel on one side of the bed and Shakespeare on the other.

'I cannot trust my own father any more,' he said shakily, 'and now I must look to you, my dear, loyal friends. In case you are afraid,' here he took a hand of each, and kissed it with great tenderness, 'I assure you both that what I hear from the servants about the sharing of my mother's bed does not displease me, though the idea took some getting used to.'

Miguel's shoulders sagged and he looked away, not wanting the invalid to see his pain.

'That is very generous-hearted of you, George,'

Shakespeare said. 'We intended to tell you ourselves, but we were waiting until you had got better, weren't we?'

'Your mother . . .' Miguel began to say, but he was so charged with emotion he could not finish, and stalked out of the room.

George frowned and picked at the linen sheet, his expression thoughtful.

'The servants also passed on the observation that, although Miguel finds it difficult to share, you do not,' he said with a sudden, challenging grin.

'I share whenever I can,' Shakespeare declared with a laugh. 'Enough of this. It's a fine day. Are you going to get up?'

George timidly got out of bed but sat on the side, weakly holding on to Shakespeare.

'My mother says you are the wisest, most profound, insightful man,' he murmured. 'Her admiration for your genius has increased as she has got to know you. Then tell me this: how can I escape the dictates of my father whom I now believe to be mad?'

'Only by going along with him,' Shakespeare said, mindful of the fate of both Romeo and Juliet in a play that was still a favourite of his from Miguel's earlier *oeuvre*. 'If you are patient, and obedient, things will fall out your way, I'm sure.'

CHAPTER TWO

—◆—

WHEN SIR GEORGE sent to the Lord Chamberlain for permission to present his son at Court 'by virtue of his precociousness', he received a short reply telling him the customary procedures had been suspended. Sir George then wrote another letter to a friend who knew the Court, asking what was going on. He heard back that the old Queen had withdrawn to Richmond Palace in Surrey and was seeing any youth who had the right breeding, solely as something to look at while she waited for death. But be warned, his correspondent added, with things as bad as they are in all matters of trade, money and business, the queue is very long.

By the time Miguel and Shakespeare took George to London to see the Queen, *Measure for Measure* was half finished and the winter was coming to an end. One or two venturesome daffodils had broken out of their buds, catkins were pricking on the ash and willow so the gaunt woods had a vague green tinge, and young George was burgeoning with a spring of his own. Four months living inside the tempestuous inner world of his mother and her lovers had not caused him to shrink away from love, but rather the contrary. He had thrived on their conflict, on their comings together and drawings apart, and developed not only a knack for dealing with such passionate unruliness but a taste for it as well.

Meanwhile, his father, who had been forced to sell off many acres of land to satisfy creditors, had sunk into a mooning depression, lightened only by the company of Miguel and Shakespeare.

'If my troubles have been of any benefit,' he said as he bade them farewell on the morning of their departure for Richmond with George, 'it is that they brought you to my house. I am a changed man, God help me, and if I had my time again I would be more like you. Do your best for my son and all of us here at Brooksby.'

Mary kept to her room that morning, pale and fading as frost. It was as if the entire substance of her life had elected to leave her.

'You will not come back,' she had said to Miguel and Shakespeare as they lay together that early dawn with the blackbirds throbbing in song outside the window. 'You will both forget me because I am not young any more.'

They gave her assurances they would return as they had departed, her heart-bound slaves, no matter whom they should meet, how the world might treat them, what golden offers they might receive; but one thing they encouraged her to do before they got back.

'Choose between us,' Miguel entreated her. 'We have talked about this between ourselves and decided we cannot go on sharing you. I speak for Will as well as myself when I say we know our feelings and have compared them closely. Both are absolute. Both have in them the danger of self-destruction if denied.'

'Then how can I choose? If one of you should die

because of me . . .' Here her small hands fluttered upwards in a spiral like two chaffinches fighting over bread. 'I would have to die myself!'

'Madam, you must decide,' Shakespeare exhorted her. 'We are no more than two shipwrecked men clinging to the same spar, with only room for one.'

'No, no,' she protested, her voice rough and cracking with exasperation, 'we are three! A trinity which is sacred to me. I even believe you give each other joy in this.'

The two men interrupted each other as they sought to disabuse her of this fallacy, but neither was being honest. Something had happened between them during the long snowbound winter at Brooksby but we will not leave the horses saddled at the door, the baggage strapped so tightly, the splitting of today's daffodils suspended, in order to describe it, but leave that mystery to unfold on the journey southward.

★

By now George had become aware that his education was an incidental part of a greater enterprise, one Miguel pursued on his own behalf. The taking up and putting down of his writing governed the rhythm of George's lessons. No matter if it were fencing or spelling, the class could be cancelled because Miguel had been overtaken by a thought which must be written out before it fled his mind.

This second place in Miguel's priorities did not cause any resentment in the pupil. He was happy to amuse himself, also to conspire with his tutor in hiding the arbitrary nature of his timetable from his father who wanted everything done post-haste. When Shakespeare had arrived and Miguel spent even more time on his other work, George had fitted in, taking a mild interest because he liked both men, but not enough to ask questions. He knew one wrote plays and poems – his mother had shown him some printed verse, *Venus and Adonis* and *The Rape of Lucrece*, but had not allowed him to read them because he was not old enough. Inevitably, these had been sought out when his mother was not looking, and he had flipped through the pages, bemused at so much high-minded talk and so little action, but there had been rewards to be found.

On the other hand, Miguel was more of a scholar and scribe. He always seemed to be reading and making notes, copying, editing, reshaping, all in all a rather mundane and clerky business.

So although he never actually saw Mr Shakespeare writing a poem or a play, he heard him talking on the subject often enough, and was able to believe he dictated most of what Miguel wrote, and if he ever sat down and wrote himself it was at some private hour when he could summon sensual demons to pen lines such as:

> His hand, as proud of such a dignity,
> Smoking with pride, march'd on to make his stand
> On her bare breast, the heart of all her land;
> > Whose ranks of blue veins, as his hand did scale,
> > Left there round turrets destitute and pale.

and, four verses later:

> His hand, that yet remains upon her breast—
> Rude ram to batter such an ivory wall!—

May feel her heart, poor citizen, distress'd,
Wounding itself to death, rise up and fall,
Beating her bulk, that his hand shakes withal.
    This moves in him more rage and lesser pity,
    To make the breach and enter this sweet city.

which George had learnt during his stolen hours with *The Rape of Lucrece*, the only literature of any kind he'd been able reliably to commit to memory, though Miguel had tried him with many authors.

Therefore it was only a minor surprise to him that clear morning when Miguel announced as they were approaching the village of Uppingham that *things had started to happen* and he urgently had to get it all down. As writing plays on horseback is impossible, they had to stop and sit by the roadside for a while. This happened another seven times before Kettering where a bargain had to be struck with a local tradesman because the delays would have quadrupled the time taken for the journey, and they continued south on a cart with planks of wood nailed across it to make a desk, an ink bottle held steady in Shakespeare's hand for Miguel's pen as he sent it flying, across the page.

'Give me a name,' Miguel cried as they breasted the top of a hill, the horses standing to take breath.

'What kind of a name?' Shakespeare asked.

'It's for the comic scenes I told you about, the ones I've got to splice in to counterbalance the virginity theme and all the references to purity and the law.'

'Low life, then?'

'Very low.'

'How about Muck?'

'Muck?' Miguel expostulated. 'We can't have a character called Muck. Try again.'

'What does he *do*?' George asked, now mildly interested.

'He's essentially a pimp.'

'Call him Bum.'

'That's the one,' Miguel declared. 'Thank you, George. We'll call him Bum, Pompey Bum.'

'Why Pompey?' Shakespeare queried.

'Wait till you hear the way he talks.'

★

The writing of those vital scenes made *Measure for Measure* classifiable as comedy, which was the description Shakespeare needed to disguise the violent attack on the Puritans. During the remainder of the journey to Saint Albans via Bedford, George christened all the other low-life characters – Elbow, Froth and Mistress Overdone, though for the last he received a box round the ear from Miguel for saying it was what the servants at Brooksby now called his mother.

By the time they came in sight of the great tower of the dilapidated abbey at Saint Albans, once a great house of the Benedictines but now dissolved like all monasteries in England, George had begun to grasp that Miguel worked for Shakespeare as a supplier of shaped information, much like a carpenter makes chairs for one who sells furniture and, as in life, in art, the retailer enjoys more power, status and reward than the craftsman.

At Saint Albans they disposed of the cart and stayed at Sumpters Yard for their last night together. In the morning their paths would divide: Shakespeare to Barnet and

London; George and Miguel to Richmond via Harrow-on-the-Hill.

Much of their time was spent collating the play over dinner, keeping gravy and wine off the pages, some of which already showed spatters and ink runs from the wet weather.

When all was done and the manuscript lay on the table in front of Miguel tied with a ribbon he'd plucked from a serving-wench's hair for luck, a black mood suddenly descended upon him. One moment he was laughing – the next he was sitting hunched up, brows driven together, muttering.

George looked questioningly at Shakespeare who put a finger to his lips, then leant over to pick up the manuscript, preparing to leave.

'I'm for my bed,' he murmured, 'I have a long day tomorrow.'

With a shout of 'NO! Not this time, you dog!' Miguel crashed both hands on top of the manuscript then wrapped his arms around it, growling, 'You've had all you're getting.'

'Come on, now,' Shakespeare said, as if to a child. 'You know it has to go with me. People are waiting for it.'

'Let them whistle!' Miguel snarled. 'Or *you* offer them something for once.'

'Is this the behaviour of an honourable man? A man who has given his word?'

Miguel lowered his head until it rested on the bundle of papers. To George's astonishment he saw tears in his eyes.

18

Shakespeare hastily leant across and stemmed them with a napkin.

'Don't make any more splotches or they won't be able to read it,' he said. 'Best to let me look after it now.'

Gently trying to prise the manuscript out of Miguel's grasp, he was almost succeeding until the author yanked it back, clutched it tightly to his chest, staggered to his feet, looked wildly about him like a cornered animal and then charged out. They heard him run up the wooden stairs and his footsteps overhead as he entered their room, bolting the door.

'What's the matter with him?' George asked.

'Is there a full moon?' Shakespeare wondered aloud. 'Whatever the reason, it's got the better of him.'

'Why is he so upset about the play?'

With a wry, pensive look, Shakespeare eased back into his chair, took his time pouring himself another cup of wine, filled and lit his pipe, then wafted a space in the clouds of smoke like a priest at an oracle.

'There are some men who cannot marry, settle down and have children,' he said, pointing upwards to the ceiling. Above it Miguel could be heard walking up and down. 'There is something in their nature that makes sharing impossible.'

'But Miguel shares,' George exclaimed, 'he shares all the time. He shares with me, he shares with you.'

'Not in things that matter,' Shakespeare replied, blowing out streams of white smoke.

'My mother doesn't matter?'

'Leaving her aside for the moment,' Shakespeare responded, all equanimity mixed with earnestness, 'she

19

being someone inviolate and sacred to both of us. I must point out to you, George, that I have a wife and three children, thereby proving my capacity for sharing.' He took the pipe out of his mouth. 'Miguel will have told you about that?'

'No, he hasn't.'

Shakespeare raised an eyebrow so it rode up the dome of his forehead towards his thinning brown hair. 'You surprise me. No matter. The case remains the same. Having a normal family life means I have no need to make my plays serve as surrogates. They are merely shows, entertainments, whereas for Miguel, in his loneliness, being allowed to help me with them has become a substitute for fatherhood. Tonight you saw what happens when he can't let go.'

It took some effort for George to follow this argument. While he was doing so Shakespeare puffed on his pipe and looked up at the ceiling.

'And, I have to say,' he mused, 'dear friend of mine though he is, when it comes to your own position, you must beware this tendency of his to cling hold of what he thinks he has created. It might eventually include yourself.'

★

When George joined Miguel at breakfast next day, Shakespeare had already left. They ate in silence for a while.

'If you could bear it, I'd like to take a look at the old abbey,' Miguel said after he had cleared his plate. 'When I came through with your father last summer he was in too much of a hurry to let me linger, and besides, he didn't want anything to get in the way of our talks about you.'

'What did you say about me?' George asked, now wary of being taken over, and suddenly struck by the oddness of people actually expressing *thoughts* about him.

'Your father did all the talking. All I did was listen,' Miguel told him, leading the way to the door. 'Don't you think it's natural for parents to always have their children in mind?'

'You wouldn't let Will put me in a play, would you?' George wanted to know, a strange nervousness at work within him. 'I don't think I'd like that.'

Miguel opened the door. 'When a sharp lad is needed for some stage mischief, you might have to watch out,' he said with a sober laugh, ushering George out into the street.

★

George did not stay long in the abbey, which was full of rubble, fallen roof timbers and bird droppings. Miguel tried to interest him in the ruins of the ancient shrine of Alban the Roman, first martyr in the isle of Britain, but the boy preferred to wait outside.

Once he had gone, Miguel joined a handful of old women who were standing amongst the fragments of the broken shrine, casting furtive glances around them, surreptitiously petitioning the saint for cures and favours. This time-hallowed practice was now forbidden, but the older people found it hard to do without.

Putting a sharp stone beneath each knee, Miguel knelt and bowed his head. Seeing him do this, the crones scuttled out clucking with fear, leaving him alone below the pigeon-haunted vault.

His prayer, made in the midst of a shrine demolished

by the hammers of Puritans, was not to any god outside himself. First, it was a ferocious attack upon his unmanageable pride. 'One moment I'm too proud to need Fame,' he said to himself, eyes on the clouds visible through the shattered roof, 'the next I'm an Angelo, my own hypocritical character. I lust after greatness as if it were a woman, but I'm worse than Angelo because I haven't got the courage to soil myself and be seen for what I am.'

One old woman, less timid than the rest because she was insane, crept over to him and warned that the sexton brought anyone found praying at the shrine before the magistrate. Miguel thanked her for her trouble, but said he had more prayers to say and this place seemed to offer him comfort.

★

Part of the abbey had been given over to use as a grammar school and, it being the start of the day, a troop of town boys came past George on their way to lessons. They began to taunt him with being unacceptably pretty.

At Brooksby, George had only his brothers and sisters for company, and he saw them infrequently because their time was spent at a dower house in a nearby village. If out, he was always guarded as Sir George's treasure, so he had little notion of how to behave when faced by a mass of hostile contemporaries and promptly hurled himself at them and was quickly felled. He was saved from too much injury by the abbey bell which was rung to summon the boys to class. But he had taken fists and boots in his face.

When Miguel came out of the building he found him covered with blood, one eye beginning to blacken, his lip and nostril damaged and bruises all over his fair complexion.

'Who did this?' he raged.

'I didn't see them,' George mumbled. 'They came up behind me.'

'Why did they attack you?'

'Thieves. I beat them off before they could rob me,' George croaked manfully, but then fell silent when he saw the disbelief in Miguel's face as he eyed George's good clothes, hat and shoes, all of which were intact.

'Well, they certainly made a mess of you, whoever they were,' Miguel said, picking him up in his arms. 'In the state you're in now, no queen would give you a second look.'

CHAPTER THREE

—◆—

As MIGUEL WAS carrying George back to the inn four constables of the town watch arrived and arrested him for behaving popishly in the parish church. At first the arrest was violent because the constables, seeing Miguel, a dark-skinned foreigner bearing off a fair English boy, believed he must be a Jew (which he was) who was taking the lad to a synagogue for human sacrifice (which he wasn't). Miguel, unable to draw his sword because he was encumbered by having George in his arms, was knocked to the ground and thrashed.

It was only when George was able to explain that Miguel was his tutor, and he himself the son of a knight, that the beating ceased. By then Miguel was barely in his senses.

At the town gaol Miguel still had to account for praying at the shrine. He found this awkward to explain because he could not even claim to be a Catholic but, as was his custom under intellectual duress, his recourse was to an oblique version of the truth.

'It was a mark of respect for a brave Englishman,' he mumbled through swollen lips. 'I have been reading the account of Alban's martyrdom given by the

Venerable Bede and I was much taken by the courage he displayed.'

This caused consternation amongst the constables. 'We were told he was a Roman,' they said, 'one of the first papists in the country.'

'Then you have been misinformed,' Miguel assured them. 'He was an Englishman through and through and I can prove it.'

The constables were persuaded to send one of their number to the Sumpters Yard for Bede's book, *The Ecclesiastical History of the English People*, which was in Miguel's baggage. This did not take long and soon the volume was on the table along with Miguel's most valuable possessions and best apparel.

'Although this great work is not written in English,' Miguel said, heading off the displeasure he could see already clouding the brows of the constables when they looked at the open page, 'it is Latin from a thousand years ago when all great artists used that language.'

Then he went through the chapter, translating line by line until the story of Alban's suffering at the hands of the evil judge, and the miracles he performed – including the conversion of a public executioner, drying up a river and making a spring gush forth from the top of a hill – took hold of the constables' imaginations.

'By God, he was a brave and powerful man!' the chief among them declared. 'Why have we never been shown this before?'

'Because Bede, the author, is cruelly neglected in his own country!' Miguel replied. 'Although read all over Europe – indeed, he is the only Englishman who Dante gives a place in his *Paradiso* – here, amongst his own people, he is virtually unknown. It's a shame and a scandal. But do not take my word for it,' he added before any of the constables could pick up on the foreignness of *Paradiso*. 'Go to a reputable scholar in the town and ask him to verify what I have read to you is on the page and I haven't been making it up. Everyone in Saint Albans should be proud of their saint, a local man of world stature and reputation. I tell you, even as far away as Constantinople and Muscovy the memory of this great English hero is respected. And, sirs, I must remind you – he was martyred BY the Romans and never one of them.'

This was enough for the constables, who were rough, good-hearted sons of Hertfordshire living only a day's ride from London. The city and its plethora of famous men had always overshadowed their region and made them feel inferior. But now they were moved to pride by the story of Alban and besides, the Jew seemed to be a solid, manly fellow, in spite of his gold earring and frizzy hair.

Once Miguel's purse had been donated, plus his best boots and clothes, and the constables had been given Bede's book to be the start of a gaol library, the prisoners were allowed to leave.

Picking up what was left of their baggage they took horse and galloped southwards, not pausing until the broken tower of the abbey was no longer visible over their shoulders.

'You were inspired! Marvellous!' George said, a grin on his damaged face. 'I thought we were going to get stuck there.'

A large post carrier appeared on the road at a fork to

London and began laboriously climbing the hill, going north. Miguel steered his horse off the road, indicating they should rest a while. Dismounting, he took pen and ink and sat cross-legged on the ground to write.

'What's this?' George cried, getting gingerly off his horse and standing stiffly, legs apart. 'Surely you haven't found another play for Uncle Will to write already?'

Miguel chuckled savagely and shook his head. 'I must have some revenge on those bastards,' he growled with his one open eye close to the paper. 'I'm writing to tell them the only other famous son their dung heap of a town has ever spawned was Nicholas Breakespeare, the only Englishman ever to be pope!' He stopped writing for a moment, thought, then became aware of the carrier's approaching rumble. 'But you may be right without knowing it, George,' he said, scribbling the last few words. 'There may be a play in it.'

Finishing the letter with a venomous full stop he folded the paper and wrote the address before running over to hand it to the carrier.

When he returned and they had mounted their horses and resumed their journey, he kept George's mind off the pain of his injuries by telling him the story of Adrian the Fourth, the only English pope whose very name, he said slyly, certainly did have a theatrical ring to it.

★

Being in no condition to journey too far that day, they looked for lodgings at Wealdstone north of Harrow-on-the-Hill, but because of the goriness of their cuts and bruises could find nowhere to take them. Giving up on that place they continued on the road to Richmond, very tired, until they came to a solitary house set on a ridge well back from the road with a sign offering accommodation.

'You'd be better off in an infirmary by the look of you,' said the host, well fitted to his work by the goodness of his temperament (though the property was no more than a rough farmhouse and outbuildings recently turned over to be a temporary inn in order to pick up the Richmond trade). 'Were you robbed on the road?'

This was a fair enough story so Miguel went along with it.

'We are on our way to the Court,' he informed the host with a touch of condescension, seeking to impress him so there would be no questions about money as it was now all in the pockets of the constables. 'We need a few days rest and recuperation before presenting ourselves.'

'There's no need to be grand with me,' the host replied. 'I've had over a hundred hopefuls staying here over the last couple of weeks, and I've ten in for tonight. They'd sleep anywhere, as long as it's cheap – even the pigsty, if I'd let them!'

That evening the rain came down. George and Miguel were glad to be under shelter, even though it was only in the barn a few yards from their horses.

Before the light went, Miguel gathered comfrey from the hedge to dress their wounds and bruises. They settled down to sleep with the rough, hairy leaves thrust down their shirts and breeches, wrapped round their heads, necks and faces, to quicken healing.

★

We will leave them in this curious guise of greenery while we follow Shakespeare down through Barnet and Islington and into the City, making one final observation before granting sleep to the afflicted as they toss and turn in the barn, scratched by the hairy herb.

If Shakespeare had known how Miguel's simple act of lying in a barn covered with leaves was creating in embryo the great scene whereby Birnam Wood comes to Dunsinane in *Macbeth*, a play that would enrich Shakespeare even beyond the limits of his greed – he might have mastered those gnawing inner urges to usurp his friend's place as true author, and remain satisfied with his lot. But the sharing of Mary's love with Miguel had made Shakespeare fall into the delusion that he was as good a man all round.

Conversely (and here we enter the mysterious woods of the lower soul), such intense propinquity to genius had made the actor slave and acolyte of what he knew instinctively was not only the provider of his meat and drink, but also the dream of his better self.

★

The reaction of Petronius Thompson, the elegant dramaturge of the Globe to the new play was more positive than Shakespeare had anticipated. The prevailing gossip was that the Queen had at last made up her mind to nominate James, King of Scotland, as her successor. The Globe's shareholders also surmised this noted homosexual to be a secret Catholic sympathizer who would look favourably on the attack against both Puritanism and marriage contained in the play.

'How d'you interpret it as an attack on marriage?' Shakespeare asked cautiously.

'Isn't that what you intended?' Petronius asked. 'If not, I'm surprised. But then, as a playwright you're so deep half the time you don't know what you're saying anyhow.'

'Why would James, if he becomes king, undermine something which binds his realm together for him?' Shakespeare demanded, the memory of many bedroom discussions with Miguel and Mary on the uses and abuses of matrimony coming to mind.

'Because he wants to get rid of his boring Danish wife and marry some Scottish duke,' Petronius replied, 'and good luck to him, I say.'

Shakespeare thought for a while. He knew how long it would take to get the play on the stage and how that must be set against how long the Queen would live. For although she had never married she had very fixed ideas about loyalty between lovers, as Robert Devereux, Earl of Essex, would have testified if his head had still been on his shoulders.

'Where did you hear James wants to marry a man?' Shakespeare asked, ready to salt the information away in that part of his memory reserved for plots to feed Miguel, but now ready to house ideas for plays of his own.

'From the Howards, who aren't his friends, I admit,' Petronius replied, 'but their intelligence on most things is excellent. And James's queen isn't keeping quiet about how she gets treated. So, let's say that we'll produce your new play . . .' He looked at a schedule on the wall of his office following a line with a finger. 'The end of March? People starting to move about, feeling more like going out, seeing something new. How would that suit you?'

'It's a good time to open,' Shakespeare observed.

'We'll do well with it, never fear. And we'll make you good money,' Petronius enthused.

Shakespeare nodded, his mind already working on other matters, running other plans for Miguel's work through his mind. There was also *All's Well That Ends Well* to think about.

'You never stop, do you?' Petronius said admiringly. 'I can see you're miles away, writing again. God knows where it all comes from but I suppose we must just be glad it keeps flowing. But now we've got an agreement, Will, there's something that intrigues me. I'm very glad to be producing the play, it's a real bonus for us and we'd do it whatever the risk, but your fellow shareholders here wonder if there's more potential political danger with it than they can imagine.'

Shakespeare frowned in puzzlement.

'What's political about lust?' he said.

'That's what it's about? Lust?'

'Pure lust.'

'Ah, but whose lust?' Petronius asked cagily. 'In the play Angelo's a stand-in for a duke, but it could be argued the Scot would only be a stand-in for a king.'

'D'you think I'm an absolute fool?' Shakespeare remonstrated. 'I make use of that neglected form, Allegory. The lead character is a devil called Angelo. An ambiguity runs through the text, but it's in words of fire. And he's everywhere, this Angelo, and everyone.'

'I love it when you talk like that. It's wonderful!' Petronius breathed. 'Thank God for ambiguity, I say. It keeps us all out of prison. And you've made me very pleased with myself, Will, because I've always said someone would hit upon the idea of adapting the old Morality play and bringing it back. It's good to be proved right now and again. I should've guessed it would be an outstanding visionary like yourself who'd do it. And aren't the times right, dear fellow? Aren't the times right?'

★

Having placed the new play – and deliberately neglected to put himself forward to be cast as Angelo – Shakespeare did the rounds of all those theatre companies and printers who owed him money.

One of these – Jackson, the owner of a back-street printing business – had failed to offer redress or compensation when Shakespeare complained about him publishing a hacked-up version of *Romeo and Juliet* with added scenes of sexual explicitness. This had sold well and, because it was unperformable, caused no great damage to the play in the theatre proper.

Shakespeare strolled to Fleet Street accompanied by four hired bullies and entered the printing house, which was packed with delivery boys and men working the presses.

Jackson, a balding man in his forties, skin ingrained with ink from years in the trade, wiped his hands on his apron and invited Shakespeare to come into another room where they could talk. Before following the printer through, Shakespeare gave the nod to the hirelings. By the time the printer had closed the door pandemonium had broken out in the print room.

'There's no need for that, Master Shakespeare,' Jackson said. 'I have the money for you.'

'But late. Four months late. So at twenty-five per cent

compound interest per month I make it eight pounds, twelve shillings.'

'What?' shrieked the printer, clutching at his head. 'That's more than I'm worth altogether!'

'Then perhaps you'd better sell up and go out of business,' Shakespeare suggested, 'because I must have all my money.'

The din from next door was still going on.

'How can I pay you now?' Jackson moaned. 'You've smashed all my presses.'

'They are skilled men. Only those parts easily repaired have been broken, and your staff will be able to limp back to work after a day or two,' Shakespeare said, tweaking the desolated printer's ear. 'Take comfort. All is not lost. But in future you must not make a bargain and then cross me. That makes me upset.'

'I'm ruined!' Jackson whimpered, his face in his hands. 'Go on, set fire to the place and be done with it!'

'No need for that yet,' Shakespeare said, opening the door and peering through at the wreckage and the bullies glowing after their work. 'But if you're not at my lodgings with the full sum by this time tomorrow I'll give it serious thought.'

The next call on his itinerary was at the house of Michael Ogg, an actor who had walked out of the cast of *Hamlet*, in which he was playing Osric, a small part, in favour of the lead in a revival of Ben Jonson's *Every Man in his Humour*.

Ogg was at home relaxing with his new German concubine and a few theatre friends, enjoying a conversation in which his success in the long-running Jonson play was frequently touched upon, when Shakespeare arrived with his myrmidons.

'Will, I tried to get hold of you to explain,' Ogg cried, forced to his knees while all his friends raced for the street, 'but I couldn't find you anywhere. Be fair, old fellow! You didn't lose a single show because of me. There was a queue of actors waiting to get into *Hamlet*.'

'A professional just doesn't do that kind of thing,' Shakespeare said, 'especially to me! Break his nose!'

The German hurled herself at the bullies as they dragged her lover to his feet before breaking his nose. Although a strongly built woman, she was easily swatted aside while the job was done.

'Swines!' she howled, taking Ogg into her arms. 'You have destroyed a master of the modern stage!'

'Madam,' Shakespeare said, leaning over and giving one of her breasts a hard squeeze, 'when this great Thespis of yours is mended, let him visit me and I'll give him work sweeping that which once he was master of: the stage.'

'Ben won't like this,' Ogg blubbered bloodily. 'The understudy's down with fever and they'll have to cancel shows. You know what Ben's like when he gets mad. I'll try to calm him down, but you mustn't blame me if he comes after you with his rapier.'

'Bugger Ben!' Shakespeare snarled. 'He shouldn't go poaching my players.'

★

By the end of a long morning's work – there were three other calls made on various defaulters – the bullies were glad to be paid off in the back room of the Greyhound near Shakespeare's Silver Street lodgings, leaving him to his thoughts and calculations.

Ben Jonson would not come for his revenge in the orthodox way, having already been in court for killing an actor in a duel and only escaping the gallows by invoking an old law whereby a man need only recite a little Latin learnt by heart to have his sentence commuted to a fine.

Jonson would undoubtedly plot a true playwright's vengeance, thorny and tortuous, thus teaching his rival lessons. This would all be grist to the plagiarist's mill. From now on Shakespeare was hell-bent upon coming into his majority, writing the real stuff rather than pretending to. He had served a profitable apprenticeship, but dreamed that once the pen of the authentic artist was in his hand, he would astonish the world. So, any risk that would bring him nearer to being the essence rather than the mirage was worth taking. Even the enmity of Jonson, that wild and dangerous man, friend in success, enemy in failure.

Shakespeare had punished Michael Ogg more than he deserved purely to entice Jonson into a battle of wits. If Shakespeare could win that contest – which would be fought out in an arena he understood – the criminal twilight of the London stage – it would be a strong encouragement towards believing he had the calibre of the worldly Jonson.

Which would leave only one final conquest to make – the unworldly Miguel.

As he contemplated the darkly dramatic complexities of all this, Shakespeare's heart began to sink – a tell-tale weakness of his when faced by the impossible. Stirring, he paced the room, talking to himself, whispering that failure could not even be contemplated. Cowardice at this critical point would kill him even more surely than Ben Jonson. To continue life wearing his present poisoned mask (when he appeared in a work by *Shakespeare* he was an actor acting in a play by a writer he was acting, which was a nightmare of mixed identities) was no longer an option.

He thought for a while about the pleasure palaces he might visit, the friends he might call out for festivity, to buoy up his sinking spirits, but the urge was not there.

He sat down and wrote a long, detailed letter home to Stratford. It was full of fondness and hope and his wife, a blurred domestic vision, kept changing places with the woman he'd left behind in two minds at Brooksby.

When he had finished, and proudly read it through, noting all the felicities of style and expression, all the levels of meaning, the subterfuges, hints and deep-laid machinations of purpose, he realized what it was he wanted to do above all others – to go and see the new batch of Iberian bears at the Bankside gardens, creatures famed for their savagery, and watch while one was baited into a foaming fury by mastiffs.

*

While Shakespeare, with sport in mind, walks down towards the river in the afternoon sun of an early English spring, one eye on the crowd for the unsheathing of a rapier or the smile of someone who might recognize him as the man of the moment, a line of thought is offered on what forces have gone to make him the strange creature he is.

It may seem to many people for someone to be a glovemaker's son in a quiet English country town is not a bad life, but outsiders give little thought to how knotty and exacting a trade it is, and how blinkered and inward-looking the citizens of such a place can be. In glove making the cut and measurements must be exact, for the hand is our most delicate instrument, far more so than the thundering foot. With our hands we write, we stroke, we tickle, we arouse, we give greetings, we clinch bargains, we wield sword and stilleto, we surrender, we make intricate artefacts.

And if something is perfectly tailored for us, no bagginess, no waste, what do we say?

It fits like a glove.

These high standards impose a heavy burden on any craftsman with more than his share of pride and conscience; especially those with a restless and turbulent disposition. Such a man was Shakespeare's father, John. He had to sew forefingers and little fingers, fingers with room for rings and arthritis. At night he dreamt of wrists and knuckles, special gloves for amputees and those with Siamese joints. Sometimes he deliberately courted disaster by making gloves that little bit too tight for those who had trouble putting their hands in their purses.

All this came out in the way he treated his son, Bill, a gauntleteer in the making. One minute his father was counselling obedience, piety and diligence, the next the boy had to watch as he truculently thumbed his nose, bit his thumb, raised two fingers at anyone who tried to control him, and deliberately did bad, dishonest work.

From the day he left his father's house and went to

seek his fortune in London as an actor, Shakespeare never again wore gloves.

For all its pretence, he saw the theatre as a bareknuckle world.

CHAPTER FOUR

———◦———

MIGUEL AND GEORGE joined the end of the queue in Richmond Park on the Ides of March 1603. By then the length was two miles and three furlongs and it was the wonder of Europe.

Each night those in the queue had to camp in order to keep their places, so there were tents, bivouacs, servants and fires. Drawn by the chance of custom from the rain-sodden entourages, came flocks of buskers, players and clowns, sellers of pies and cordials, whores and gypsies. Keeping this raggle-taggle in order had become such a problem to the royal guard a whipping post and pillory had been erected in the park.

Foreign visitors came to gape at the sight of the sons of the English gentry queueing in thousands to attract the eye of the old, enfeebled queen. It was, as the Venetian ambassador put it, like a sullen serpent with its head in the present and its tail in the past.

With the aim of reducing the queue, chamberlains rode up and down its length twice a day, weeding out those youths who were so ugly, malformed or defective they could have no chance.

After one such scrutiny, a chamberlain who had

looked hard at George as he passed, returned and called him out.

'You're a Possible,' he said quietly. 'If you want to get to the front, treat me right. If you'd like to go before the Queen when she's at her best – which is between eleven and twelve – treat me right. Am I speaking in a way you understand?'

George had learnt a few things since leaving Brooksby and was able to affirm he had received the chamberlain's message. 'However,' he added, 'if it is a matter of money, I must talk to my guardian.'

'Doesn't have to be money, lad,' the chamberlain smirked. 'There are other items of value you have I can see just standing here. And don't forget, you need to get a move on. She can't last long.' Then he rode off to join his companions.

George passed on what had been said.

'There's a rogue who'll take pennies off a dead man's eyes,' Miguel said grimly. 'But, even if we wanted to buy his services, we have no money until either your father sends us his letter of credit, which I've written asking him to do . . .' he tailed off, watching the chamberlain stop and summon another youth out of the queue further down '. . . or Will responds to my call for help, which is probably our better chance. The money I borrowed [from the host at the guesthouse where they had licked their wounds] has nearly gone.'

George stood close to Miguel who put his cloak round him. The boy's teeth were chattering in the cold wind coming across the park and his nose was running.

'I'll never forgive my father for subjecting me to this,' he seethed. 'Why can't he put his affairs in order? We're

supposed to be wealthy people! And look where he's
landed me! Living in a muddy field, pestered by pimps
and pederasts.'

'We'll find a way,' Miguel said, holding him tighter.
'Plenty of families are feeling the pinch these days. Look
around you.'

'But why did I have to end up with a father like
mine?' George fulminated. 'Why couldn't I have had
someone like Will?'

Miguel drew in his breath as though stabbed, and
George felt the arm round his shoulder go limp.

Aware he'd said something wrong, the boy peered
up from under the cloak and smiled winningly. 'You'd
make a good father as well, of course. You're very clever,
you know a lot, you've been everywhere, and I'm very
very fond of you,' he said, seeking to undo some of
the harm, 'but let's admit it,' he continued blithely,
'you're not a patch on Will when it comes to making a
fortune.'

★

When Shakespeare got back to his lodgings he found two
messages nailed to his door. One was Miguel's letter
asking for money to be sent to Richmond, the other was
a child's toy lance snapped in half and tied together in a
cross, with this verse attached:

> Do not assume, O quivering reed,
> Escape is now thy only need;
> A shilling's worth of English grave
> The parish offers, murthering slave;
> Hell is what to shake thy weapon at.

Exhilarated and fortified as he was by an afternoon at the bear-baiting, Shakespeare's courage immediately drained away and his knees turned to water. Rushing into his room he fell over a pile of his clothes and possessions left behind the door. As he groped in the heap he realized the intruders had also emptied their bladders and bowels all over it.

He gagged, wandering around the room with his head in his hands. It had been his intention to recruit a good, strong bodyguard that very evening but Jonson had struck back immediately. If he was going to react so quickly, and with such force, Shakespeare would need his man right away and safe lodgings. Without waiting to clear up he went out to see to these needs.

As he came down into the street Ben Jonson was waiting for him, leaning against the door. He was glowering, pop-eyed, leaden-cheeked, in company with the same four bullies who had worked for Shakespeare that morning.

'These fellows gave your name as a reference, Will,' Jonson said, his arms round the shoulders of two of them. 'I didn't have time to check with you if they were any good, but they've done well enough for me so far, haven't you, lads?'

The bullies howled with laughter, pointing at Shakespeare and slapping their knees.

'They've got so warm working hard on a job I gave them I've decided to buy them a cooling drink. Won't you join us?'

Shakespeare could not meet the cold hostility of Jonson's eye. He looked down, but not before glancing along the street to see if any chance of escape presented itself.

Jonson took his arms from round the necks of the bullies and stepped forward, thrusting his face into Shakespeare's. His bottle nose gleamed, his breath stank of onions, his pale cheeks had an unnatural hue, his big brown eyes bulged with animosity.

'While you've been sitting on your arse watching dumb creatures being tormented,' he grated, 'I've had to go on stage for Ogg because there was no one else who knew the lines. I was hauled away from my dinner to do it. Needless to say, I was not at my best. In fact, the audience laughed at me when they were not supposed to be laughing, but crying. You know how that can hurt. Also I know you can guess just what harm this has done my reputation. I am now not only a fool, but a man who cannot protect those who earn his bread for him. These unjust opinions, which will give me headaches for weeks to come, I have you to thank for.'

Grabbing two handfuls of the long, silky hair over Shakespeare's ears, he held him fast. 'You'll die when you hear this. I was so bad in my own play they've cancelled all the performances until they can track down the understudy and bring him back to London. That means pain for me, and loss.'

Jonson's head came forward abruptly and crashed into Shakespeare's high-domed brow. As he reeled back, the bullies gathered round and laid into him.

'That's enough,' Jonson cried after ten or so good blows had been struck. 'We don't want our second-best maker of plays dead before his time.'

Elbowing the bullies aside he offered Shakespeare his hand to help him to his feet.

'Now fair is fair, we'll say no more about it, Will,' he said jovially. 'They didn't break your writing arm, I hope?'

While the bullies chortled, Jonson held Shakespeare's right hand in his as if it were a child's, gently giving each finger a testing pull.

How was he to know this painless, mildly derisive action, akin to taking off an invisible glove, was one no man should ever undertake against the person of the adult William Shakespeare?

Outnumbered, outflanked, outwitted though he was, nothing could stop the explosion.

Shakespeare went black in the face.

Blood flooded his eyeballs.

A scream came out of his throat.

He went berserk.

Those bystanders enjoying the entertainment provided by this one-sided brawl soon had cause to regret their idle interest. Having bitten Jonson savagely in the face, clawed his eyes and rendered him *hors de combat* with a crunching blow to the windpipe, the maddened Shakespeare hurled the howling playwright at the bullies as they charged, seized a cudgel from one, felled two with consecutive blows, then, as the others ran off down the street bawling 'Lunatic at large!' he turned on the spectators and belaboured anyone within range.

★

That night he went back across the bridge to Bankside, but this time in a closed carriage and accompanied by the silent, muscle-bound Connah, his new servant. The destination was not the beargarden, the theatres, or the lodgings of his friends. Amongst all the houses of pleasure on the waterfront of Southwark only one guaranteed forgetfulness.

During the hours since the spasm of violence Shakespeare had built up his defences against both his enemies and himself. It must never happen again, he had vowed while scurrying around the City looking over his shoulder expecting arrest. I must change my ways. Move away from the mad, dark world of the theatre into better company. Return to Brooksby! To sweet, gentle Mary!

Tonight was to be a farewell to his old life.

As the carriage passed the Swan Theatre in Paris Street, Shakespeare held the curtain back a little and watched the huge running shadows of the lightboys against the curved wall. He shuddered, seeing those giant images of flight. All the performances he'd watched on that stage! Where were they now? And those that had been of plays in his name – why, they were doubly ephemeral.

The carriage rolled along dark streets studded with rosily torchlit doorways: the Variorum of Venus, Ballzan-all Inn, Sarah's Seraglio, Silken Jane's, all places he had frequented in the past after shows, both in celebration and in sorrow.

Once the horses had turned away from the river again the dark was complete. No lights showed in the unconsecrated cemetery where many of the whores he'd known lay buried. He took grim comfort in the thought that none of the women where he was going would have to worry about ending up in that dismal plot. They were better cared for.

The carriage stopped. Shakespeare waited while Connah got out and checked that all was safe in the alley. When he rapped on the carriage with the hilt of his cutlass, Shakespeare stepped out. Quickly crossing the pavement he entered the porch.

He did not have to knock. Their arrival had been observed and he had been recognized. Once inside, Connah was shown to a side booth where servants could rest while they waited.

The church of Saints Boris and Gleb had been the place of worship for London's Russian community for two hundred years, its onion domes a well-known part of the south bank's skyline. When the Baltic trade declined because of continuous wars in Poland, Denmark and Sweden, the congregation decreased and the church fell into disrepair and was eventually put up for sale.

A sharp entrepreneur saw how its smallness and intimate proportions recommended it for conversion into an exclusive palace of pleasure. The necessary alterations were done without damaging the fabric and all the frescoes showing the lives of Russian Orthodox saints kept intact because they added a saltily metaphysical dimension to the church's new function. Even the bells remained hung. For an extra sum a client could have them rung to mark the high point of his endeavours.

Shakespeare had only been able to afford visits here now and then over the last couple of years. Known and respected as a quietish client, one of those who could control his excesses, he was the kind of customer who kept the staff of the emporium sane. Tonight, however, he was a different man – one whose real animal strength had been freed from the cage inside his psyche. Though this strength scared him when he thought about it coolly, in his heart he found a new manly self-respect stirring. That awesome power was *his*. It could be called upon in an emergency.

'Is it to be the Phocas Room again, sir?' he was asked by one of the matrons in the narthex.

'No, not this time,' Shakespeare replied, 'give me a moment to think.'

On every occasion he had felt rich enough to visit Boris and Gleb's he had found himself economizing as soon he was through the door, alarmed by how much it was going to cost him. On the scale of charges, the Phocas Room was near the bottom; the drinks were cheaper, the beauties not quite the best.

That was not the only reason he always chose it, however. After a visit there with a defiant Miguel after *Troilus and Cressida* had failed, the story of Saint Phocas's suffering★ painted on the walls had become the inspiration for the famous first scene of the fifth act of *Hamlet*, and the line which had already entered the folklore of London: 'Alas, poor Yorick! I knew him, Horatio.'

★ Phocas was a market gardener at Sinope in Pontius on the shores of the Black Sea. The local governor sent troops to kill all Christians on this part of the coast. A squad of soldiers called at the market garden and said they were looking for someone called Phocas who was reputed to be a Christian. Phocas did not admit his identity but invited them to stay the night. While they slept he went and dug his own grave. In the morning he told the soldiers he was the man they were looking for. They slew him with regret.

'Have you made up your mind yet, sir?' the matron asked, seeing Shakespeare was in some sort of reverie.

'Tonight it has to be Basil the Blessed!' he declared with sudden heat, as if the decision had made itself. 'To hell with the expense.'

The matron raised her eyebrows and murmured that the gentleman was obviously intent on only the sweetest of delights, and how he had come just at the right time of the evening to enjoy all that was fresh and lovely.

So saying, she led him into the body of the church.

*

It was a mistake, of course. For a man who had always held back from the deeper part of his nature (in case he found it shallow) to imagine he could tempt the beast in his personal pit only hours after its first furious bound out of darkness was ill advised.

As soon as the music played and the incense was lit he knew the creature was demanding to be let out again. When sacrificial meat was handed to him in the form of nobly born fourteen-year-old violet-eyed Hyrcanian virgin twins of such surpassing exquisiteness they had to be kept hidden from every eye but their first and last client, Shakespeare became no more than the bonestrewn earth on which his predator prowled.

The staff of the Basil the Blessed room were taken aback by the girls' screams for help. They had not been expecting Master Shakespeare to cause them problems as many of the ravenous clients from the law courts, the clergy and the merchant houses did. And because it was a booking for all night, once the musicians had started, the drinks, sweetmeats, illustrated books and equipment laid out, the staff had settled down to play cards.

It took six of them to drag Shakespeare off the trembling, deflowered girls. As he lay pinioned on the bed, eyes staring, froth on his lips, Sir Nigel Main arrived at the church, having spent hours finding him. Once the jittery staff had been cleared from the chamber, taking the sobbing Hyrcanians with them, Sir Nigel sat on the bed and waved a piece of paper under Shakespeare's nose.

'Know what this is, Will?' he said. 'Prepare for your life to be changed at a stroke.'

Shakespeare looked vaguely at the paper, his mind torn and turbulent.

'This is the first specific commission for a new play ever awarded by the Crown,' Sir Nigel announced grandly. 'And it's got your name on it!'

Still in his wilderness, Shakespeare could only manage a grunt to indicate he had half understood.

'What she wants you to write about won't come as any surprise. Death! Isn't that wonderful?'

'Oh,' Shakespeare murmured, sitting up, 'that shouldn't be too difficult.'

'That's what I thought. When I heard what she wanted I jumped straight in and put your name forward.'

'How kind you are,' Shakespeare murmured.

'But she wants it in two parts, like your *Henry IV*. Death will be dealt with in Part One ...' Sir Nigel paused, teasingly. 'Come on. Don't you want to know what the second is?'

Shakespeare stood up groggily, one hand on Sir

Nigel's shoulder. 'Tell me, do,' he whispered, eyes wandering round and round the circular frescoed wall where a shaggy, barefoot Basil the Blessed, having raided a cobbler's shop was handing out shoes to an infinitely long queue of the poor.

'When you get into these places you really let yourself go, don't you?' Sir Nigel said wonderingly. 'I'm not sure that's a good idea for a man in your position. But who am I to preach, eh?'

'What must I do, Nigel?' Shakespeare whined as the real world thudded back into place. 'Don't torment me.'

'I thought you, as a good Christian, would have guessed by now,' Sir Nigel chuckled. 'If the first part is death then the second must be resurrection!' Then he burst out laughing, rubbing his hands together. 'Miguel would love to hear this. He'll lend you a hand with the deep stuff. How is he, by the way?'

'Fine, fine,' Shakespeare mumbled. 'But what's all this about resurrection?'

Sir Nigel patted the dome. 'She means you're somehow to bring her back from the dead when she dies,' he said.

CHAPTER FIVE

———— ◆ ————

WHEN GEORGE SHUFFLED forward to be looked at by the Queen he was past caring whether she would like what she saw or not. Elizabeth sat in the shadows, her ravaged face hidden behind a fan while chamberlains herded the youths along a corridor and into the room one by one. Staring mournfully into the faces of her country's youth, she twisted the golden ring she wore as symbol of her marriage to the nation, making it press upon an arthritic knuckle.

'I don't want anything religious,' she said to Shakespeare who was standing beside her. 'Nothing to do with Lazarus or anyone like that.'

'I understand, ma'am.'

'It must be a secular resurrection. You'll have to sort out what that means.'

'Yes, ma'am,' came the obsequious reply. 'That shouldn't pose too many problems.'

'Really?' the Queen snapped, waving to indicate that she'd finished looking at George and he should be moved out. 'In these sectarian times, I'd have thought it could pose hundreds!'

'Which is why you're being paid so much money to

do it, Master Shakespeare!' added Cecil, the First Secretary, a bright-eyed, grey, hunchback dwarf in furs who
stood on the other side of the Queen with his arms full
of documents.

With the usher's hand already on his elbow, George
cried, 'Will! It *is* you! I thought I recognized your voice
but I couldn't believe it,' and rushed forward. He was
grabbed and held before he could get far, but excitement
brightened his tired face and its beauty was now more
noticeable.

Until then, overwhelmed by the occasion, his concentration on pleasing the Queen, disquieted to find himself
in the presence of the powerful First Secretary, the Lord
Cecil, Shakespeare had been blind to who the boy was,
failing to identify the shivering ragamuffin as George.

'Oh . . . I forgot you might be here . . .' Shakespeare
muttered, looking away. 'I'll catch up with you later,' he
added stiffly. 'Don't bother me now.'

Miguel had heard these exchanges from outside the
door. Peering over the crossed pikes of the guards he
waved to Shakespeare and called out, 'Have you brought
the money?'

'What's going on here?' Cecil demanded to know, his
pointed face sharp with annoyance. 'Do your creditors
pursue you even as far as this?'

'Friends of a sort from Leicestershire,' Shakespeare
explained nervously.

'Did you arrange to meet here?' Cecil asked sus-
piciously, long, ivory-white fingers drumming on the
documents held to his pigeon chest.

'No, no, sir. I did not expect to see them for some
time, and then, elsewhere.'

'What do they want of you?'

'They have been asking me for help.'

'Then give it to them!' Cecil snapped, leaning down to whisper something to the Queen.

'This one? Truly? Are you sure?' she said, her eyes on George who had been cast down by Shakespeare's cursoriness. 'Very well. If you say so,' Elizabeth continued. 'Master Shakespeare, since you're such a friend of this lad, bring him to me again this evening. I'd like to have another look at him. But see he gets a good bath and wears better clothes. I want to see him at his best.'

With that she got to her feet, stood for a while to steady herself, then took Cecil's arm and left Shakespeare and George together amidst a crowd of buzzing officials who wanted to know everything about the lad who'd shed such a ray of warming light into the gloom of the Queen's mortality.

★

The inaugural meeting of The Sons of the Virgin Queen took place at Richmond Palace on 22 March, three days after George's appointment as *page intime* of the Bedchamber.

Cecil chaired the meeting. The first item on the agenda was Elizabeth's health. The physicians calculated she would be dead before the end of the month.

The second item was the formation of the movement itself, which was a simple matter because there was no constitution and no paperwork. The organization would never formally exist.

Third was a proposal which had the members both puzzled and upset.

'Once she's dead,' Cecil said in his high, penetrating voice, 'the tradition of celebrating the date of her accession as a holy day will be discontinued.'

A murmur of protest came from the people around the long table.

Someone called out this would be burying Elizabeth too deep.

'The people will carry on doing it, no matter what we say!' said another.

'Then they will have to be stopped,' Cecil replied coolly. 'Whoever becomes monarch must not feel the realm is being governed from the grave.' He paused, scanning the faces around the table, then added, 'Even though that is what we intend.'

The members laughed and applauded.

In a room close by, Miguel heard the noise. He looked across at Shakespeare.

'They sound lively,' he said. 'Let's hope they're still in a good frame of mind by the time we get in.'

'I still say you should have told me what was going on!' Shakespeare hissed.

'I had to swear an oath of secrecy,' Miguel replied. 'Cecil doesn't take kindly to those who disobey him.'

Shakespeare shuddered, hands on knees to steady himself as he heard the door of the hall where the meeting was being held open.

'And you're positive he doesn't know about our arrangement?' Shakespeare quavered.

'Which arrangement is that, Will?'

'You know what I mean!'

'We seem to have several arrangements,' Miguel said,

standing up as Sir Nigel Main them down the corridor to conduct them into the hall.

'About you writing all the plays!' Shakespeare hissed.

'Oh, don't worry. I'd never tell anyone about that,' Miguel said comfortingly, straightening his ruff.

Sir Nigel was now at the door, summoning them with smiling courtesy. As they walked three abreast along the corridor with him in the middle, he linked arms, pulling them closer.

'Thankfully, the atmosphere you'll walk into with so many stirred and lively folk gathered before the tragedy begins cannot be a strange one to someone like you, Will, so I don't know why you're trembling,' he murmured. 'Keep your head, my friend. Don't be overawed. Secretary Cecil has a sharp manner, but he is a perceptive man, and remember: he is the one who chose you for this great venture.'

'I haven't had time to do anything about the commission yet,' Shakespeare pointed out apprehensively. 'It'll need a lot of thought and preparation.'

'That is only a part of the whole design,' Sir Nigel replied, 'though an important one.'

'But with the Queen fading I must hurry,' Shakespeare went on agitatedly. 'There's no time to lose.'

'The Queen will never fade,' Sir Nigel said steelily, bringing them to a halt in front of the doors, behind which they could hear a passionate harangue being given, with clamours of agreement and dissent. He held them both at arm's length, looked deep into their eyes and advised them not to take too much notice of the jumpy, argumentative state of the members. 'Things will settle down once we get down to the detailed business,' he promised. 'You must appreciate that even though every one in there is used to high matters of state and great events, at this terrible time they are not fully in possession of themselves. Their hearts and loves are being slowly racked as she is taken from us, for never was any woman, any mother, any wife, any monarch loved as she has been.'

Shakespeare let out a whimper and put his hands to his face.

'Come, come, Will. No more of that,' Sir Nigel said sternly. 'I'm surprised at you. I thought our Sophocles had all these emotions strongly under control so he could write clearly. Don't let me down in front of the members. From now on we must be firm and resolute. There's no room for tears.'

'I think he weeps because this is all happening only a couple of days after he received the commission,' Miguel observed. 'You'll have to work fast, eh, Will? Have you got it in you?'

'I have an English heart!' Shakespeare retorted. 'Which is more than you have!'

'Be true brothers,' Sir Nigel said soothingly. 'Once all is revealed, you will see how closely you will have to work together. Submerge rivalries and disharmonious thoughts about each other. Now, in you go. Make me proud.'

The doors were opened and they entered the hall.

★

George sat on a stool beside the Queen's bed while physicians, bishops, secretaries, and sundry others milled around her.

56

He had nothing to do.

The work of Elizabeth's *page intime* did not seem to exist. All he had done since his appointment was move into quarters, visit the tailor, and have a short interview with a senior lawyer on Cecil's staff. Otherwise George's whole time had been spent sitting beside the Queen while the Court swept clear the path to her tomb.

The lawyer had warned him that if the Queen should happen to mention anything to do with the succession during a private talk or when she was rambling, this was not to be discussed but immediately reported to the First Secretary.

Later on, not long after George had been given the news his father, mother, brothers and sisters had all arrived at Richmond to share his good fortune, Elizabeth rallied strongly, sat up in bed, ordered everyone except George out of the room, then told him to stand in the light from the window.

'What thoughts are going through your head, boy?' she asked him.

'So much has happened to me, I don't know what to think yet, ma'am,' George answered.

Elizabeth nodded, a smile of approval on her hollowed face. 'A good answer. Those who told me you were slow-witted made too much of it.' She lay back on the pillows as a fit of tiredness passed through her body, murmuring, 'I hope that won't get in the way. Can you sing?'

George said that he could. He gave the first verse of 'Robin and Marion' but Elizabeth had fallen asleep before the end of the chorus. After a quarter of an hour she woke, peered at him and asked who he was. When George identified himself she struggled to sit up, sighed heavily, told him to pull back the curtain to let more of the sunshine in, then ordered him to recite.

'I'm not very good at the Ancients, ma'am,' George said.

'Then you should be,' Elizabeth scolded him. 'Isn't your tutor teaching you properly?'

'He says I haven't the mind for it.'

'Do you agree with him?'

'I do, ma'am, very much.'

Elizabeth laughed briefly, drawing the coverlet around her as cold struck into her marrow.

'Then what can you do?' she asked shakily.

'Some of Shakespeare,' George replied, adding proudly, 'and I know how to do it properly because he has just spent the winter at our house.'

'Indeed?' the Queen said with a strange little grin.

'Should I proceed, ma'am?'

'Pray do, but quietly.'

George recited the verses he had by heart from 'The Rape Of Lucrece'.

★

For the Queen's dying words to have been heard only by an eleven-year-old page was a great nuisance to those who must administer her will. When George was interrogated by Cecil himself, the account he gave made the First Secretary frown.

'Boy, what you tell me must be communicated to Parliament, and to the courts of all other kingdoms, so I must be certain of what you're saying. If you're not telling the truth it will go hard with you.'

'It is only the truth, my lord. I swear it.'

'Let us go over it again to be certain,' Cecil said patiently, looking at his notes. 'When you'd finished your poetry and Her Majesty took the stroke, you definitely remember her saying, "What a pity Mary's lump favours his sinister side."?'

'Yes, my lord.'

'Have you any idea what she meant?'

'No, my lord. As I said, she wept a little, then stared at me, wagged her finger and said, "And you must look to be Frenchified." Then she gave a big groan and cried: "Stuart dumpling, it's yours!" and died.'

Cecil pursed his lips, scrutinizing George's face intently. 'Do you have any idea what a Stuart dumpling might be?' he asked. 'Or even a suet dumpling?'

George shook his head.

'You must answer me with *words*,' Cecil said carefully, 'so I can swear on my Christian oath as to your meaning, if called upon to do so.'

'I do not know what a Stuart dumpling is.'

'But you know well enough what a *dumpling* is,' Cecil suggested. 'Everyone knows that.'

'I do, my lord.'

'For the record – what is it?'

'It is something to be eaten, a round thing.'

'Leaving that aside now – am I right to deduce from your answers that until this day you did not know what a Stuart is?'

'I still don't.'

'Answer my question directly!' Cecil snapped. 'Did you up to this time know what a *Stuart* is?'

'I have never known what a Stuart is,' George complied. 'Was that wrong of me?'

'Nothing is ever wrong about the truth,' Cecil declared as he sanded what he had written, 'but you might think it to be something to do with the kitchen, a *stew*, or *art*, or art of stewing, and it is none of these.'

'May I now be told what a Stuart is?'

Cecil chuckled, his unearthly blue eyes twinkling. 'We will all find that out soon enough,' he said with an elvish grin. 'But until you are examined by the Privy Council you must remain ignorant of the meaning. Meanwhile we will have to hold you incommunicado.'

'I don't know what that is either, my lord.'

Cecil sighed and gathered his papers, muttering under his breath as he left the room, 'I suppose it will take two dumplings to make a pair.'

CHAPTER SIX

———•◆•———

GEORGE'S INCARCERATION AT Richmond Palace lasted three days. During this time England went into a convulsion of grief. There was a deal of hectic rushing up and down between London and Edinburgh. Thousands upon thousands of services, meetings and confabulations throbbed throughout the nation – in the Parliament, the towns and cities and ports, the merchant houses, the country houses, the churches, mines and farms, the ditches, gaols and dungeons. Although the times had been troubled and poor of late, everyone except the fanatical Catholics realized a splendour had left the land. Amongst people of every kind the dominant feeling was rich, resonant gloom, plus a fatalistic confidence that everything would now go rapidly downhill.

In his confinement these dark, destructive obsequies passed George by. Those put to guard him were told to control their own grief and look cheerful in case their demeanour affected the boy's testimony.

At first George was simply bewildered with both life and himself. As he was being led away to the room to be shut up until his appearance before the Privy Council, Cecil had whispered to him that the Queen's will had been altered to make special provisions for him.

The fortunes of the Villiers family were now saved.

It was generally agreed, Cecil had added, all this had been accomplished by George, single handed, and his father would be proud of him.

Now, here he was, held in a small room up near the palace roof, under surveillance day and night by men who had orders not to speak to him for any reason whatsoever. Nor was he permitted to write. Every communication he made had to be by gesture.

This wall of silence, coming as it did after a period of much privation, then excitement, made George feel more than a little mad. There was nothing to hold onto, no friendly face, no familiar voice.

Where was Miguel?

Where was Uncle Will?

Frederick II, the Holy Roman Emperor (*Stupor Mundi* to his contemporaries) kept a new-born child in a cell where it never heard human speech to see if it would grow up speaking Hebrew. That poor child died because it was deprived of language. The warm, good women giving it suck were dumb. The kind and thoughtful gaolers were dumb. So, to all intents and purposes, the entire universe was dumb.

In spite of George's recent success in the talking world, the sudden denial of human contact through speech plunged him into despair. After all, if no one will talk to you when you have achieved something remarkable, when else will they bother? And his isolation started to fill his mind with the grave and its attractions, his instincts working along the same lines as the Emperor's guinea pig. Also, a sharp sense of slipping back into the bad old times further complicated his feelings. Until six months ago George had been the one at Brooksby who was *watched*, then along came Miguel and Shakespeare who were so involved in what they were doing they never watched him because they had something important to do themselves. Now he was back to being watched and they were not there to comfort him with their healthy self-absorption.

His greatest enemy in that room was fixed in the ceiling – a huge circular mirror decorated round the periphery with golden leaves and fruit. When George lay on his bed and looked up he saw himself horribly, hopelessly alone.

At first his tears brought no one to the door. After all, with the whole nation weeping for the dead Queen, why should his lamentations call for special attention? However, when the sound of George breaking his heart did not reduce, and he did not touch food or drink, or take sleep, the gaolers sent a report to Cecil.

The First Secretary's life was one of perpetual business, and these current days were the most busy. He had people to see and meetings to attend day and night, but he found time to mount the stair with one of his coolest and most astute agents to see George.

The date of that interview was 28 March; the time ten o'clock at night – one hour *after* the end of the inaugural meeting of The Sons of the Virgin Queen (for brevity's sake we will now refer to it as the SVQ) where we left Miguel and Shakespeare and to which we will now return.

★

Test by tribunal was not a new experience for either the playwright or the plagiarist. Miguel had appeared before the Inquisition, the examining board of several mosques and Arab universities, courts martial, the secret enclave of the Monorydian Cabal, and many others: Shakespeare had stood in front of actors at rehearsals trying to justify scripts he was blamed for having written when he hadn't, making excuses when the parts Miguel had created were deemed unperformable and the lines unsayable.

Standing between two tall, branched taper-holders, he listened while Miguel gave the members a report on his mission to Brooksby. It made Shakespeare's head whirl to listen. He'd been duped for so long – he, an experienced actor, taken in! How had everyone known he would follow Miguel there? Because they knew about the arrangement? But as he listened to the details, he realized how George was the focus of concern, and Miguel had assured Cecil the famous friend would come to visit him, and be persuaded to stay, thus providing George with the theatre's sparky, relevant wisdom to go alongside Miguel's strength of learning.

But one member sitting close by was distracting Shakespeare as he tried to follow the overall gist of what was going on. Hunched forward, broad, plumed hat tilted over, elbows on the table, the member kept clasping and unclasping hands which quivered like a pair of hum-mingbirds.

Shakespeare knew those hands.

He knew those fluttering fingers.

He could *hear* them whirring in his heart!

A reflection of her face under the hat's brim was in

the polished elm of the table top, her eyes two dark, blurred hollows. Slowly lifting her head as if it were a painful weight, Mary looked up and two lances of vibrating sorrow were hurled at him.

'Oh, watch over my son, Will! Let him come to no harm!' she whispered.

Shakespeare turned away, making a panicky warning noise but Miguel was too involved with giving his report to take any notice.

'Mary's here!' he whispered.

'Hold your tongue!' Cecil commanded.

Shakespeare dared not look at Mary again. But when he looked at others round the table, some of them returned his frightened gaze with womanly understanding, though every one wore a man's broad-brimmed, plumed black hat and male clothes.

After the fight at Silver Street, the ravishment at Boris and Gleb's, the news of the commission followed by the rush to Richmond, the meeting with Elizabeth, her immediate death, the revelations of what had been going on behind his back at Brooksby, suddenly it was all too much for Shakespeare's mind. Once, he had prided himself upon coolness. That had been broken down and now he was at the mercy of events, urges and visions.

He rapidly overheated again. The dreadful thought struck him this was his trial. Miguel was making his case against him. Women were in the jury. Women he had wronged. His wife, left at home as too dull and stupid to grace his arm, while he spread his seed in London and Leicestershire. Mary, whom he had sworn to love to the exclusion of all others. The Hyrcanian girls, holding on to each other as he rampaged over their bodies like a starved wolf. Elizabeth whom he had killed by accepting her commission.

'Without death how can there be resurrection?' he said aloud. 'It was your choice, madam, not mine!'

Miguel paused in what he was saying. Cecil turned and glared, then his manner softened.

'How hard you work at your craft, Master Shakespeare. But try to keep it for later, eh?'

The members laughed, looking at him from under their hats. But when he looked round the table he realized it was not the sound of mockery, but understanding.

'Are you quite well, old friend?' Miguel whispered, touching Shakespeare's arm. 'I have to press on.'

Shakespeare smiled wanly, then nodded his head.

Miguel resumed what he had been saying.

It was as if he had made an exit, then come back onto the stage in a marvellous costume. All eyes were on him. Miguel had the words, but Shakespeare had somehow upstaged him. Those eyes on him which had female light were now older, more knowing than the women on his conscience. They did not accuse, only appraise. As he heard Miguel describing to the members the good work done at Brooksby, giving him the credit for all that was useful, fear faded, his heart warmed. With Mary near, his friend lauding him, he could begin to divine the purpose of this strange meeting and how it made sense for him to be there.

George was to be moulded into a great man of a particular kind.

Shakespeare had been chosen as the best form of

influence available in these testing times. This eminence, this compliment from the mighty, he shared with Miguel.

But it was clear to him their secret would only be kept within this context, and from now on he would have to be the silent servant of the state, a force greater and even more tangled than himself. And he would have to learn not to ask too many questions.

★

Cecil was gentle with George, who lay on his bed, deathly pale and staring at his reflection in the ceiling mirror.

'I have asked the members of the Privy Council to meet in haste so you might be released,' Cecil said, patting the boy's hand, which hung limp and ice-cold over the side of the bed. 'But you will have to speak for yourself when questioned. Can you do that?'

George made no reply.

Moving away from the bed, Cecil slipped quietly behind a screen hiding the door and spoke to Mary who was waiting there, her eye to a peephole.

'Are we building the future on a weak foundation, do you think?' he whispered. 'Will he be strong enough for the work?'

The answer he received seemed to comfort him and he returned to the bed, picking up George's hand and chafing it between his own.

'Within the hour you shall have hot almond tart just as you like it,' he murmured close to the boy's ear, 'with raspberry syrup.'

George's eyes flickered momentarily, then resumed their blank stare. Cecil looked round at Mary who made a gesture that now all would be well and they should leave.

Outside in the corridor Cecil leant his hunch against the wall and ran a thoughtful fingertip over his lips.

'You're sure?' he asked Mary.

'I've seen him like this before. He appears to buckle but it is only a means of taking time to adjust,' came the soft reply. 'Something simple and familiar will bring him round.'

Cecil's pale, narrow face gleamed in the rushlight.

'I have done all I can,' he said, holding out both his little hands. 'This is his moment. He must be ready to take it. But whether he does so or not, madam, I now lay claim to mine.'

Mary shuddered, unable to touch the delicate quill-like fingers.

'If your lordship could wait a day,' she said in a low, apologetic voice. 'Tonight would not be the best of times.'

'That doesn't worry me,' Cecil trilled, arching his back. 'With a woman of your nature it is almost an inducement. The Privy Council meets in half an hour. Go and wait in my chamber.'

'As your lordship commands,' she said.

Cecil froze, glaring at her like a ruffled, misshapen falcon.

'Show some liking for the idea, lady! Remember what was agreed. I do not work for nothing.'

'I have not forgotten, my lord.'

'I know you well enough, who you are and what you are! You may think all the power is now yours because of your child. But nothing will work without me. And somehow I must have some of your loyalty.'

'My lord, I have no such power over anyone, and you know my loyalty full well, and have often had it proved.'

'You have power, though it's possible you may not always know how much,' Cecil rasped. 'Possession can be complete, shutting out the original self, so I have read. You know my needs as a sinful man who bears mighty burdens. You carry others in your carcase, greater women than yourself, friends and opponents of mine who would make lesser men tremble! But not me! I can deal with the dead, as I have shown. And treachery by prayer, by the force of spirit and belief, is a force your Jesuits have often thrown against me.'

Mary calmly walked up and down as Cecil ranted on, shoulders twitching, forefinger stabbing.

'You should realize woman, this power of yours does not make me afraid. I have good power, here, in the temporal world, but I also have skills and arts in yours. I can fence with your allies well enough. Many's the time we have fought together and I have won!'

'My truest ally is innocence!' Mary cried suddenly. 'I cannot understand your lordship's anger. All this was settled between us, and with perfect understanding, so I thought. But now you seem to need me to suffer more than the thing itself, which is enough. Please, let me be quiet for a while and gather my wits.'

'I shall expect warmth and good giving tonight, madam! You will respond. Eve, our mother, was only a milkmaid and you're no better,' Cecil scoffed. 'You forget how long I have watched you. And remember as I made George, so I can destroy him.'

He paused, watching colour rise up Mary's cheek. As

a wily and subtle exponent of torture's uses, he calculated the threat to George had moved her necessarily towards carnal desire. In the strange mind encased in his crooked body, born and brought up in power, never openly mocked by anyone except a god-queen, Cecil had this one gaping flaw: he could not see how women were repelled by either his violence or deformity. The submission by females, high and low, whom he took by the force of his colossal power in England, he mistook for evidence of his attractiveness; their groans of horror for cries of ecstasy.

To all who served him, his aides and officers, his wife and family, his network of agents and spies, this was a sacred blindness, an essential and undetachable component of his genius without which it could not work.

★

While a smiling and re-invigorated George, replete with hot almond tart smothered in raspberry syrup, gave his truthful testimony to the Privy Council, Shakespeare and Miguel were given a room close to Cecil's to wait for a full briefing on the management of George's future.

'Will, before you start, let me apologize,' Miguel said, sitting down, taking off his boots and resting his feet on the window sill. 'Cecil said I had to keep quiet until now. It'll be a relief to get this off my chest. D'you remember finding me washed up on Dover Beach the day after the Armada passed? You were on tour, taking a stroll . . .'

'Would I ever forget? Changed my life.'

'Well, I wasn't a half-drowned enemy. I hadn't fallen overboard. Cecil already had me on his pay-roll. He recruited me while I was working undercover for the Holy See in Sardinia. I was waiting for you that day.'

Shakespeare's eyes bulged.

His fingers twitched uncontrollably.

'Hold on,' Miguel said, shifting into a more defensive position, 'you might as well hear it all before you blow up.'

'What shitty behaviour!' Shakespeare screamed. 'All the risks I took harbouring you! I could've been hanged!'

'Quite right – but Cecil had you spotted as a future partner for me. He knew how kind-hearted you are,' Miguel said, smiling warily, 'and I'd made conditions before I agreed to work for him. One was I'd be given a chance to cut my teeth as a playwright in the English theatre.'

Shakespeare clasped his hands together, fingers interwoven, fighting back the black rage which threatened to engulf him. Out of his tormented struggle came a calm, rather controlled question as self-interest gained the upper hand: 'What was the matter with Spanish or Sardinian theatre, may I ask?'

'The language wasn't strong and flexible enough for what I wanted to say. And I didn't want fame, which I held in contempt, only facilities for dramatical experiment. You'll remember how rough my first efforts were . . . well, you should remember. *Titus Andronicus*? It still gives me nightmares. I was finding my way, taking short cuts, too interested in effects, no substance, too many compromises.'

'But we're soulmates, Miguel . . . you could have told me. I genuinely thought I'd saved your life, I've been quite proud of what we've managed to achieve together from virtually nothing. Now, I find out I've been a dupe all along – an unknowing assistant to a common spy.'

'Would you have understood if I'd told you? I like this kind of thing – the excitement, the complexity, the involvement with life and death. I enjoy the high stakes, the danger, not quite knowing how it will all turn out. Espionage feeds me. These people are stimulating.'

'I have to go along with it now, I suppose,' Shakespeare sighed.

Miguel shrugged, his eyes on a horned moon butting clouds. 'Do you imagine monarchs die in a vacuum? There's nothing unusual in the steps taken here,' he said, a touch dreamily. 'I've seen it happen many times. Now and then these grand strategies work for a while.'

'I'm not sure I want to spend valuable years of my . . . our creative life looking after George!' Shakespeare whined. 'We should be doing our best work now, not thinking about him. Anyhow, you'll have to look after all this other business. It's not my milieu.'

'Well, it's mine, so you're bound to go along with it if you want us to carry on working together,' Miguel advised sardonically. 'I get much more out of them than they get out of me. And you get much more out of me than I get out of you!'

Shakespeare nodded humbly, then asked why Mary had been at the meeting.

'You imagined it during that little upset of yours.'

'Mary was there!'

'As George's mother, she ought to have been, perhaps, but only men were there.'

'She spoke to me! And there were other women there, old women! Who are we working for?'

'Ourselves,' Miguel told him, putting a strong arm round his shoulder.

CHAPTER SEVEN

———◆———

FOR SEVERAL HOURS Mary sat on a bench outside Cecil's bedchamber. With her were two guards, a bodyservant and a clerk copying documents. They did not spare her blushes. As she sat, still, quiet and dignified, her mind on George's future, they harassed her with leers and nudges.

Cecil arrived at two o'clock, jubilant, not at all fatigued, flitting excitedly into the room like a bat.

'All is accomplished! They have accepted the Scot! We go forward! Bring hot wine and cakes,' he shrilled, waving a long key on a lanyard of silver twine and offering Mary an arm. 'Madam, let us enter into our own.'

Once Cecil had unlocked the door with jovial ceremony, Mary allowed herself to be ushered into the bedchamber. With head raised, eyes fixed, she stood by the bed like a marble statue, cold to the marrow from sitting so long but no part of her trembled. Emotionally, she was chilled and impenetrable as stone.

Being so braced for a grim experience, she took no immediate interest in her surroundings. Until now a determined hope that strength, grace and forgiveness would be granted her to see this thing through had kept her going. During doleful contemplations over those long

73

hours of waiting for Cecil she had encountered the option of death, influenced by reading stories of noble, high-minded heroines from the past – the Roman matron Lucrece being not the least of them. But she had laid this puffed-up melodrama aside. It made no sense to a woman who felt herself no more than a birch wood for strong winds to blow through, some warm, some freezing cold, some clean, some foetid. And although Cecil was physically hideous to her, she had consented to take him upon the advice of certain women who had proposed the best reasons for doing so.

As for Cecil, he was in high spirits, smiling, chattering, fussing over her, taking lights and furs from servants at the door, youthfully excited, a goblin anticipating a glorious treat. He warbled snatches of song to her, bowed, pranced, chucked her under the chin, called her fond names.

For a long time she could not look him in the eye, taking refuge in the sights the room offered. Images of the dead queen stood everywhere: Elizabeth in black and pearls; in hunting garb; in orange and sequins; in Greek classical dress; as a mermaid with a ship in one hand; Elizabeth, Elizabeth, Elizabeth! Statues, busts, figures, paintings, miniatures, medallions, tapestries! Even the full-length mirror was painted with her likeness as if she stood somewhere, being reflected.

'Sit, my summer flower,' Cecil said, setting down a tray on which a jug of heated wine stood wreathed with spiced steam. 'You are looking at my treasures. Wherever I go, they go with me.'

Mary sat with the cup of wine warming her chilled hands, her mind newly numb. All thoughts had been banished except, 'With HER so firmly lodged in Cecil's favour, when all is done, what good nature will there be left for me?'

Over the bed was a painting in a dark wood frame. The composition was of two serene, smiling young women, naked to the waist, sat side by side on a shawl, arms crossed over as they squeezed each other's nipples into the mouths of babes. At their feet stretched a deerhound, its head laid sideways on its paws. The background was a snowbound valley, bare poplars, a frozen stream, a naked orchard, and two black, saw-toothed crags topped with ice.

'You are admiring my Corregio,' Cecil observed, blowing air through his fine, close-set nostrils on to the nape of her neck, and sitting close so his spindly thigh lay alongside hers. 'Can you guess what it represents?'

Mary suggested it might be an illustration of some old Olympian legend.

'No, no, use your eyes,' Cecil chided her. 'These are Christians. If you look carefully in the valley there are three faint crosses.'

Mary stared at the bodies of the two women. The artist had made no attempt to disguise the sensual joy he took in his work. It reached out from under the stillness of the two figures on the canvas. They had been put there with such a lascivious brush the icy background only served to accentuate the artist's delight in the flesh of womankind.

'First, leaving aside the question *who* they are for a moment, *what* are they, these two bountiful lovelies?' Cecil whispered, taking Mary's hand. 'Open up your mind. Regard!'

A thought struck her – the painting was the only representation in the room not of Elizabeth.

Her calm broke and she shivered for the first time, gulping at the hot wine.

'Are they sisters?'

Cecil burst out laughing, his small, sharp teeth glistening. 'No, no! Not sisters. MOTHERS, my forget-me-not!' he told her brightly. 'Haven't you worked it out yet? On the right is Mary with the infant Jesus. On the left is her friend Elizabeth with the infant John the Baptist.'

Mary's defences crumbled a little further. Even in the rôle history had denied the dead queen, that of motherhood, this demon had her triumphant.

'I knew tonight I would need a Mary for my Elizabeth,' Cecil tinkled, his lips cool and dry against her ear. 'Elizabeth and Mary. Mary and Elizabeth. Both queens of hearts and sorrows. We had such blood. The people loved Mary's death. We had dancing in shrouds and fireworks. Will we raise as much hell under the sheets, my lady?'

He cocked his head to one side and pointed at the clasp at the top of her dress, grinning with steel-eyed affability. 'Off! Off!' he chanted. 'Let's see what's hidden under there. Why, in what a fearful stew you tremble. More! More! Quiver! Quiver! We have worked hard for this, you and I!'

Mary rose to her feet in fright, all resolution, all vows of self-sacrifice dented. The act of copulation had never held any special terror for her. She was always well above it. But she had heard the stories about Cecil's mania, a hundred lurid tales of ambushes, perverse lecheries practised on farm girls, gentlewomen and duchesses. When he struck, he liked to make his points, and he could lose control like a stoat scenting a rabbit's fear.

While waiting in the room with the guards, the bodyservant and the copy clerk had advised her as they mocked her: never provoke the gnome. Resist the dwarf and die. When *Microgibbous* bites run for an antidote. If *Roberto il Diavolo* thinks he's cast a spell, best fake enchantment.

In view of these warnings, she had taken the precaution of divesting herself of the crucifix and tiny piece of fabric tied to it which she wore on her breast; a handkerchief's corner dipped in the blood of the Jesuit, John Southwell, during his Smithfield martyrdom. She had been taken there by Sir George as a last attempt to swing her away from Rome when her conversion became known to him. This precious talisman was now hidden behind a loose board in the lavatory with the crucifix.

'Stir yourself,' Cecil said briskly, unbuttoning his tunic, a garment tailored to emphasize rather than conceal his hunch. 'In the morning I must leave your embraces early. There is much to do and much to talk about. But before we start, put this back round your neck.'

He held a clenched fist under her nose, then opened it to reveal the crucifix on its chain and the pathetic shred of brown cloth attached to it.

'Behold!' he crowed gaily. 'It will be much sweeter for me if you wear them!'

*

Mary's paying-off of Cecil was observed through the eyes of the deerhound at Elizabeth's feet in the Corregio by the copy clerk who was an agent of the Spanish ambassador. He made several copies of his report (naturally enough) and sold one later on to the Danes who were interested in any move Cecil made towards a compromise with the Catholic states. Another copy was sent to the French when the ambassador was collecting information about the new star in the English political firmament of 1614, Sir George Villiers, the king's up-and-coming favourite.

The copy clerk's presence behind the panelling was known to Cecil, in fact he'd placed him there, often. It was the man's task to wait with a bladder full of milk attached by tubes to shower-head holes in the nipples of the two women in the picture. When Cecil's frenzy peaked, the clerk had to squeeze the bladder and spray the room with a fine mist of milk, while also striking a deep-toned gong which was a family heirloom brought back from the Russian steppes by a Welsh ancestor of the First Secretary, once used by Cossacks to summon their pony herds in from grass for the start of the raiding season.

It was a task less thankless than copying documents and it gave the spy perfect opportunities for surveillance, but there was little real commercial advantage because Cecil (a happily married Christian) never cared to hide his sexual playfulness, however wicked. Wherever he went, whoever he lay with, scores of ribald accounts went on the London espionage market. This state of affairs had been going on so long the information was only bought by the ambassadors because it made entertaining reading, infinitely preferable to long-winded reports from the House of Commons.

And to Cecil himself it seemed the reputation he

gained increased rather than damaged his personal power. It was an effective cloak for activities on a grander scale and of greater moment. Often those who wished to keep Cecil's true objectives firmly in their sights were sent off on a tangent.

One final interesting feature of the copy clerk's part in our story is that he was, by coincidence, an inveterate playgoer who had seen everything new on the London stage for the last ten or twelve years. It had certainly affected the way he expressed himself, which, in general, was of higher quality than the laboured observations of most spies active at this time. *Enter* and *exeunt* come in for a lot of repetitive comic use in his written reports. His favourite Shakespeare play was *The Comedy of Errors*, one of Miguel's crude, early pieces when he was just getting on top of the language, resorting to plenty of Anglo-Saxon street fighting and Punch-and-Judyish knockabout farce. The scene nearest the spy's heart was the infamous misogynistic second of the third act. The report quotes large, half-digested gobbets from the text when describing the ravishment of Mary by the insatiable homunculous, remarking how she always managed to end up in a position with hands crossed on her breast like a funerary monument. 'Teach sin the carriage of a holy saint' the spy-voyeur employs, also 'She'll burn a week longer than the whole world' also 'I could find out countries in her' and 'Where stood Belgia, the Netherlands?'

★

Richmond Palace that mad March night was a place ridden with requiems, swollen with dreams – Cecil and Mary in one room, she always at the point of breaking

but always strong, he with his upcurved satyr's wand 'a
reaper's hook with his bait tied halfway up the handle,'
the spy wrote, referring to the unusual placement of
Cecil's scrotum (a deformity mentioned many times in
contemporary documents).

Nonetheless, thoughts of Richmond Palace (now
demolished like lives and loves past) have a creative feel
to them and fine visions rise in the mind: evil and good
furiously chasing each other like wild wolves; Cecil's
nightlong, dog-frequent lust shadowed by white rain and
august Glorianas; Miguel and Shakespeare next door –
with the superplagiarist unsure of his first *coup d'imagination* (had that been Mary at the SVQ meeting, *playing* a
man or *being* a man?) – and young George up near the
roof, sleeping off the almond tart, having by his testimony
to the Privy Council set England on the deepening road
to disgust, rage, rebellion and civil war.

CHAPTER EIGHT

———◆———

WHEN THE VILLIERS family left Richmond to return home, Miguel and Shakespeare accompanied them. Only the three lovers knew the full arrangements made by the SVQ for George's future.

First, while passing through the vale of puberty, and for a year or so afterwards, he should be sent away to school with other boys. This would toughen him up, provide rudimentary skills in dealing with his own sex, and extend his horizons beyond Brooksby. Miguel would live nearby and continue as tutor. His bosom friend, the famous poet and playwright, would always be visiting to provide *ad hoc* guidance and special instruction by means of the drama.

Second, George would go to France to be given a final polish and finished. The SVQ would decide when the time was right.

Third, the weakness revealed when George had been shut up in silence must be remedied. Cecil believed that even if all went well and the whole stratagem was successful in every part, George would have to bear times of piercing loss and loneliness during his life. As he put it when writing to Shakespeare with rough outlines for three instructive plays for George: 'Pinnacles are savage, sharp and isolated places.'

As to the question of precisely when George would be supplied to the King, Cecil had told them it had been decided James should be given a good long period to forget his coarser, more benighted and barbarous court in the north, reject his existing friends and favourites, become further alienated from Queen Anne and, with advancing age, start to crave for the quintessence of youth.

'When we make our move,' Cecil said, 'the ground must have been properly prepared, and adjustments made in our commonwealth. The new king will depend on those who are wise in ruling this larger, richer, more complicated nation.'

Here he had paused, looking along his thin nose, eyes concentrating into a cold squint. 'But George must be ready when the time is ready. He must be irresistible. We will not have more than a couple of chances before our enemies deduce what we are about. Whatever you do, don't bring me a clumsy, awkward dolt full of flaws back from France. He must be an infallible argument against age and death. A perfect refuge from the weariness of government and the pain of politics.'

★

No one who reads the great tragedies can doubt that the period 1604–14 (the time of George's preparation for greatness) was not only a harvest grown from *Hamlet*'s seed, but also when two hands worked on some of the texts published under the name of Shakespeare. The shift in emphasis from true theatre to schoolroom sketch is there to mark the deterioration, also the variation in quality as Shakespeare tried his hand at writing under Miguel's supervision. So we switch from the glories of *Othello, Macbeth,* and *Lear,* and the marvellous love song of *Anthony and Cleopatra* to the banalities of *Coriolanus, Timon* and *Pericles* – what we will call (after the boarding school where our hero was sent) the Billesdon Collusaries.

The overworked Miguel obviously gave Shakespeare whole scenes of these three plays to write, and the joins with the inspired work of the master show up like bad cloth sewn to good.

In the commissioning documents for 'a set of instructive dramas', Cecil specified the first should concern itself with 'the ruin of a noble soul through pride and haughtiness' and 'the subject should be a man brought to eminence by his own class but who deserts it and is thereby destroyed.'

Miguel dug up the story of *Coriolanus* from antiquity and when he could find time from writing his own work, helped Shakespeare cobble the play together. Watching this process during visits to the farmhouse where the two men worked, George could not help conclude it was Shakespeare who was the generative power in the writing and Miguel more the editor, for one was always correcting the other and not vice versa.

This was a disastrous first experiment in full two-handed co-operation and most of the apprentice's work was taken out as soon as actors got the plays into rehearsal. But they still stand as achievements of a sort, especially in the creation of that trio of beautiful, tender and majestic women – Volumnia, Virgilia and Valeria – all, one cannot help suspecting, aspects of Mary Villiers. Although she was no more than fifteen miles away at Brooksby, both

Miguel and Shakespeare felt her absence keenly and spent many hours every week on horseback (where, one must remember, the writing of plays is impossible) taking turns to ride over and be with her.

Whether the recollection of the moral in *Coriolanus* (Ben Jonson gave it the title 'Pride Goes Before Decline and Fall' after attending the disastrous opening night) was effective in preventing George from making a bid for absolute power from his position of favourite later on we can only guess. But the fact remains that in spite of having King James eating out of his hand, he always kept his ambition in check.

In *Timon of Athens* the learner's hand is starting to run away with itself, upsetting the balance of both structure and language. One can only sympathize with Miguel's predicament. He was living in two writing worlds since the return from Richmond. In one he rode with Lear's madness, the witches and ghosts of Macbeth, the voluptuous splendours of Cleopatra. In the other, he was saddled with Shakespeare.

Cecil, observing how James, the new king, was guilty of lax and feckless philanthropy and capricious, indeed frantic, infatuation with all sorts, insisted the second play should attack these faults. The character of the rich Lord Timon with his rosy illusions and indiscriminate good nature and open-handedness is the result. He likes all but loves no one. What he needs as a ruler is a strong, exclusive bond with one other person, otherwise he will fall into the trap of alienation when confronted with ingratitude. If Timon only had a true soul-mate, someone capable of reversing the swing of his angered soul towards harsh hatred of mankind, his tragedy would have been averted.

Before we come to *Pericles*, the last of the Billesdon Collusaries, it should be noted when it was written – a time when the dangers of love-madness between Cecil's three agents in Leicestershire had risen with frightening force, outdoing anything they had ever experienced in youth. The long emotional adventure of these three people, all of whom were forty-five and over, was as much a lesson to young George on the power of love as anything that would happen to him later.

He watched them suffer. He felt them yearn. And as the tension bound his mother, Miguel and Shakespeare tighter and tighter together, he found himself hoping they would either consummate this passion of life in an out-burst of violence, which was how it always seemed to happen in the plays being written under his nose, or they would flee from each other and find peace elsewhere.

What appears to be the total disintegration of Miguel's genius in *Pericles* is attributable to the two male lovers being so battered by jealousy, when it was written, they could no longer work together. *Pericles* is virtually all the work of Shakespeare.

Cecil had wanted a play about loss 'in which a man who has everything ends up with nothing.' The trouble started at the Billesdon farmhouse when Miguel, having found the story in Lawrence Twine's *Patterne of Painful Adventures*, a book just published, handed over the writing of the first two acts to Shakespeare saying, 'You should be able to do this one. You were a man of nothing until I made you into something.'

The ensuing fight rolled all round the farm, Shakespeare displaying the terrifying berserk rage and strength which had felled Ben Jonson and the bullies. The farmer who was renting them the accommodation finally had to help George pull them both out of a stinking pool in the middle of the farmyard's vast dungheap in which they were trying to drown each other.

Soon afterwards, when forgiveness had been exchanged, Shakespeare, having had moments of doubt about what he was writing, and feeling rather lost, thought it best to show Miguel a section of dialogue for *Pericles*, on which he needed help.

Fresh from a few days of bliss with Mary at Brooksby, when he had penned the death scene in *Anthony and Cleopatra* (based on a proposal for Mary and himself to end it all magnificently rather than continue with sharing her), Miguel lost patience, condemned Shakespeare's work outright, and said it wasn't good enough for an arse-wipe.

This time Shakespeare fled rather than release his demon.

Yet, by an act of staggering misjudgement and generosity on Miguel's part, *Pericles* went forward to join the others in their glory; Shakespeare's wooden verse and numbing excesses lying side by side with the smallest shoots of loveliness later grafted on the text by Miguel when printers balked at the play's vileness on the page and demanded some rewrites.

★

Sir George had been kept ignorant of the SVQ's grand plan. Apart from chagrin at having been virtually ignored at Richmond, he was delighted at the course of events, which had fulfilled *his* grand plan. The Exchequer made a number of substantial capital grants, as well as paying off all his debts, and future income was assured him as sole recipient of the import dues on pepper. All these gifts were made ostensibly for George's good who, so the Privy Council informed the proud father, had become in Elizabeth's last hours an angelic mirage of the son she had always yearned for, a king to rule her people when she had gone.

Sir George was given only a few years to enjoy these benefits. With everything in place for a prosperous and easy future, his lands his own, the harvests improving, he took ill after sampling too heavily a tun of imported Portuguese red *charnigo* and died of a protracted cerebral paralysis known to medicine as far back as the Roman Galen's time as *Ultima Elysium*.

George was at Cade's Academy for the Scions of Gentlemen at Billesdon by then and was called home with Miguel to attend the deathbed. This was no morbid affair because Sir George's condition, whereby the brain was locked at a high point of intoxication, kept him monstrously cheerful and boisterous to the end. He had always been blessed with a strong, loud countryman's voice but it was said his last words, a chorus from the old Leicestershire folksong, 'Put pleasures near my hand' were so powerfully roared out they could be heard four fields away.

Brooksby then passed to Sir George's eldest son and Mary moved a few miles eastwards and occupied a dower house at Goadby Marwood, a muddy hamlet even more removed from the greater world than Brooksby.

The man Mary married by arrangement after Sir George's death was Sir William Reyner, who was old, impotent and Cecil's appointee. He need not concern us too much, though his understanding of Mary's emotional needs was exemplary.

As dawn broke, Miguel would reluctantly leave Mary after a long, long post-coital kiss as if drawing power from her lips, take bread and milk from the kitchen, pick up his tray of pens, ink, paper, drying sand, candles in winter and, with a bundle of source books under his arm, cross the garden to his little wooden factory of words, rain or shine, snowdrift or thunder. There he would work until noon when, as if by a heavenly sign, all inspiration dried up. Often he would emerge with thirty sheets in his hand, unmarked by alterations or excisions, evidence of a full, firm flow untroubled by interruptions.

Then he would find Mary and take rest with her before the midday meal. They would talk only about themselves, their love, their jealousies, joys, forgivenesses, rages, the frequent pain of their separations, her indecision, her choices, sometimes about George and his progress, but never about what Miguel had been doing tucked away in the shed at the corner of the garden. That was merely his *work*, something secret he did for Cecil, himself, and the world outside Mary did not have to know about – except, somehow, though the substance was a mystery, it was for her he had striven.

In his turn, Miguel never encouraged her to get too close to the point of his pen. Although he talked to her endlessly, it was always about reality and not about what he might make out of it. Even his passion was a straight, live thing, not full of similes and metaphors. When

Miguel was alone with Mary, the poetic persona was voiceless and secondary, only coming into its own when she had gone and he was left in the afterglow of her presence. Then it became a power in the land of his mind.

Because the pattern of her past life was a semi-public one as lady of the manor, its course, shape and progress made discernible by her class and status, he tended to dominate their pillow talk with accounts of his childhood, youth, journeys and adventurers so she would not have to keep going over old ground or ever have to justify herself to him. Provided the heat of her love didn't cool he was happy to let her be silent for the most part and listen, except to speak of love as it was happening.

And she was so amazed that one man could have done and seen so much, it did not occur to her he might have any need to elaborate and enrich such a life by writing anything about it. As far as Mary was concerned, the fabrications and fictions of the imagination were best left to those who needed the exercise – people like dear, adoring Shakespeare, who'd had such a quiet, uneventful upbringing in an English country town, going nowhere, seeing very little but the mossy wheel of parish life turning through season after season; and had grown to adulthood with a desperate need to dramatize every little thing so existence could have some zest and meaning.

CHAPTER NINE

———◆———

GEORGE, A BOY now used to walking with giants, queens and dwarves, could find no time or liking for his head-master, the Reverend Cade. He was repelled by the melancholy of the little man and his attentively worrisome ways. In addition Mr Cade's sepulchrally bass voice annoyed him, coming from nowhere (his chest was as shallow and thin as a pullet's) always following him through the school, booming 'George! Where is our dear George Vee?'

Cade enthused over the new arrival to such an extent the other pupils could not help but take umbrage. George's academic work was marked differently, using a confidential standard. His poor performance in every subject taught at the academy was excused and his prowess in games lauded. This, coupled with the privilege of having two private tutors in attendance who took the favoured student to taverns and market days and kept him from church, created dissension and envy in the school.

It was left to Mrs Marjorie Cade, a strong, tall young woman, half her husband's age, not uncomely in a slightly horsey way, to minister to the boys as matron.

George arrived at Billesdon at a crucial time in the

Reverend Cade's life. His school had become successful and in fashion, with a long waiting list for places. It was at this high point in his career an ironic fate decreed he should be struck down by a sense of escalating personal sin. The remedy he found was to hand over all questions of discipline and management of the boys to his wife. For his own part, he confessed to being unfit to govern others until his salvation was quite worked out. One function he retained: to teach Divinity, the very subject which had led him down the deadly nightshade path of purple Christian gloom.

George's arrival at Billesdon apparelled in the archangelic radiance of early adolescence and armed with a character reference from the dying John Whitgift, Archbishop of Canterbury, (MA Cantab – Peterhouse, BD, DD, SVQ) coincided with Cade's descent into the pit of spiritual depression.

Marjorie Cade fell prey to George's good looks from the moment he arrived. Running his life was a delight. Sometimes she picked on him in order to have a long private moment to apologize. Time spent alone in the surgery cupboard patching up the boy's wounds after fights was drawn out to its limit. She insisted on supervising his bath. There were intimate exchanges when she sat at the foot of his bed (the only one not in a dormitory) explaining human nature, and the need of all human folk for contact and comfort.

In doing this every detail of the Lord Cecil's requirements were not only met but exceeded, for the First Secretary had worked hard on finding a school with all the right elements to bring George perfectly to the point when a boy, firm in his Englishness, is ready to be

Frenchified. The needs stipulated by Cecil, Marjorie could understand and satisfy; those unwritten, she and her husband met without knowing it.

Into this fertile gap Cecil had carefully inserted George with his tutors. But it was Marjorie who had been chosen first, then her husband. Although Cade was left in no doubt that George was the most important pupil he had, he was never apprized of the predeterminations behind the boy's future. Nor did he know the extent to which his wife had occupied the vacuum left behind by his lapse into religious mania.

Behind his back, she had agreed with the SVQ that once George had established control over the king, the school would close.

This sacrifice, which would be handsomely compensated, was essential to the political health of the nation, wiping out records of the gaffes, idiocies, embarrassments and disorders which always accompany the years of adolescence in boys.

*

The school itself was small, no more than twenty pupils drawn from good families, but it was big enough to dominate the village of Billesdon. A constant procession of frowning parents, time-wasting relatives, specialist teachers of music, geometry and natural science, lawyers, Catholic priests disguised as tinkers, ministers, Leicester town whores for the hedge initiation of boys who had started pestering servants, came into the village to visit the students. If ever a stranger appeared at the end of the long, rutted main street the villagers would know that nine times out of ten it would be Academy business had brought them there.

Living quietly in such a place was not an easy matter for a famous gentleman playwright and a foreign Jew. At first Shakespeare and Miguel were bothered by the congenital nosiness of the peasantry. Matters were made worse by the frequent jealous rows and fights at home, spilling over into the Fox and Hounds Inn, the only place of resort other than Cade's living quarters at the school house – a purgatorial social venue for anyone with no interest in the recent history of the English Church or a taste for the contents of Fox's *Book of Martyrs*.

'What Christian Need Fear Death?' was chalked on the outside of Cade's parlour door and 'Me!' on the inside. Once, when Miguel and Shakespeare had to attend the weekly meeting to discuss George's progress and Marjorie was called away, Cade appeared covered in whitewash with earthworms in his ears, crying 'Woe unto thee, Babylon' and had to be restrained from cutting his wrists. At other times he could be gentle and charming, deferring to Miguel whom he instinctively recognized as a superior mind.

This was the man selected by the SVQ to teach George the principles of Divinity, with Marjorie, Miguel and Shakespeare standing by to pick up the pieces. The design is plain enough: to besmirch religious excess with lunacy, but in the middle of George's time at Billesdon it went askew.

It was in the short interregnum between kings Macbeth and Lear, when Miguel was suffering from the withdrawal of his creative demiurge, that Mary came down to Billesdon for her son's confirmation. Shakespeare was not there, having gone to London with the script of *Macbeth* and thence home to Stratford for a while on family business. To the amazement of the local vicar, Whitgift's successor as Archbishop of Canterbury, Richard Bancroft (MA Cantab – Christ's and Jesus BD, DD, SVQ) had elected to come all the way from London to perform the ceremony himself, and the loyal, humble vicar was further puzzled by Bancroft insisting a special questioning of George's knowledge of the catechism be held by himself in the vestry, in camera.

But had the vicar been there he would have noticed nothing untoward. George knew his creed and ten commandments and delivered them faultlessly, though without evincing any great interest in the content.

Later, when the Archbishop had laid hands on the heads of all the other candidates, George came up for his turn. As Bancroft put his hands on George's head a convulsion seized the prelate, making him sway, then utter an incoherent cry. The congregation of clergy and layfolk leant forward, craning for a closer look – the episcopalians suspicious of the influence pentecostal sects with their shaking, and speaking in tongues were having on the church hierarchy, while those of presbyterian persuasion suspected sabotage by pro-papal demons.

What had actually assailed the unfortunate Bancroft was the first attack of kidney stone, an ailment which would kill him a year later.

It could not have happened at a worse time for the Archbishop. He had recently been heavily criticized for anti-Puritan bias and sympathies with Catholics. Cecil had urged him to find immediate means of pleasing the King, who was still angry over the Gunpowder Plot and increasingly intolerant of all forms of intolerance. The Archbishop had been thus frog-marched into the ranks of the ecumenical SVQ and George's confirmation into the national church was his first mission on their behalf, one he could not afford to botch.

With George's head clutched in his hands, the tormented Bancroft could not stop himself giving vent to Marian oaths: 'Mother of God!' 'By our Lady!' and so on.

With his neck being violently twisted and turned by the pain-racked Archbishop, George struggled to look up, encountering the furious glare of Cade who was aflame with indignation, and his mother's glowing eyes raised in an ecstatic swoon at hearing the Virgin's name spoken so hotly in open church, a practice long banned in England (where another Virgin had cunningly taken her place).

All this motion and emotion! All this vicarious suffering, for him!

Then light flooded in. He reeled with the power of the sudden insight into where he was.

In a spiritual company where he was centre.

In a structure built for a holy purpose.

In a field, in a shire, in a land, in a world crammed with hope for his soul, a part of himself he had not yet learnt to value!

Letting out a wail of guilt he seized the Archbishop's hands, kept them clamped to the sides of his head by bracing all his strength against the tumultuous writhing of the sick man, and cried out his need.

'O Lord, make me thine!'

This was accepted with relieved alleluias and mutterings

by the disturbed congregation. Bancroft's spasm ended
and he was just able to finish intoning the proper text and
declare George confirmed before collapsing into a dead
faint.

★

Afterwards Mary took George out to dinner at the Fox
and Hounds, telling Miguel she wanted to have some
time alone with her son on this day of days.

'Have you ever wondered why I have never discussed
matters of religion with you?' she asked.

'Because you knew it was hopeless,' George replied
bitterly. 'How blind I've been! I feel I've cheated everyone who cares for me. When I think of poor father and
what a disappointment I must have been to him. Virtually
a heathen!'

'You must never think that,' Mary said. 'He was very
proud of you. But he left all matters of faith to me. He
said it was women's work. But I say religion is for the
later years. Don't worry about it now. Be young. That is
a prayer God always hears.'

It would be a pleasure to be able to say George took
his mother's advice to heart, but that was not in him.
Instead he took only the first part seriously – the care of
his soul should be left to her – and then promptly asked
what she would do with it.

'Keep it safe until a certain day,' she replied
mysteriously.

'When will that be, Mother? I feel something newly
alive in me *now*.'

'Suppress it,' Mary urged him. 'My prayers will keep
you pure in the sight of God, no matter what sewers they

make you wade through, what poisons they put in your mind.'

Seeing the fog of doubt swirl into his eyes she took his hands, passionately kissed them, then went to his lips.

It had been a strange day for George. Revelations had crowded into a space within himself he had never known existed until now. However, he could account for each new moment of clarity – where it had come from, and why it had appeared.

But the erection which sprang up at his mother's touch had no explanation.

★

The following Wednesday afternoon was a regular period for Miguel to give George tuition in the military arts. They were fencing with rapiers when the pupil managed to slip under the teacher's guard and scratch his upper arm. As Miguel looked down in surprise, ready to laugh it off as an accident, George drew back for a further thrust but this time to the heart. Parrying it to one side, Miguel wrested the rapier away in his gloved hand.

'What are you trying to do?' he roared. 'I wasn't ready.'

'Leave her alone!' George hissed.

Miguel, who had the impression George approved, even enjoyed, having him as his mother's lover, and believed the reference was probably to Mrs Cade who had increasingly showed both of them signs of favour, guffawed.

'You have no rival in me,' he said, meaning it kindly enough.

George turned on his heel and ran off in hot tears.

'Next time be more choosy!' Miguel yelled after him. 'You can have her as far as I'm concerned, you young fool!'

That night George ran away.

It was June, when the light lasts. When everyone had gone to bed he crept out of the school and headed north on foot for Goadby Marwood, keeping away from the road, using woodland tracks and following a stream he knew led in the right direction. By ten o'clock the light was fading and he had only covered five of the fifteen miles. A moon came out and helped him see where he was going but as the trees thickened and the stream dived beneath overhanging bushes, he became confused, unable to trust his sense of direction.

It was not a cold night. Without thinking, he followed a procedure Miguel had taught him: scraping out a hollow away from the wind, laying out a system of long twigs in a star with his bed at the centre. If tripped over or trodden upon by an intruder, this would waken him. Then he covered himself with leaves, settling down to sleep with a stout stick in his hand.

The woods were full of owls, nightingales and night-jars. George quickly fell asleep, the smell of moss and decaying vegetation rank in his nostrils.

While in the throes of an outrageous dream about his mother, from which (so he later claimed) he was struggling to break as any good Christian would, he was wakened by sharp movement amongst the long twigs he had laid over his body.

Remaining still, he strained to see what had disturbed him but could not discern anything, although he could hear whispers. These got closer, the owners of the voices still invisible. When they were less than a yard away George saw a few moving outlines of heads and shoulders against a piece of moonlight admitted by the canopy of trees.

If he had not previously been in the toils of a frightening dream which made him amazed at the strangeness of his own mind, and greatly relieved to be out of it, he would have been frightened by now; but these human shapes, even if they were supernatural, were his deliverers from shame.

'I'm here,' he said from under the leaves. 'What do you want?'

There were some low chuckles.

'Is that George de Villiers?' a deep, rasping voice asked.

'There's no *de*,' George replied. 'Who are you?'

'Friends.'

George slowly sat up. He saw the flash of teeth and eyes and felt hands on his face and shoulders. Four dark figures squatted around him.

'You hid well,' one said. 'It was a hard job to find you.'

George made to stand up but the hands held him down.

'No, sleep on. We'll watch over you till morning,' another said in a voice edged with authority. Then they lay beside him, one at his head, one at his feet, and one on either side, and covered themselves with leaves.

'If you're robbers, I have nothing for you to steal,' George told them. 'If you're murderers, what can I say?'

'We don't murder boys,' came the reply. 'Go back to sleep.'

Years later, when recounting the story, George said the strangest thing of all on this night of strangeness was he was able to obey and go straight back to sleep without fear.

Upon thinking about it he wondered whether the unusual smell of the men, one of fragrant, fermented corn, had sent him off.

★

When he woke in the morning he found a small fire burning and bread cooking on sticks. Beside the fire was an earthenware pot of clean water.

His nocturnal visitors were nowhere to be seen. The places where they had lain in the leaves were still visible, pressed down, and the pleasant smell still lingered. Some shavings from the sticks they had cleaned to wrap dough around were by the fire, but nothing else.

George walked up and down between the trees for quite a while looking for the men, then ate the bread and drank the water.

It was while he was pissing on the fire to put it out he heard laughter above his head. Looking up he saw four black men clad cap-à-pie in black sitting in the branches of a tree.

'Miguel has taught you some useful things,' the largest of them, a broad man with a head of close-cropped grey hair and protruding ears called out, rocking the tree with extraordinary strength.

As one, the four jumped out of the tree, landed on the soft leaves, rolled forward in a tumble, then sprang to their feet like acrobats finishing a trick.

CHAPTER TEN

———◆———

I<small>N THE YEAR</small> of George's birth, Queen Elizabeth had given Robert Cecil his first commissions in Council.

There were two. One was the prosecution of Sir John Perrot who, while Lord Deputy of Ireland, was too often drunk, making lewd, disparaging remarks about the monarch while in his cups. Cecil had him tried, condemned to death and put in the Tower where he died of natural causes before the headsman could have him.

The second was to supervise the unloading of a ship. This may sound an almost humiliating task for a rising star in the government but this was no ordinary vessel and getting her cargo safely off no common dockside problem.

The *Madre de Deus* was an enormous Portuguese carrack of 1,600 tons and seven decks, one of the largest vessels afloat. She had been captured by English warships sent on a privateering expedition by a company of shareholders which included the Queen and Sir Walter Raleigh.

The carrack was heading home from Luanda in Angola towards Portugal when she was captured. Her outward trading destination had been the East Indies where a vast cargo of silks, spices, carpets and jewels, including a huge uncut diamond, had been taken on.

From the moment she was boarded incessant thieving had taken place. Before the ship came to berth in England, £29,000 worth of valuables (a massive sum in those days) had already been looted and hordes of criminals, merchants, speculators, goldsmiths and jewellers were streaming down to Dartmouth for the main pickings (which included three-quarters of a million pounds of pepper – dream of the import dues on that, Sir George!) the remaining cargo being worth a further £140,000.

Cecil did his best to control the mayhem when the great ship came into port. But the heat of anticipation, the hysterical, orgiastic greed, was nearly uncontrollable. Unable to guard the vessel from mobs of investors, merchants, felons of all kinds who invaded her – permits to board, genuine and forged, having been touted throughout the southern counties – Cecil managed to get the Queen's share off and away to London.

For the rest, the ship was pillaged and stripped to her ribs.

While this was going on, a consignment of African slaves lay chained and starving below the water line on the lowest deck, ignored by the frenzied speculators because, by law, they could not be sold in England and therefore had no commercial value. When Cecil did his final inspection in search of anything left he could sell, having not put much aside for himself, being more anxious to serve the Queen's interests than his own, he discovered the Africans.

It was late on a cold September day with a strong wet wind blowing in from the sea when he entered the hold.

In the darkness he heard moaning and the rattling of chains, smelled strong odours, and assumed he had found livestock. Then, by the light of his torch, he saw the rows of Africans as they lay shivering in their fetters, begging for food and drink, prostrated in ordure. They had not been fed since the loot-laden sailors who had captured the ship made off immediately upon reaching dry land.

Cecil described the sight to his father as 'the argument and proof of man's ineradicable Evil,' a scene of pitiable human misery so terrible nothing could touch his opinions on the subject again. From that day on, his mercy was always tempered with stern policy. 'For a better world,' he wrote, 'find better laws beyond manhood, and fair rulers who can be maintained above the greed of their subjects.'

Of 547 African men and women on the *Madre de Deus*, 377 were already dead and decomposing in their fetters. Another 68 were to die within seven days.

The surviving 102 he took as his portion. Moving them off the ship by night, he had them transported under cover to his father's estate in Hertfordshire where 92 were nursed back to health, the others dying of England's winter ailments. Of those who survived, 22 were sold in Antwerp; 12 in Paris; 18 were given back to their original owners as part of a diplomatic deal when Elizabeth was encouraging the Portuguese to accept a unified crown with Spain (Cecil's financial loss was compensated by the Crown), and another 40 formed the corps of Cecil's Night Riders.

Now, after fifteen years in the dangerous world of European politics, the unmarked graves of those of them who had given their lives on missions for the English state lay scattered throughout the home islands, France, Iberia, the German and Italian states, the Netherlands, Turkey and North Africa. There was even one in the Vatican cemetery for heathens and unbaptized infants.

Only four of the original human cargo of the *Madre de Deus* were now left alive, the Hollehtoh brothers.

These were the men who stood laughing in front of George in the woods that summer morning, picking dead leaves out of their hair.

★

In reply to George's heated demand they should immediately identify themselves, the senior of the four explained this was not possible.

'We have no names, except amongst ourselves, and our numbers would mean nothing to you,' he said.

'Nonsense!' George expostulated. 'Everyone must be able to give a name and say who they are.'

'Not necessarily so,' the senior murmured, shaking his head with a curious rolling motion.

'Who sent you after me?'

'Aho! That would be telling. But you have been given a choice: either you can go back to school and resume your lessons, or you can go to your mother for seven days and sort out your feelings for her. Take a moment to think about it.'

George was so dumbfounded these four strangers knew his innermost secrets he had to lean against a tree.

'Who told you about this?' he managed to say.

'Miguel, of course.'

'You know Miguel?'

'Would he tell us such intimate things about a boy he loves if we didn't? Besides, you tried to kill him.'

'Now I will kill him!' George shouted, leaping up and running back towards Billesdon the way he'd come through the wood.

Even though George was running flat out, weaving through the trees, he found the Riders jogging alongside him.

Unable to draw away, George threw himself to the ground, screaming.

The Riders squatted round him, waiting until he had exhausted himself.

'Now, let's talk about your dilemma,' the grey-headed senior said soothingly. 'Why did you run away from school?'

'I want my mother!' George howled.

'Before I set out on a five-day journey to see some-one, I'd be sure they were where I was going,' the senior Rider said thoughtfully. 'Your mother's gone to Berwick-on-Tweed.'

George refused to believe this and insisted on going to Goadby Marwood. The Riders took him to where five magnificent black horses were tethered in a nearby glade and rode the ten miles north with him along the wood-land tracks to his home.

Whenever they came upon anyone along the way the Riders rolled white silk masks down from under the brims of their hats.

George noted fear in the eyes of the people they passed, which surprised him. Whatever these men were, and however interfering, they seemed harmless.

'Who are you, really?' he asked when they were about

to cross the main Melton Mowbray to Grantham road and the Riders were bringing their masks down again because a mounted party was approaching.

'You asked the question once!' the senior Rider snapped in a voice he had not used before, 'and we said we were friends. Let that satisfy you, boy!'

When they reached Goadby Marwood the Riders waited down the lane while George went into the house. He found everything shut up. A gardener told him his step-father had gone to London and his mother had left for Berwick-on-Tweed the previous day.

Disconsolate he returned to where he had left the Riders but they had gone.

The horse he had ridden had been left for him with a note thrust under the crupper which read: THE PLACE FOR UNBELIEVERS IS SCHOOL.

★

On their way through Billesdon the Riders called in to the farmhouse, told Miguel George was on his way back, and warned him Cecil would be angry once he heard George had run away. Lord Cecil would need to see an improvement, and evidence the boy possessed the calibre and mettle to absorb change.

'You've got me into a lot of trouble,' Miguel told George when he rode in. 'You can't just walk off like that. Where did you get the horse?'

'Some black men gave it me.'

'Black men? What black men?'

'They know you and Uncle Will.'

'First, you try to kill me, then you run off, then you

do some horse-stealing and come back here to tell a pack of lies. What's the matter with you these days?'

'I don't know,' George replied, getting off the horse.

'The punishment for boys who run away is a beating in front of the whole school,' Miguel said, forcing himself to speak coldly. 'Cade will be waiting.'

George was aghast. 'Me? Beaten? By him? In front of everyone?' he stuttered furiously. 'I refuse!'

'Since we've been here you've had to watch other boys being beaten for running away,' Miguel said sternly. 'Why should you be treated differently?'

'They were only homesick!'

'If that's such a little thing, what great issue drove you to it?'

George hesitated.

'Go on, spit it out! Surely it can't have been because you're in love with Marjorie Cade? Why run away from her? She'd welcome you with open arms.'

George stared.

'Marjorie Cade? What are you talking about?'

Miguel could not help but be convinced by the boy's puzzlement. 'Nothing, nothing,' he muttered. 'I shouldn't have mentioned Marjorie Cade.'

'I see the confusion!' George said. 'What a relief! So, Miguel, you're having an affair with Marjorie Cade! I'm not surprised. She's a very beautiful woman. Am I to assume it's all over between you and Mother?'

Miguel did not answer. His mind was going over the written report the Riders had wanted off him for Cecil. In it he had stated George had run away from school because he had a passion for the headmaster's wife. This was first love, in the nature of an adolescent infatuation, and could not be requited. In his view, the offence of running away was not only understandable but pardonable.

George wrongly interpreted Miguel's silence as an admission both his own guesses were right.

With Miguel besotted by Mrs Cade and out of the competition for his mother, his only remaining rival was Uncle Will.

Feeling much happier he embraced his tutor and patted his cheek.

'Marjorie Cade is the kind of woman you need at your age,' he said, 'someone a little younger, who's got patience; and as for my mother, well, the three of you couldn't go on like that for ever, could you? To be honest, I think she's had you in second place behind Uncle Will for a while but I notice she's even starting to get tired of him as well.'

He grinned and gave Miguel another hug, then took his hand, pulling him towards the door. 'Come on, I want to get this beating over with,' he said cheerfully. 'Let's find Cade and I'll show you how a man can take his punishment.'

CHAPTER ELEVEN

———◆———

THE REVEREND CADE demurred at the prospect of scourging his most prized pupil, but when George insisted he should have his just punishment, and in the proper prescribed manner, the headmaster had no choice. But being poised on the edge of an abysmal Christian despair at this time, he declared himself an invalid and delegated the distasteful business of carrying out the punishment to his wife.

Although unenthusiastic, she obeyed her husband's command and found herself laying into George's bare backside with a rope's end (Cade had been a naval midshipman before taking holy orders) in front of the assembled school. Unaccountably, she experienced pleasurable sensations while at her task. A strange headiness took hold of her as the rope's end whistled and the boy's buttocks shuddered.

George behaved well, not flinching or crying out. As he stalked stiffly through the audience of boys on his way to the exit, a tiny glitter of moisture in his eye, he whispered aloud, 'Feeble!' a defiance expected of the brave at Cade's Academy.

★

At the time George was at Billesdon, Cecil was in the throes of building his new house at Hatfield on the site of the Bishop of Ely's palace. Only one part of the original edifice was left standing at the western end and it was here, while Mary was at dinner with four aged ladies, she felt the blows of the rope's end. (When George had been attacked by the boys of Saint Albans' Grammar School his mother, who had been picking daffodils at Brooksby, was thrown to the ground by her womb's psychokinetic power and battered from within. Knowing him to be in danger she had immediately sent a servant south on a fast horse to find out what had happened.)

'Not again!' she cried, muffling her pain with a napkin. 'Who's hurting him this time?'

'Your boy and his flea bites!' said the oldest woman in a dry, cracked voice. She was a bent crone, wrinkled as a walnut shell, and sat nodding next to Mary, her elbows on the table. 'You jump every time he stubs his toe. God knows what you'll go through before he's finished.'

'Why is he suffering now?' Mary moaned. 'Where are those wretched men? They should be taking care of him.'

'You expect too much of men,' the most lissom of the women said, picking Mary's spoon up off the floor, 'and who in their right mind would choose a playwright and a spoilt rabbi for the job?'

'They were Cecil's choice,' Mary sighed, relieved that the blows had ceased, 'not that my heart hasn't regretted it since.'

'Ach, woman, you're too soft, even though your heart can do more somersaults than a tumbler!' said the youngest (though she was over sixty, her face was ravaged by forces other than Time). A small, lively, red-wigged woman with an impatient, imperious air, she spoke in a voice swirling with accents of France and north of the border. Clutching her lap-dog to her breast she fed it bits from her plate, mimicking the animal's deep growls of pleasure.

'If your son is to help us he'll need a heart as supple and strong as yours, Mary,' she mused.

'His heart will always be his own, I hope,' came the passionate reply. 'That is what I have taught him, and ordered his tutors to teach him.'

'And it must be made of steel!' laughed the woman with the lap-dog, holding it up in the air and kissing its wet nose. 'How will he endure the embraces of my unnatural son otherwise?'

★

The tradition of English gentlemanly behaviour goes back a long way. The idea of executing upper-class women was offensive even to the Anglo-Saxons.

It was only when the English burned Joan of Arc in 1431, having bought her from the Burgundians for 10,000 francs, that this cultural prohibition wavered. Even then, some nobles and soldiers protested because Joan had the right to be treated as a captured war leader, someone who should have been ransomed.

The arguments publicly put forward in favour of her destruction were as follows: having been originally a farm girl she fell outside the definition of a lady; she was French; and, the strongest and most interesting point of all, she was a witch. These implicitly weak arguments were shored up by the Church in England and by France adding the charge of heresy. The Maid had heard voices summoning her to drive out France's enemies. The bishops of both countries agreed these voices must come from a diabolical source, possibly because the English had the upper hand in the war at the time.

But these spurious justifications can be swept aside. They were contrived in order to disguise the actual purpose behind the death of Joan. It is clear she was a human sacrifice in the style of Homeric Greece.

Iphigenia, offered up on the altar so her father Agamemnon's fleet becalmed at Aulis could have a wind to sail to the Trojan War, is her classical counterpart. Both virgins, both precious to kings, both put on the altar for the purposes of military and political propaganda, both confirmations of the power of witchcraft in the popular mind, and both sacrificial deaths to satisfy the deep-seated belief that a divine Creator in male image resents the competition of a human creator in female, and is best petitioned by shedding the blood of potential mothers.

This regrettable return to ancient practices occurred then in European history because the revival of Greek learning which underpinned the burgeoning Renaissance was not restricted to unearthing forgotten philosophers but also included reading the work of Greek playwrights who put cruel but effective sacrificial rituals at the heart of their tragedies. In addition, Wycliffe's translation of the Bible into English had been in circulation for fifty years. In the books of the Old Testament human sacrifice is shown as an act of obedience to a god whose needs and morality are incomprehensible.

When the reading of Wycliffe's translation was subsequently condemned, the network of Christian witches in

England took this to be a sign that the sacrifice of males was an old error of the Jews and the direct cause of their persecution by their own god, Jehovah. They saw how male sacrifice was only useful in earthbound political causes, notably war or secular disputes with no spiritual dimension.

The Maid of Orleans became a burnt offering in Rouen's marketplace during this confusing intellectual aftermath among English witches. When Henry the Sixth's forces were driven out of France shortly afterwards, the efficacy of human sacrifice fell into doubt and disrepute and was put aside. England then collapsed into civil strife during the Wars of the Roses in which bloodletting was exclusively male and had no religious or spiritual purpose at all.

The wave of witchcraft that rose in England and Scotland after the break with Rome and the Dissolution of the Monasteries came as a result of disenchantment with a Christianity dominated by academic doctrine. The Church had patently failed to prove itself a custodian of a living faith and the organization now lay in pieces, its principles and truths tossed into the gutter. Many said this had happened because the fathers and doctors of the Church had increasingly shut their minds to the older faiths, thereby losing their roots in the pre-Christian earth. After all, they argued, without the Creation there could never had been a Crucifixion.

On 19 May, 1536, Anne Boleyn, the first queen of four to be sacrificed in England during the New Age of the Witch, was beheaded on Tower Green. After her came Catherine Howard in 1542, Jane Grey in 1554, and then, the most famous of them all, Mary Stuart in 1587.

Then what are these women doing at dinner with Mary Villiers at Hatfield in 1609?

Certain courtesies survive even an age of spiritual mayhem. One remaining in use during the fifty years when the four queens were offered up to appease the male Creator was the age-old dispensation whereby eminent and influential folk condemned to death were allowed to pay someone else to suffer in their place. There have always been poor people willing to make this sacrifice, who will sell the only precious thing they have, life itself, in order to feed their children or dependents. A little theatre work with make-up, a wig and costume does the rest.

When the axe fell at the execution of Mary Stuart and the head dropped into the basket, the wig the stand-in was wearing fell off, revealing a grey, close-cropped skull belonging to a woman twenty years older than Mary. This caused more horror and consternation than the decapitation itself. All two hundred people round the scaffold in the great hall of Fotheringhay Castle that day knew Mary was vain about her hair and had it combed three times a day.

Sir Amias Paulet, Mary's keeper, fell out of favour immediately after the execution, not, as has been claimed by historians, because Queen Elizabeth felt guilt and remorse but for the sake of a spot of glue.

*

Shortly after her accession, Queen Elizabeth brought together the three queens who had already fallen to the sacrificial axe (even though their actual deaths were by proxy, the destruction of their influence had been absolute), and formed them into a caucus of councillors to help her rule the English nation, bedevilled as it was by a suspicion of women in power which was more or less reasonable at the time.

Elizabeth's sister Mary, by her infatuation with that super-mysogynist the Catholic King Philip of Spain, had salted the earth for female rulers, and if it had not been for the strange sexuality of the Cecils, father and son, who needed a very powerful female to abase themselves to while mortifying scores of others, it is certain Elizabeth would never have been given the crown. Elizabeth was able to add the Cecils to the three queens at the Old Palace at Hatfield and thereby create the seedbed from which the SVQ would spring.

CHAPTER TWELVE

—◆—

THE CALL FOR George to go to France with his 'two lerned tutars' (sic) came in the shape of a pass sent by the Privy Council direct to the Globe Theatre just as *Coriolanus*, *Timon* and *Pericles*, in consecutive performances were about to begin in a light April shower.

It was eight in the morning and George, Miguel and Shakespeare were in the audience, waiting for the show to start. Six in the evening was the time it would finish, all being well.

The idea of doing the three plays one after the other had been Cecil's, now Lord Treasurer to King James. He had provided a sum for Shakespeare's company at the Globe to mount the production, giving as reason the government's desire to improve the moral and artistic standards of the London stage, which were currently thought to be at a low ebb.

To any of the London *cognoscenti* outside the SVQ, this represented a credible motive. Unless the theatre subtly mocked one's enemies or cunningly praised one's friends, it was condemned as shallow, whore-ridden and insolent. It was always offending foreigners, someone at Court or the religious community. Jonson, and the playwrights Marston and Chapman had been put in prison for mocking the Scots in *Eastward Ho!* a few years back, but the lesson had only been partially learnt. Satire still hummed beneath the surface of most plays written, but the wise trick was to set a piece a long way back and the historical Greek and Roman background of the Collusaries defended them against any charge of sedition even better than tenth-century Scotland and Holinshed's revered chronicle had *Macbeth*.

However, the playgoers of London, being as perverse and unimprovable as they were, had given *Coriolanus*, *Timon* and *Pericles* the thumbs down when first produced and it seemed an act of either defiance, contempt or commercial madness to revive them, especially in this marathon form.

As George waited with Miguel and Shakespeare for the first play to start, he was one of fifty-seven in a theatre which could hold twelve hundred. And it was as well he didn't know this ordeal had been designed for his benefit. The prospect of a whole day on an uncomfortable bench watching sheeted actors rant had not been George's idea of the best entertainment London had to offer. After yet another long winter at Cade's Academy George was ready for anything that was trivial and amusing. Even one of Ben Jonson's new masques, full of nubile girls painted gold and singing 'Come to me and sport, ye sons of Onan,' would have struck him as too serious. Also the action would undoubtedly be poisoned with *poetry*, and of poetry George had had more than enough.

The Privy Council pass 'to repair unto France and parts beyond the seas to gain experience' was delivered by Sir Thomas Campion, the new husband allocated to Mary by the SVQ, Sir William having died recently in a plumbing accident.

★

As *Coriolanus* was about to begin, a large party of wealthy but soberly dressed men and four women in heavily veiled mourning black, one of them very infirm, came onto the stage, each carrying a small stool. They sat in a horseshoe, leaving only the front of the apron open.

The walk-on actors in the opening crowd scene (the stage direction is clearly Shakework: 'Enter a company of mutinous Citizens, with staves, clubs, and other weapons') entered and began squeezing themselves between those ensconced on the stage, something they were loath to do because the hunchbacked Lord Treasurer and many of the most powerful men in the land had been immediately recognized amongst the new arrivals.

Something else to disconcert the players during the performance was the lack of attention they received from those seated on the stage. Instead of following the action and listening to the speeches with eyes on the actors, all of them sat staring at George in the audience, watching his reactions and whispering amongst themselves.

Twelve hours is a long time for an actor to be under the discipline of the stage. Many of them had parts in all three plays and were forced to see the whole day through. By the time *Pericles* was reached, several of the performers had become so emboldened by drink in the dressing room and the uncaring sourness afflicting any production doomed to fail, they turned against the party on the stage, regardless of who they were.

One of the most popular Green Room stories for

many years afterwards, right up to the demise of the theatre in 1642 when Parliament closed them all down, recalled this occasion.

Ned Morris, who was playing the Third Fisherman in the opening scene of Act Two of *Pericles*, is reputed to have thrown his net over Sir Thomas Smith, Master of the Court of Requests, rolled him off the edge of the stage and cried in a loud voice, 'Here's a slippery cod, indeed!'★

★

By the time *Timon*, the second play, began, the theatre was full. News had got to Westminster, Whitehall and the Inns of Court that anyone who was anyone, or wanted to be anyone, needed to be in the audience at the Globe with Lord Treasurer Cecil and his party, also the great length of the performance and the low standard of catering nearby made it advisable for people to bring their own food and drink. Servants arrived with hampers, cloths were hung over balconies, bottles were opened. The theatre management, having now sold every seat in the house and made a handsome profit, ignored the noise and inconvenience caused by this enormous picnic, deciding it was wiser to be lax so the audience would keep in a good humour during their long stay.

★ Morris was found guilty of petty treason, had nose and ears slit and spent a year in prison, but pops up again in 1624, playing a pawn in Thomas Middleton's anti-Spanish satire *The Game of Chess*, the most successful play of its time. George, by then Duke of Buckingham, is represented as a new chess piece, the White Duke. The Spanish ambassador, Black Rook, protested to King James and Middleton was gaoled.

Besides, all the officers and magistrates who might prosecute the company for unruliness were in the audience.

The second scene of the first act of *Timon* has a very ragged join between crowd hysteria in the opening scene and a noble banquet which follows. At this point in the text Miguel had taken up the pen once again, tormented by Shakespeare's inability to blend sense, music and blank verse. Suddenly the rhythms smooth, the thoughts ride the verse well and work, the characters charm, and the bumpy discomfort of Shakespeare's apprentice doggerel is exchanged for the art of the master.

Until this transition took place, Miguel was hunched as low as he could in his seat, collar pulled up, his beard clamped between his knees, shuddering with shame. Beside him, Shakespeare sat upright and beamed, casting his eye round the audience to encounter anyone who might recognize him.

'Rough stuff!' an old gentleman grumbled from behind. 'He must have written this when he had a sore head.'

Shakespeare leant over to Miguel and raised an oddly sympathetic half-moon eyebrow.

'I told you the banquet came in too early,' he whispered. 'They need time to quieten down and absorb everything I've put in the opening. As you often say, Miguel, very little sinks in during the first ten minutes of any play, no matter how well it's done. Ideas of any real weight have to force their way through during the half-hour that follows. Isn't that right?'

Miguel shuddered again refusing to look at the stage. Though the audience was beginning to fall under the charm of his verse, he was past being able to feel pleased. He cursed himself for being so uncritical and easy on Shakespeare. But life had been impossible at the time *Timon* was being written in Billesdon. *Macbeth* had been marching round in his head with witches, ghosts, murder and massacre in attendance, waiting to be written. A yearning to be away from Athens and into the grim, grey castle of Dunsinane where Lady Mary's double waited, plucking her nipple from the boneless gums of their never-to-be-born child had always been powerfully at work.

Often the switch from what he didn't care about to what he did care about had been beyond his intellectual control. Then, he had been forced to let the situation dictate, leaving Shakespeare to get on with duping himself. All Miguel could do was make the odd suggestion here and there, mention a few ground rules, steering the rapidly inflating beginner away from unmanageable but sensational devices (Shakespeare had wanted a whale in *Timon* – Greece is in the Mediterranean, not the Atlantic, Miguel had reminded him) while all the time keeping the best time and energy for what meant more to him.

So, *Timon* was a play which lay under interdict in Miguel's mind. He could not bring himself to watch it with a whole heart. When he saw it performed for the first time he had not been able to look Shakespeare in the eye afterwards, not because he felt ashamed but because he might get the urge to kill him.

Therefore Miguel was not expecting it when this play of all plays created a moment which dazzled him.

On Cecil's orders, the company had taken a lot of trouble over the banquet in Timon's house, providing the actors with *practical* food. The newly-arrived courtiers in the audience, anxious to please the great as ever, began offering the party of notables on stage a share of their picnic.

So, the banquet and the picnic began to be one. Members of the audience climbed onto the stage to pour Timon and his guests real wine, then tasted a spoonful of confection from the table. With the play continuing, actors began to move off and back on to the stage, saying their lines, returning with oysters and cold woodcock, but all done decorously, without disturbing the play's progress.

A *frisson* of tender excitement accompanied this strange consummation. Indeed, the hum of talk which customarily went on below the actors' lines abated. Through the medium of the play, the audience was watching and listening to itself.

This soon had Miguel sitting up, hair on end, gazing round him with eyes wide open, his fingers scrabbling for his notebook. As he tried to find words for the metaphysical thrill in the air, he observed the infirm lady in black being carried off the stage.

At once he knew it was a moment of death born out of revelation. An insight had razored some poor female away from life at exactly the point of mortal comprehension. She had seen truth, then been sent flying back to the void she had come from at birth.

Scribbling frantically, he tripped over people's feet as he got up and stumbled along the gallery to where he could look down on the woman as she was carried through the crowded pit.

Her veil had fallen aside. Staring up at him from sunken eyes was a hag.

Then the head rolled back and forth and Miguel heard her say quite clearly in a loud, cracked voice, 'Ye gods, sisters, let not our boy attend too many long plays. Today's visit to the theatre has come close to killing Anne Boleyn.'

★

One member of the audience which got this glimpse of pure theatrical actuality as it passed by was George – but he missed its point. He was so beaten down by his mother's steadfast refusal to enter an incestuous relationship he had, of late, become very hard of heart, and could give no vision access to his mind. All he wanted was to be away to France where he could forget the humiliations of rejection and enjoy life in a lighter, wilder vein.

★

Mary was not only the mother of children, the mistress of lovers, and the wife of husbands. She had another string to the bow of her beauty, her capacity for emotional metamorphosis.

This knack had been encouraged. As soon as her mother had noticed it at work in her daughter she had taken advice from Doctor Dee, the brilliant court astrologer, who had verified and consolidated her natural talent.

This was the reason she had been chosen by the queens in 1588 to bring forth a beautiful male child. Another reason was Mary had already proved able to bear healthy male children who survived.

123

A sire was provided in the handsome, fiery shape of Robert Devereux, the brave second Earl of Essex, then twenty-four and in his sexual prime – he had impregnated four female servants by the time he was sixteen. Devereux had been brought up in the Cecil household and taught to know his duty.

Elizabeth had been in love with Devereux in 1591, as she had been with his step-father, Robert Dudley, Earl of Leicester. When young Devereux secretly married without Elizabeth's permission it was at the time the five queens were deep in discussion with the Cecils about the future. Elizabeth put Devereux forward as a candidate in a spirit of pique and revenge on Devereux's young wife and Devereux himself, for the committee of five queens had agreed that once Mary was made pregnant it would be better if the natural father ceased to exist.

Devereux was given command of a force which was sent to help Henri of Navarre in his fight for the French throne, the most dangerous expedition Elizabeth could find. But the qualities in the man himself – a strong survival instinct matched with marvellous physique and athleticism – brought him through the ill-fated campaign. It took ten years and many more perilous commissions in Ireland and Spain before legitimate assassination was resorted to and Devereux was put down.

By the time of his execution in 1601 Devereux knew about the committee of five queens and the part he had played in the creation of George. One of his closest friends was Miguel, then in the household of Sir Nigel Main in London. It was no accident that Devereux, having worked out what was behind his constant posting to danger spots, arranged for Shakespeare's *Richard II* to be performed in the city. This was not, as most commentators have opined, to show a monarch being rightfully deposed – in this case so Devereux could be king (an absurd notion) – but to put on the stage a weak homosexual king dominated by a favourite, the very situation he knew the five queens were conspiring to bring about in England if Elizabeth should die. This was already the state of affairs the committee had engineered in Spain and Portugal (now unified and at peace with England for the first time in years) with Philip the Third on the throne, a man like James, a deeply religious fool, despotic but ineffective, besotted by a favourite, Francisco Gomez de Sandoval y Rojas, the scheming Duke of Lerma.

Once it was realized how much Devereux knew and how furiously indignant he was as a consequence, Cecil moved swiftly to engineer a tiny, forlorn, containable rebellion of tavern drunks that could be blamed on Devereux, then had him tried for high treason and his head on the block in just over a fortnight.

Miguel wrote *Julius Caesar* in the wake of Devereux's execution. A strong, brave man, shown with all his weaknesses intact, murdered by conspirators.

Although already in Cecil's pay, Miguel had not revealed to his master he was the author of the plays which were being produced under the name of Shakespeare. When Shakespeare was interrogated by the Master of the Revels, the Lord Chamberlain and Cecil about the meaning of *Julius Caesar* he was so obviously lost Cecil began to suspect another hand. Under interrogation, Shakespeare admitted Miguel helped him a little with meanings, structure and groundwork, but the writing was his own.

Now Cecil had found a means to control the work of Shakespeare – through his own agent, and he did not hesitate to use it to air ideas and put concepts into circulation for the sake of the nation's political health. The plays became a sounding board.

The reason Shakespeare was never imprisoned like his contemporaries was because Cecil and Miguel always agreed just how far the plays could go before they were written, though the arrangement between Miguel and Shakespeare was never fully revealed to Cecil, who was satisfied with the explanation he had been given. After all, he had what power he needed over this important part of the theatre's work and he seldom strayed further than his needs.

Miguel did not find the work of serving Cecil incompatible with writing plays, or unpleasant, and much of his espionage experience was fed into characters and plots, as we have seen. It was only when Cecil arranged for him to be chosen by Sir George as tutor and he went to Brooksby and met Mary, that the strategy for the feminization of all the major European powers was unfolded to him.

He was not told how vast the design was, nor how far developed, but he soon worked it out and, as details of the plan fell into place, he matched it with the creation of incurably flawed male characters in the tragedies bowed before strong females whose will, ambition, innocence or truth recommend them for the direct exercise of political power.

Even if he had wanted to pull out and disappear once all was clear to him, it was too late. He had fallen in love

with the woman from whose womb the English part of
the metamorphosis would proceed, and, more impor-
tantly, he had become convinced, given the mess Europe
was presently in with its wars of religion, that the five
queens deserved a chance of success.

★

So, as George sets off home to make preparations and
have a final few days with his mother before setting out
with Miguel and Shakespeare for France, singularly unim-
proved by the Collusaries and untouched by any form of
metaphysics, we must cast a glance in the direction of
King James.

He is now a man of forty-four, ripe for the most
profound emotional madness. Although on the throne of
England now for seven years, and the Scottish for thirty-
one, the five queens have effectively controlled his life
since he was thirteen when Cecil (père) arranged for the
boy's psyche to be overwhelmed by a clever, charming
pederast, the superbly good-looking and Frenchified Esmé
Stewart, a kinsman and client of Mary, Queen of Scots'
friends, the Guises, who was sent to Edinburgh on this
mission of seduction in 1579. Within a few months the
task was completed and Esmé reigned over young James
in Scotland for ten years, reaping lands, rents and duke-
doms until his behaviour roused the Scottish lords and
presbyters to drive him out.

In this early experiment the rôles were reversed –
James was the catamite, and Esmé the king. The five
queens analysed both males closely watching how the
relationship worked, isolating the gaps in education, the

crucial weaknesses, the defensive strength between the two against the world, the intricacies of male to male obsession.

When Esmé finally disappeared, swallowed up in France with his gains, the five queens had learnt a great deal about managing such an affair from the outside.

Robert Carr, James's present favourite, had much of the fractious greed and instability of Esmé. Although designed as a progression and improvement upon that first love, Carr had proved a bad choice. Rancorous, wild, crazed with his own importance, hating those he could not charm, loathed by the English, the well-built Scot had driven James close to madness several times, even sending him to the arms of his wife for comfort.

One good feature of the relationship was its durability, however. There were fights but the protagonists returned in peace, forgave, resumed their *mariage des hommes*. By the time George received the summons to go to be Frenchified, James and Carr had been lovers for over three years and were still going strong.

The king of Britain had a heart that thrived on affection. When the time came for the SVQ to take him over completely, that would have to be catered for. George could not return from France as a heartless, brittle jewel – which is the defence he had adopted to disguise his disappointment with incest – he would have to be awake to feelings, and skilful in their management.

James was no libertine, no aesthete living solely off moments of exquisite excitement. What he needed was a *spouse*.

CHAPTER THIRTEEN

———◆———

'TIME YOU HAVE in hand has to be set against time you have spent, time that will be taken away from you, and time which you must lose,' Mary said to George as they left the churchyard in Billesdon after the funeral of the Reverend Cade.

Marjorie, who stood by the lych-gate, her widow's weeds blowing in the wind, saying farewell to those who had attended the ceremony, heard these words as she curtsied and shook Mary's hand.

'Do you understand what your mother is saying, George?' she asked, leaning over so he could see the brightness of her eyes beneath the veil. 'I would also add – time you need not waste. Remember Mr Cade. A great mind o'erthrown by unnecessary worry. Go out into the world and find its adventures. Let the end look after itself.'

George felt the pressure of her gloved hand and caught a whiff of musky perfume. Marjorie was now standing side by side with his mother, both women looking down at him with rueful expressions as if the waste Marjorie had mentioned was already under way and showed in his face.

'His last words, as he lay in my arms, were, "Give the boys a holiday",' Marjorie recounted, her arms folded beneath and uplifting her breasts as if to present a salver full of sorrow. 'Even then, in the midst of the apoplectic seizure, I discover, he was quoting the Ancients. Miguel, to whom I was describing Anthony's final hours, and who has been so very good to me in my grief, was able to give me the source as Anaxagoras, the Greek thinker who first identified *mind* as the primary cause of all change.'

'Miguel is already back at Billesdon? He told me he was going to Peterborough for books to take to France!' Mary interposed, a sharper note in her voice.

'He's been and come back,' Marjorie informed her. 'Didn't you see him at the door of the church? He's been such a comfort to me. My husband respected that man so much. What a good choice you made for your dear son's tutor.'

George's heart went cold again as he saw his mother in the grip of jealousy. Then the scene at the lych-gate was broken, curt goodbyes given, and they were half-running towards the carriage.

'Oh, mother, don't be so flagrant!' George complained. 'She's laughing at you. Walk slower, be more dignified about it.'

'About what?' Mary demanded, hardly able to speak.

'Miguel's been bedding her ever since we came to this place.'

Mary stopped in the middle of the street and cuffed him. Other guests from the funeral stared at the sight, then hurried on.

'That won't change anything, will it?' George sneered.

'And Uncle Will's been sleeping with her too, on and off.'

Mary struck another blow which George took full on the face.

'You're nothing to either of them, but everything to me,' he declared, then knelt in the mud. 'I don't want to go to France with them. I want to be with you.'

Mary laughed and walked down the street, leaving him on his knees in the mud. By the time he caught up with her she had got into the carriage and instructed the driver to go to the farm where her lovers lodged.

'Don't go there, mother,' George pleaded. 'They'll only deny it.'

'Perhaps because what you say isn't true!' Mary retorted.

'They're a pair of practiced liars! If you'd seen what I've seen . . .'

'There's nothing you've seen that I haven't,' Mary seethed, staring at the miserable hovels alongside the road and the filthy children playing on the verges. 'You've done a lot of damage, George. Once I've found out the truth, or lack of it, we'll have to sit down and talk things over sensibly.'

'Things that will take a very long time to settle, I hope,' George mumbled, edging himself closer to her in the cramped seat. 'If you won't come to France with me, I won't go.'

'Nonsense! What young man of eighteen wants to spend all his time with his mother?'

'*Moi*! See, I speak French already. Why should I bother to go there!'

'Then you'll be a mummy's boy.'

'Mummy's man, so it please you.'

Mary sighed and lay back in the seat, letting him kiss her.

'We've discussed this, George,' she said when he had retreated and laid his head on her shoulder. 'A lot of trouble has been taken to rid you of this disorderliness.'

'How can it be disorderly for a son to love his mother?'

'We're talking about *how*, George, *how*.'

After George's first declaration of love, Mary had consulted Cecil. He had taken the opportunity to shower her with unusual compliments, saying how he could not be surprised anyone should fall into such a deep dependence on her. However, he saw the sense in her concern. George's instincts needed to be controlled. They must be made supple as well as strong.

He arranged for her to visit Doctor Forman at Lambeth. The famous love-sorcerer was at the height of his powers. As cabalist, astrologer and angel-magician, he was an expert in all forms of obsessive attachment. It had not taken him long to ascertain the cause of George's passion.

'He is acting on his dead father's behalf,' he told Mary. 'There is guilt at work, which we must keep active as a means of wooing him back to a more proper obedience. Why should he feel the need to fill his father's place? Have you been lubricious?'

Forman had a strong intuition he was in the final year of his life. His great ambition had always been to become a gentleman. He had achieved this, which was a miracle considering the nature of his business. Prosperity and fame had come late, but by now the whole shape of his career showed a satisfying curve. His good reputation partly rested on his refusal to pull punches.

The consultation fee the SVQ were paying him was going to be used to buy a fashionable burial plot, so he pressed on with the truth even a mite harder than usual, unmoved by Mary's signs of umbrage.

'If you're loath to tell me whether you are virtuous or not, I can easily find out. To conjure your dead husband up is only an hour's work,' threatened Forman, with a pop-eyed, insistent smile. 'No doubt he'll know if you had lovers.'

'Do your powers truly go that far?' Mary asked, alarmed.

'Madam, I have been called many things in my time,' he told her proudly, big eyes glinting with memories. 'My house has been wrecked. I have been thrown in prison, condemned by more courts than I care to think about – but no one has ever said I was dishonest. Diabolical, perhaps. Dishonest, never.'

'And whom have you raised from the dead?'

'That I may not tell. By inner law of my profession, all summonings are confidential. If not, the spirits would never come, would they? But to prove one untellable truth, use another. If I say my only failure of late has been to bring back a certain king's mother . . .'

Mary stared at him fearfully.

'I note your terror, madam. When it came to finding her spirit, she was not where I thought she must be,' Forman said, spreading his powder-stained workman's hands in a gesture of surprise. 'Simply not there. Where is she, I wonder? And, d'you know, I received not a farthing from the Scot for all my hard work. No result, no money, he told me.'

Mary then hastened to make a full confession of her amours, which pleased the old magician. His immediate response was to invite her into his bedroom, which she refused, saying she did not find him attractive enough.

'The truth is always best,' he said with a wry smile on his small, shapely lips, 'even when it hurts. Lord Cecil tells me your son must be put to young females, older females, yourself excluded by consanguinity, not young men, older men . . .' here he screwed up his failing eyes and held a sheet of notes closer '. . . so long as they be not attractive.' He put down the list and smiled. 'Why, in that case, I would do!'

The consulting room was piled high with arcane books, countless pages packed with cryptic information recipes and formulae; boxes overflowing with amulets, chemicals, metals, powders, animal skeletons, bottles, branches, bunches of herbs, feathers, weapons and suits of second-hand clothes stacked up to the ceiling. After three hours in the cramped womb-like cavity at the centre of all this sorcerous paraphernalia, Mary had been given exactly what she expected – an antidote potion for George to take which would cure his incestuous desire.

With a heavy heart Mary had put it in her bag and left, thinking to herself once out of the door, All that learning and what does one come away with? The same as if some girl had gone to a mountebank in the market. And she'd thrown the bottle of love-antidote into the bushes at the side of the road, the memory of Sir George's near-lethal concoction of boiled linseed and lambs' fries uppermost in her mind.

Doctor Forman's previous visitor had been Shakespeare. He had accompanied Mary to London, then left her to go to the sorcerer's house in Lambeth alone, saying he had a shareholder's meeting at the Globe to attend. But this was a false trail. He had made his own appointment with Forman, preceeding hers. Now he waited in the garden, screened by bushes, and saw Mary toss the bottle away.

When she had gone he went over and picked it up, took out the stopper, sniffed it, frowned, then carefully poured the contents onto the ground.

What Shakespeare had asked Doctor Forman to do was much more of a challenge than Mary's problem with an incestuous son. Forman had never been asked to attempt this piece of magic before.

The conjurations took time. While they were gestating, Forman had sent Shakespeare out for a walk for a couple of hours.

Too excited to amble around, Shakespeare had stayed close to the house. When he saw Mary arrive and go in he had immediately become jealous, assuming she must be going to see Forman to obtain something to make Miguel love her more – for Shakespeare loved her far too much already.

Only one craving put this love in its shadow.

It was to satisfy this greater, more imperious need that he had consulted the necromancer.

★

Mary knew Miguel was not at the farmhouse when she arrived. They had passed him on the road. George had been so intent on snuggling up to his mother he had not looked out of the window and seen him.

'Wait in the carriage,' she said. 'It would be better if you're not involved. I'll deal with this alone.'

'No, I want to come in,' George said. 'I'm not going to miss it if you're going to haul them over the coals.'

'This is not for your entertainment,' Mary told him. 'What the Cade woman said may or may not be true.'

'It is! They dine with her, then they dance obscenely, then . . .'

'You're making this up, my son. I find that very sad.'

'All the boys know. Ask them! We've watched through the window, listened at the door.'

'Noble behaviour indeed!'

'One can't help but hear them, the noise they make slobbering over each other.'

The conversation continued awhile in this vein, Mary's eyes getting harder by the minute. Eventually she said, 'Enough! Am I to judge men on the say-so of a child?'

'I am no child, mother. I haven't been for five years. Nor am I a virgin. I know what needs to be done, and I'm not afraid,' George declared passionately. 'Let them say what they like. I don't care. All lovers should be brave. We should be brave and not care what people think.'

'They went that far with your education?' Mary said, slightly taken aback. 'No one told them not to, I suppose.'

'I found out for myself,' George replied hotly, 'and what a murky, brutish business it is with someone you

don't love. One might as well just lie there and cudgel
each other.'

'That much is true, but a common fate,' Mary replied
wistfully. 'To love exactly within choice is a rare
privilege.'

'Then rarity will be the object of my life. And where
will I find anyone rarer than you?'

'Oh, you will, you will,' she murmured, squeezing his
hand. 'One day you will discover all my limitations.'

George shook his head wildly. 'See how those scoun-
drels have undermined you! Let anyone dare attach a
scrap of blame to my Mary and I'll kill them! Allow me
to take revenge on these filthy rogues! And when I have
stretched them out in their own blood, reward me with
the kind of love you once gave them.'

'In the name of God put that thought out of your
mind!' she gasped, quivering fingers flying to her throat
as if a noose had tightened there.

'How d'you know it wasn't God put it *in* my mind?'
George said cunningly. 'I tell you, my darling Mary, it
feels like a divine inspiration to me.'

'You must call me mother,' she said, abashed but
impressed by the compliment which was beyond George's
usual range of thought. 'Those men have taught you to
be far too bold.'

'My boldness, as you call it, brings your woman's
name to my lips. Now we are speaking honestly. All that
nursery talk can go.'

The carriage drew up at the gate of the farmyard.
Cows were waiting, shoulder to shoulder, to be milked.
Forbidding George to follow her, Mary picked up her
skirts, went round the fence to the cottage where Miguel

and Shakespeare had their lodgings, opened the door, then went over to the yard, pulled back the gate and drove the cattle across an expanse of mud and into the cottage. When she had got them all in she returned to the carriage, where George was laughing triumphantly, and told the driver to take the road to Goadby Marwood.

As the horses were being turned, Miguel arrived, doffing his hat at the carriage window.

'I'll be able to receive you shortly, madam,' he said courteously, 'pray grant me a moment to tidy up before you come in.'

Mary summoned up the strength to fix him with a haughty, aristocratic glare. 'Purely out of interest, not that it matters to me one way or the other – have you been sleeping with George's matron?'

'Not sleeping!' George guffawed. 'They never sleep!'

A chorus of frantic mooing and bawling was now coming from the cottage as the cows began to feel too confined. Miguel looked across to where one had pushed its horned head out of a ground floor window and was munching a manuscript. He knew exactly what it was: the draft of an opening scene Shakespeare had sent from London which Miguel had left on the kitchen table.

'Excuse me, madam, we will have to speak about this later,' he said, making a low bow, 'otherwise today's milk will be soured.'

★

The last week Miguel spent at Goadby Marwood before conducting George to London and travelling down to Dover with Shakespeare to embark for France was a time when the rivers flowing into his creative sea began rising from different springs.

Twenty years living and working in England had wrought changes in him. The previous width and breadth of his imagination was narrowing down to this island people and their future, and he felt the stricture. As a poet at heart who had turned to plays so the world between the lines could open up, he was turning back to his original discipline – the mysterious religion of the Word, shorn of actor, stage, entrances, exits – and audience.

He could not get time alone with Mary. George followed her everywhere, claiming her time and company, even sleeping across her door like a dog and driving Miguel away whenever he approached. When he complained, Mary told him that since she was soon to be separated from them both, it would be only right to spend her time with the one who would miss her influence most.

Here Miguel could not agree with her.

If it was a matter of influence he could show her play after play, sonnet after sonnet, all full of her effect upon him.

But they were Shakespeare's and since George had turned against his tutors and their manner of making a living, it would be to Miguel's disadvantage to claim the authorship now. Instead, he joined in George's scathing attacks on writing and its sins, with Shakespeare as the target. Claiming the rôle of scholar and researcher for himself, he abused the creator, mocked Shakespeare's antipathy to truth, honour and logic. Any betrayal of his art he could undertake, he did so, anything vile he could allege as to the characters of authors to cheapen and degrade them, he came out with, pathetically desperate to be taken back into Mary's arms again.

As he sat in the shed working furiously on a rambling mish-mash of ancient British history plaited from raw strips unrelated in time or place ripped out of Boccacio, Holinshed and *Westward for Smelts* (a mish-mash in itself, published six years ago), Miguel cursed Cecil and his demand for yet another play at short notice, this time something stirringly patriotic to keep George in touch with his proper loyalties during the initial shock of living in France, that home of civilized sophistication – England's traditional enemy.

What he wanted to write about now was not the rust and moth of History but the vital, despotic power of love: the cruelty and selfishness of it, the strength which brought forth such pain, the glorious misery of his passion. Instead, with only a week to spend with Mary, he had to push puppets around the stage in his mind, Britons and Romans chanting dislocated poetry within a ludicrously convoluted plot, all because Cecil wanted to see a draft of the new play before their departure for France.

The work became harder and harder. He felt his powers failing, his pen faltering. Sitting in the shed, that sweltering wooden box in the corner of the garden he started to stifle, to experience self-disgust, to allocate to himself the contempt he had previously reserved for Shakespeare. He was worthless, a subtle thief armed with scissors, an outsider, an outcast, a sea-robber preying on the plate fleet of European thought, a parasite without an original idea in his head.

When he found the Reverend Cade sitting in the sun beside the shed one morning, Miguel was not taken aback or horrified, having been party to the fake funeral. The whole population of the village had also been involved in this cure by appeasement of the sad necromaniac's longings, hoping to preserve the existence of the school so essential to Billesdon's economy.

With an eye to something he might make out of the story for the resurrection play Queen Elizabeth had commissioned – Cecil had given Shakespeare an order to hold back from writing it until the best conditions for its reception prevailed – Miguel had asked Marjorie to send him word at Goadby Marwood as soon as the success or failure of this therapy was known. In place of the message, Cade had come himself, getting up at dawn and walking the fifteen miles from Billesdon through the woods singing joyfully at the top of his voice.

Cade had been through the Valley of the Shadow of Death (even in a simulacrum it was frightening enough, the disinterment had taken a good half-hour of frantic digging), and his arrival at Goadby Marwood coincided with the high point of Miguel's anguish at leaving, even losing, Mary, who now seemed to be more valuable than life itself.

No better person could have arrived at this crucial time.

'Anthony! Are you well?' Miguel cried, taking his hand and noticing some warmth. 'It worked then?'

'Miguel, I had to come!' Cade cried. 'What a wonderful day to be alive! I have so much to be thankful for, and so many to thank. All those people who took part, but you most of all. Not only did you come up with the idea of acting out my death and having me inhumed with full obsequies, but before that you tried so hard to argue me out of my pernicious morbidity. The hours you spent trying to persuade me only Nature redeems, and I, in my obduracy, refused to pay heed . . .' Cade clutched Miguel's hands, overcome. 'Accept undying gratitude from one who can say it with absolute sincerity. You'll be pleased to know I now embrace pantheism. Walking through the countryside this morning I saw so many benevolent powers and spirits at work. Shall we talk about it?'

'Give yourself time, Anthony,' Miguel said with kind firmness. 'There's no need to rush into something else. Perhaps it would be better if you came in and gave me a hand with a few scene outlines I'm doing for Will. You're quite good on Celtic history, as I remember. What d'you know about King Cymbeline and his fight against the Romans?'

Opening the door of the cramped little shed he invited Cade to step inside. He paled immediately, stepping back with panic in his eyes.

'How thoughtless of me,' Miguel said, shutting the door. 'What an experience being buried alive must have been! When you're fully recovered you must tell me all about it. The thoughts you had. The sensations. Or would that be too painful so soon?'

'For you, my friend, I will relive it all,' Cade averred. 'It can be the first step in rebuilding my courage.'

While Miguel looked fondly at the reborn schoolteacher, the name for an important character in *Cymbeline* who already had many long speeches but no ascription alongside in the text, came swimming into Miguel's mind. (Of late even baptizing his fictions had been a problem.)

'*Posthumous Leonatus,*' he hummed under his breath. 'That'll do nicely.'

With this gift hot in his hand, and being hopeful the name might bring more in its wake, Miguel suggested Cade might like to rest in the garden until he could have some time with him.

A servant brought food and drink from the house. Then the traveller who had come back from 'that bourne from which no traveller returns' ate and drank with a hearty appetite, watching the bees go in and out of the towering foxgloves, listening to birdsong, inhaling the warm fragrances of lavender, rosemary and honeysuckle.

CHAPTER FOURTEEN

WHEN MIGUEL BROUGHT Cade into the house during the late afternoon, forgetting he had not let Mary and George into the secret of the headmaster's counterfeit funeral beforehand, he was ill-prepared for their shrieks of fear and horror.

While Cade stood and blushed – he was far too happy to feel unwanted – Miguel gave a rapid, indeed, gabbled and garbled explanation of what had taken place.

'Healing? What would you know about healing?' Mary cried. 'Mr Cade took a terrible risk letting you loose upon his predicaments. Stick to your books and your swords and horses, you swaggering ape! And why bring him here to torment us with your pranks? By God, if only your employment were in my hands alone!'

George heard this outburst and seized upon it. 'Why can't you send him away? Let's be done with him, mother! Uncle Will and I are far better off in France without such a burden.'

Mary came up short, realizing she had said too much. Cade was listening closely, waiting to speak in Miguel's defence.

'Of course I'm delighted to see you alive and well,

Mr Cade,' she said with mustered calm. 'In the past your affliction has worried us all, sir, though we know it arose from piety.'

'Not piety, madam,' Cade replied, 'selfishness was at the root of it. All I cared about was my own precious soul. What an unworthy consideration that seems now! As for the future, I am going to speak to Mr Shakespeare and ask him to find me a place in his theatre company.'

'Then you would be stupid, sir!' George retorted, 'for the theatre only teaches sane men to be mad over nothing.'

'Silence, boy! What do you know about life and death? Anything at all?' Cade shouted, reverting to old classroom habits. 'The playhouse is the crucible of the re-created world. My brother Miguel and I have discussed this all morning and agreed! Nothing takes us closer to Nature than the divine artifice of theatre, as my comrade here will confirm.'

Then, having made his speech with many glances towards Miguel seeking approval, Cade went quiet, remembering where he was, realizing how he had spoken out of turn. Bowing an apology for his presumption and forwardness, he sidled away and stood half-hidden behind the open door of the room.

'You would do well not to take a decision affecting your future career too lightly,' Mary advised him, drawing George's fire, for he was now stuttering with anger. 'Men of the cloth belong in the pulpit, not on the stage.'

'Now that I have recovered my wits, I have turned my back on that calling,' Cade said in a low voice, 'and I'm heartily glad to have done so.'

(This was not strictly true. The fake funeral at Billesdon had reached the sharp ears of the church authorities and Cade had been immediately suspended pending a charge of holding the holy sacraments up to ridicule. An order for his arrest had been issued. He was now a wanted man on the run.)

'So, sir,' George jeeringly interjected, 'you have given up your life, your living and your wife because of this filthy, treacherous charlatan Jew!'

Cade raised his head, put on a proud, dignified air, stepped out from behind the door, crossed to the window where the light was better, then stalked up and down with the palm of his right hand pressed against his forehead, sighing heavily, a man in the thrall of great feeling.

'Speak no ill of my wife!' he suddenly declaimed. 'No woman has suffered more for her husband's sake. Without Miguel's support I doubt if she could have endured the course of my derangement. That she had the good sense to accept his strong arm is a cause for rejoicing, not scorn.'

George was about to launch a riposte but Mary held him back, impressed by the nobility of Cade's sentiments (though he was, of course, beginning to act), her love for Miguel mysteriously beginning to play freely again as she heard him praised.

'If this is true, then you have cause enough to thank your friend, and it is greatly to his credit he has helped you return to the world,' she said, gracefully giving Cade her hand, who promptly kissed it with fervour.

'It is a great honour and advantage for your son to be accompanied by such a wise and civilized teacher,' he said warmly. 'A wiser, more ingenious and generous man never lived. And his heart is yours, and yours alone. How many nights we have sat together over our books, prising apart the Psalms, dissecting Deuteronomy, eviscerating the Epistles of Paul, and the poor man has not been able to see the page, blinded by remembrances of your beauty.'

Mary was startled by the burst of pleasure Cade's intimate remark gave her. Rosy colour entered her cheek and her eyes went brighter as she glanced swiftly at Miguel to see if he was annoyed by this revelation.

He wasn't. In fact he looked rather proud in a sheepish way.

Mary's pleasure quickly retracted. She suspected Cade had been rehearsed.

'If you will excuse us, we have much to do,' she said, putting some distance between herself and Cade. 'Do keep us informed of your progress.'

George suddenly undammed a flood of abuse, laying his tongue on every vile oath and disgusting swearword he could find in his vocabulary, all directed against Miguel who stood still and grim as a statue, smile scraped from his face. Mary hurriedly left the room, one hand gripping George's wrist, pulling him after her. As she dragged him down the corridor, ignoring his pleas to be released so he could get his sword and run the lying, upstart, blasphemer through, she wondered whether Miguel could find a dramatical cure for George's obsessive affection in the same way as he had Cade's. They must talk about it. If something was not done to alleviate this condition of curdled, fermenting child-love, a toxic passion that was now hurting George physically and causing her much sympathetic pain, Cecil would soon interpret the signs and work out what had happened.

Then everything would be in jeopardy. Even the four

queens would not be able to protect her. Knowing far too much, and having been chosen in the first place for her rock-like ambition, she would probably have to be silenced.

It had been impossible not to respond to the temptation of George's limpet-like baby love in its magnificent adult form and she acknowledged to herself she'd been guilty of a particularly coy weakness which had encouraged him. But now George's feelings had to be diverted from her towards someone or something else.

It had crossed her mind after the disappointment with Doctor Forman that Miguel might introduce George to astrology, necromancy, magic and alchemy, subjects held in great awe and respect which seemed to soak up the vitality of those who studied them, especially men with too much energy, but George was no scholar.

Nor was he ever going to be fit to meddle in anything metaphysical.

*

'A youth in love with his mother is never going to be a fit consort for a king, especially one who has been so cold towards his own,' Miguel whispered to Mary, eyes on the shrubs and bushes in case George had woken from his sleep of emotional exhaustion and was already creeping up on him, sword in hand, through the dark of the garden.

'His pain possesses me,' Mary lamented. 'I can't feel anything on my own behalf. And that pain I have is his. So I suffer twice, and my own love for him is being turned. If this goes on, before long I'll go mad. This has to be remedied before you go away, otherwise I will never be able to carry the scheme through. My life will become impossible.'

'Some of the fault is your own,' Miguel chided her.

'True. I should have seen what was happening. But don't insist on my blame. Liberate him. Liberate me!'

'Are you sure you mean – completely?'

Mary let out a soft, stifled, frightened sound, the alarm call of a dove. The idea of George ending up with no love for her at all was too cruel to contemplate.

'Reduce it, calm it down,' she said plaintively, 'bring back proportion, balance, all the things you're always talking about. Having learnt so much from Will about stagecraft since you've been together, and proved what you can do with Cade, can't you think of a means to bring George to his senses?'

Miguel sat forward, elbows on knees, shaking his head so Mary could see the starlight on the bald patch that was beginning to show in his curls.

'That was an experiment,' he said. 'Although it appears to have cured Cade's melancholy, he's almost worse off – an outlaw. His school will be taken from him; knowing Marjorie she'll get it somehow . . .'

Mary suppressed the spurt of jealous anger triggered by 'knowing Marjorie', and argued that Cade had the best of the bargain – his sanity. Armed with that he could work his way back into better times, the return of his living, his wife.

'No. The theatre has got him,' Miguel corrected her. 'The cure has become the obsession.' He thought for a while, staring gloomily at the backs of his hands, then looked up. 'Perhaps that's the way to do it? Replace one obsession with another. On the other hand, we could wait and see how separation affects him. Time and distance are love's greatest healers. But then, meanwhile, he might actually kill me. You wouldn't want that, would you?'

It was well past midnight and still warm, the air fragrant. A moon had come out. In the corner of the walled garden, the shed stood like an obeliscal image brooding timelessly over the scene. They dared not go to bed together because George might wake in the night and prowl about with his naked blade, as he had been doing since their return to Goadby Marwood.

'*Amore al fresco, tempostoso, nocturno, e primo placere di gioventu del mondo*,' Miguel whispered in her ear, his arm stealing round her waist.

'Who wrote that?' Mary asked, leaning into him. 'Virgil?'

'I did,' he breathed, 'just now.'

'Will had better watch out or you'll steal his crown,' Mary said with a soft laugh, allowing him to ease her to the ground.

*

During the thousands of lessons Miguel had given Shakespeare about theatre, by example in the first stage of their relationship and now directly as Will struggled to become a dramatist in his own right, it had always been stressed that the true mystery of the craft lay in the audience, not the players.

As Miguel made love to Mary on a bed of chamomile between low box hedges there was an audience, both mysterious and crafty, each member of it bringing something of their own to the ritual.

On the top of the wall, hidden by overhanging beech boughs, the four Hollehtoh brothers sat in their long Night Rider capes, carrying out their surveillance duties for Cecil. Their master had received so many reports on this affair one more would not interest him, so their concentration was lax, almost idling.

'How old is Miguel now?' the senior asked hoarsely, the dust of several counties in his throat.

'Forty-five, at least. He told me last time we shared a cup together in Shoreditch he has to be careful not to use up all his vital sparks on *hlanganana* because it affects his brain.'

'Tonight he doesn't seem to care about that. Perhaps he's done all his thinking for the day. Strange how he cannot help crying out yet she is silent.'

'That has always been her way. Miguel tells me she is all-powerful, like a god. Her silence is that of the stars and the heavens. Once a man is up there amongst it, he hears music, and must sing.'

In the opposite corner of the garden, peering from the small window in the shed, having conquered his memory of the coffin, Cade watched also.

Like the Night Riders, it was not the first time he had seen Miguel occupied this way. On previous occasions Miguel had been with Marjorie whom Cade had never been able to approach sexually because she was his wife and as a Christian he could not bring himself to contaminate her with the evil implicit in the act. When she had complained that no woman could endure being unsexed by Scripture, he had agreed to turn his head away while she gratified her evil instincts elsewhere. This had let Cade off the hook and driven him into the mad melancholy of death. It was an irony Miguel should be the means to find a way to bring him back into the living world.

However, there was something insulting about the animal persistence of the man, Cade thought as he glared out. For all Miguel's charity, all his concern, he was a slave to this rooting between the thighs of women. What was he so desperate to find?

These cogitations were far from the mind of Sir Thomas, Mary's new husband, wakened by an importunate bladder, who had found the pot under the bed full to the top and decided to piss out of the window. Any man who finds himself faced by the sight of moonlit lovers grappling while his own penis lies useless in his hand can only resort to the blackest of thoughts. To save himself he raised sweet memories, smiled, forgave old wounds and betrayals again in his mind, ruefully rubbed himself up and down a little, then sat on the window ledge.

The last member of the audience arrived as the lovers' climax came.

Shakespeare's horse had lamed five miles away and he had been forced to walk the rest of the road. Entering the garden he looked up towards Mary's room to see if a light was burning. It was, so he knew she was alone, for that was always the signal.

In his baggage was a book of one hundred and fifty-four sonnets recently published under the name of William Shakespeare. Armed with these marvellously passionate poems by Miguel, he planned to make the most dashing of entrances, bowl Mary over with the ardent declaration that he could not think of going to

France without a final night in her arms, then bed her till long after the sun had risen.

He was so intent on his design he stumbled over the bodies on the ground between the low box hedges. Until then he had been in another play, a play he had carried in his imagination all the way up the Great North Road. Suddenly that romance collapsed and something darker and more dangerous took its place.

The Night Riders slipped down off the wall and pulled Shakespeare away as he manically battered Miguel's head with the book of sonnets, which was a presentation copy bound in brass and ebony.

Because he was so enraged, and Miguel and Mary were screaming at him to stop, it was difficult for anyone to hear what Shakespeare was shouting as the blows rained down. The tongue he spoke in, and fluently, was Spanish, a language he did not know. Most curious of all, he repeatedly yowled, '*Lanzasacudiendo!*' as he crashed blows down on Miguel with the heavy book.

The Hollehtoh brothers, who were trained to listen for useful information above the din of street and tavern brawl or pitched battle, gave each other puzzled looks as they pulled the attacker off and gave Miguel time to get to his feet and defend himself.

Over the years they had mastered all the main European languages, so they understood *Lanzasacudiendo* and it seemed very strange to them in construction, and even stranger in the use to which it was being put. Why was Shakespeare calling Miguel Shakespeare in Spanish (or Spearshake if the inversion of noun and verb is followed pedantically), while trying to beat his brains out?

When they melted back into the darkness, they

conferred in a nearby spinney before taking horse for London to inform Cecil of what they had witnessed, and give their interpretation.

They knew Will had no grasp of any foreign language. Because he wished to appear to have the trappings of a gentleman with a classical education he'd learnt a few Latin and Greek tags. Now, here he was, roaring out Spanish as if he had received the gift of tongues like one of the apostles at Pentecost. If England's foremost playwright was ejaculating in the tongue of the King's enemies, it was their duty to report it.

The sorting out that took place between the three lovers was a long, fumbling, shamefaced business during which a slow retreat to the house took place with grudging apologies, lacunas full of tension, and calls to forget.

George had slept through it all, but not unscathed. A most powerful wet dream had exploded at the moment of his mother's silent joy in the garden, one so strong and sweet the exhaustion which followed made him sink even deeper into slumber.

*

Doctor Forman's success in performing a transfer of natural talent from one living being to another was the crowning achievement of his life. As an adept and accomplished necromancer he had often raised spirits from the dead, but not exchanged them between the living. It had cost Shakespeare a huge sum, but in terms of self-respect it had been worth it. The self he now possessed was that of genius. Shakespeare had taken the lot, been made whole – the actor, the plagiarist, the entrepreneur, the gentleman, the playwright and poet, were now all his.

But as with all meddling in the occult, not everything had been under control. What had always mattered most to Shakespeare was to *be* Miguel, with all the strength of his character. Riding up to Leicestershire from London after the operation at Forman's house, Shakespeare had been in a delirium of delight, feeling the new power working in his mind, until Connah, his man – and a duller, more limited and mundane brute cannot be imagined – began to ply him with surly questions about the approaching theatre season in London and why a new play by his master was not included, whereas Jonson had one, Tourneur another etc., the implication being – was Connah's employment safe?

Shakespeare had been caught off-guard by the anger, envy and resentment which had unexpectedly boiled up inside him. Where did these feelings come from? He had been changed, improved, moved upwards many notches on the moral scale. Why had this grossness, this baseness of nature lingered on?

By the time they reached Stamford, Shakespeare had come to realize the transfer did not include the parts of Miguel he secretly admired above the rest. It was only the creative talent he had received, not the character to go with it.

CHAPTER FIFTEEN

SHAKESPEARE WROTE HIS first complete play under his own steam in three days of passionate sulking at Goadby Marwood, hiding himself away in a nearby copse and using a tree stump as a table. Cecil's order to begin work on the resurrection play arrived on the Tuesday (specifically excluding the Iberian Peninsula as a setting for the piece) and by Friday *The Winter's Tale*, that marvel of sick jealousy, murderous madness and pastoral pleasures was finished, its famous dénouement, the bringing to life of Queen Hermione's marble statue by the sheer force and magic of redeeming love, flying from Shakespeare's quill like quicksilver as gnats danced round his head.

With recent events in mind, the atmosphere had been such that no one dared intrude on another's privacy, so Shakespeare was left strictly alone while the genius Doctor Forman had grafted onto his stock burst into rapid flower. But although he had been given the genius of Miguel, he had not received the gift of either his learning, his experience or the eye of his travels. When it came to choosing a location for his play, he followed the original (the story was torn bleeding out of Greene's *Pandosto* in

156

the usual Miguelian manner) and left it in Sicily and Bohemia.

If Miguel had done the plundering of this old book (a technique that went hand in hand with his genius), he would have known the lay of both lands, having fought over them – in Sicily as an underground agent working for the local partisans against the Spanish occupation forces, in Bohemia as a mercenary with the Habsburgs pursuing Hussite Protestant rebels through the forests of the Elbe in the campaign of 1584–5, and thus would never have made the mistake Shakespeare did when he set Scene 111, Act 111 of the play in 'A desert country near the sea' in Bohemia, because he would have known it not to have coast or arid zone.

This lapse aside – which can be forgiven when one considers the majesty, power and poetical variety of the overall achievement – it is impossible to distinguish between the writings of Miguel at this period and Shakespeare.

Miguel had also taken refuge from the heartache of imminent parting and recent upsets in work, avoiding George, spending his time saving *Cymbeline*, still editing long tracts of Will's turgid pre-Forman labours in the shed, unaware of what was going on in the copse less than quarter of a mile away.

A feeling of reproach and uneasiness was in the air at Goadby Marwood during those last few days. Everyone needed time to get their breath back before parting with England and Mary and, after the débâcle in the garden, no one was sure it was the right time to go. George clung to his mother, refusing to share her time with anyone.

She did not resist but sat it out, talking, comforting, admonishing, preparing him for his adventure.

Only Miguel had travelled beyond the seas before and knew what to expect.

★

When *Cymbeline* and *The Winter's Tale* were shown to Cecil for approval at Whitehall before being taken to the Globe, the hunchback made them sit with him while he read both through, his sharp eyes darting from Shakespeare to Miguel and back again each time he raised his head from the page.

After four hours of silent scrutiny, the only interruptions being coughs and sniffles as he suffered with a springtime cold, he sat back and wheezed, 'I am astonished on two counts. First that the same man can have written both of these, one being so superior to the other, and second that such wonderful work,' here he tapped the manuscript of *The Winter's Tale* with a tapered fingernail, 'can have been done in such a short time. I didn't expect it to be delivered for six months or so. Are you sure you didn't have it hidden in a drawer?'

'No, my lord,' Shakespeare replied boldy. 'There is only fresh work in that play. It came out in a rush, as my friend here will witness.'

'I will never completely understand how you fellows work,' Cecil mused, wiping his long nose with a handkerchief while giving Miguel a scornful look. 'Don't you ever aspire to rise above being his assistant to writing something for yourself?'

Miguel smiled tightly and said he was happy to go along with things as they were, adding, 'To make a small contribution to good work is better than being wholly responsible for bad.'

'Very praiseworthy, perhaps, but beware of envy should it ever arise. People change, you know, suddenly they want different things, especially at your time of life.'

'He has learnt to share,' Shakespeare said sententiously, 'and I benefit greatly by his informed criticism and wide experience. We're always honest with each other.'

'May it ever be so,' Cecil said, handing them the plays with a twinkle of amusement. 'In this world two heads are always better than one. Well done. You have kept your bargain and I am delighted.' He reached out a hand and gave Shakespeare's a congratulatory shake. 'Once this play is seen, and that statue comes to life, our people will begin to open up again. Suspicion, cynicism, defeat, that sense of disappointment we have suffered since She died will start to evaporate. Change will begin. The Female principle will step down off its lonely pedestal and mix with the people. Perhaps Hermione can be made to look very like Her Majesty?'

'At what stage of life?' Shakespeare asked anxiously. 'I have constructed the queen with a true likeness in mind, flesh and blood.'

'In her mature beauty, as in the play, of course!' Cecil snapped. 'I'd expect even a man who'd just written a masterpiece in such short order to have enough wit left to follow the simple line of my reasoning. Do you know what we are about? What great matters you are part of?'

'My obedience . . . my duty, can be read in my play,' Shakespeare faltered. 'The broader issues I take on trust from your lordship.'

'The queen will be played by a boy,' Miguel pointed out in a polite undertone. 'The degree of verisimilitude will be governed by that.'

'Not this part!' Cecil retorted. 'Tradition will have to go out of the window. Get a woman to do it. A beautiful, intelligent, wise woman.'

'If we do that, they'll call her a whore,' Shakespeare said. 'We can't have the queen being called a whore.'

'They're all whores, aren't they?' Cecil stated, his humped shoulder twitching. 'We're not fighting a war against whoredom. That's too deep inside us all. We need to buy and sell our favours, and always will. What we seek is flexibility, a respect for the flux, without war, without pedantry, the blood-heat of woman warming all our statecraft. Queens have always been whores, bought and sold. The only one who wasn't . . .' he paused and a fond but sly smile came to his pale lips, 'we will call Hermione and leave it at that.'

*

At Dover Shakespeare was compelled by his inner creative power to start work again.

In the room they shared, Miguel wrote out what Shakespeare had dictated between mouthfuls during dinner and expressed amazement yet again at the improvement in his writing, then proceeded to carp over this word and that, making small alterations and shifts in sense.

Shakespeare protested, but he was now literally in Miguel's hands, having lost the use of his own. Theatrical luck, being the meddling bitch she is, plus the physiological influence of moral conscience entangled in the genius taken from Miguel, had induced the temporary resurgence of a dormant condition, Glover's Palsy, an ailment passed from father to son in the trade.

At the Globe, while praises were being heaped upon him by fellow actors and shareholders, deserved for the first time (or were they?), Shakespeare had had to stand with his hands hanging uselessly by his side, unable to respond to the effusions of his admirers while they declared *The Winter's Tale* to be one of the most beautiful pieces of theatre he'd ever made, though they had to admit to not being as taken with *Cymbeline*, even with Imogen being such a peach of a part, but only a lad would be playing that anyway.

Only Miguel could take from Shakespeare's mouth the fruit of Forman's magic and write it down in its proper form. As the verse rolled, and Miguel scribbled, a strange, disturbing, geminated music issued, and Shakespeare suffered intensely as his rival's pen did the work of writing down what was Miguel's in origin but Shakespeare's by sorcerous piracy.

But there was no other way of doing it. Connah was illiterate. George had made it clear he wanted no more to do with the theatre or writing of any sort, and Cade, who had joined the party as unpaid servant to get beyond the reach of the courts, was so eager to be involved with anything which smacked of the stage, he was as much use as a wild horse at a ploughing match.

Shakespeare's chagrin worsened when he discovered Miguel's emendations and rewriting, some of which involved the construction of entire scenes and new characters, showed there had been no diminishment in his own ability at all. He was rewriting to the same high standard Shakespeare was now writing.

Enraged, Shakespeare threw the beginning of the new play in the fire. Miguel was appalled at the waste, burning his hand as he tried to retrieve the pages. Immediately the Glover's Palsy went on the retreat. Within an hour Shakespeare had the use of his hands again and could hold a pen.

Before sailing from Dover, he wrote a letter of complaint to Doctor Forman, claiming compensation. The sum he demanded was double the fee originally paid for the transfer magic, 'For I had reason to look forward not only to my benefit, but to his loss. Until meeting you I had thought it impossible to empty a bottle yet leave it full. Also you have stirred up dangerous parts of my past to cripple me which destroys any gain I might have had. Add to this the humiliation and pest of impotence caused by sucking all the strength from my loins into my imagination, and you will be able to estimate how much your work has gone awry and how wronged I am by you.'

The letter, written on 25 August, 1610 was found in Forman's daybook after his death. There was no indication in his accounts of any repayment to Shakespeare, but we do have Forman's review of *The Winter's Tale* at the Globe, dated 15 May 1611. Attending the performance might have given him some professional satisfaction, but the play could also have been Shakespeare's revenge. Within a few months of seeing it Forman was dead of a fig-shaped ulcer which had its beginning about that time. The ulcer burst while he was rowing a boat on the Thames on 8 September, which was Saint Adrian's Day, a martyr whose severed hand performed miracles of healing.

★

As the merchant ship *Jupiter* left Dover harbour – George, Miguel, Shakespeare, Cade and Connah aboard – and sailed into the open sea, it was watched from the beach by the four queens who were sunning themselves, having long ago abandoned the court fashion of keeping their complexions pale. So much of their time had been spent in the gardens of Hatfield and the countryside around during the unusually hot spring weather England had enjoyed that year, they could now be mistaken for gypsies sitting on the shingle, their shawls thrown aside, their bracelets glittering, arms and heads bared.

The *Jupiter* moved slowly, having to tack because the light breeze was against them, blowing up the Channel from the south-west.

George could be seen standing in the stern, shading his eyes.

'Our darling boy's not been to sea before,' Anne croaked, stroking an egg-shaped black pebble she had found. 'It would teach him a thing or two if they could hit rough water before they get to the mouth of the Loire. That would strengthen his stomach so he can cope with some of those spicy French dishes they cook up over there.'

On the top of the white cliffs, the Night Riders stood with their horses, keeping an eye on the old women on the beach, having escorted them down from Hatfield the previous day.

They loved it when their work brought them to the coast where lighthouses could remind them of *Oruffu*, their long-necked giraffe god. A mood of meditation was on them now as they looked down at the four nut-brown old women chatting on the stony beach.

The brothers knew what the four queens would be talking about down there beside the blue-grey sea. The same as yesterday, and the day before, and the day before that; a topic they had gnawed on all the way down from Hertfordshire, their seamless parley humming along as the carriage wheels passed through the smooth ruts of the London to Dover road.

Men and the wickedness of men was the mental meat and drink of these weathered ladies.

To the Night Riders far above, picking up the cadences of the four queens' conversation on the warm, rising breeze, it was a chant they might have heard in their desert homeland, a moon-bound murmur from the womb.

★

George and Miguel were still on the stern of the *Jupiter*, their feet wider spread because the ship was beginning to take the swell.

Each had his own thoughts as the sight of Albion's bone-white cliffs diminished.

Miguel's thoughts were still back in Goadby Marwood with his love, her loveliness rising to his mind like a gull from the surface of the sea. George was already responding to the lure of adventure, the turbulence of the immediate past blown from his mind by the salt wind and the beat of the waves on the *Jupiter*'s bow.

Meanwhile, Shakespeare sat groaning in the wooden U of the ship's well, echoing the voice of the straining timbers, already regretting his departure from dry land, feeling the world shudder and roll unfamiliarly on its axis, his head pressed against a stanchion, trying to escape into sleep and dreams.

★

Further down the coast a fast schooner set sail from Winchelsea on a course to intercept the *Jupiter*, carrying coded instructions for Miguel from Cecil.

The orders were urgent, composed only that morning in a new cypher based on the 154 sonnets published under Shakespeare's name.

This code had been developed at Miguel's request, 'So new poetry can have practical use in our trade. I'm sure Will wouldn't grudge us. Also, the book isn't printed in France, I've unpacked his and left it behind. I carry the whole sequence in my head where he seemed to want it kept . . .' he had written, still smarting from the loss of his tenderest expressions of love for Mary, for George, even for himself, to Shakespeare's lust for fame.

When Miguel opened the letter it was a sequence of Roman and Arabic numbers which he could relate to the sonnets and then assemble the message. The first group was the sonnet number, the second the line, the third the word.

For a while he sat decoding in a corner with pencil and paper, then went to the *Jupiter*'s skipper and told him to alter course for Honfleur and the mouth of the River Seine.

CHAPTER SIXTEEN

THE *JUPITER* CAME into Honfleur on the evening tide. Shakespeare's seasickness had been so severe he was immediately transferred to Les Écorcheurs, a waterfront inn, and put to bed where he fell into a deep healing sleep.

On this spring night, his first in a foreign country, George was very excited. He wished the darkness away so he could see everything more clearly. Strolling round the harbour with Miguel and Cade he peered into every lit window, examined every craft which had a torch aboard, commented on all that was different from home: a purple headscarf; a basket on the gunwhale of a fishing boat deck; the shape of an anchor; the sound of the language swiftly spoken.

The tide was now half out, exposing mud banks that gleamed beneath the moon. Miguel, George and Cade came round the final corner of the sea wall to find a huge cargo barge lying slightly tipped to one side on the mud, connected to the harbour wall by a wide gangway of planks.

Musicians sat in the stern of the barge beneath an enormous flag with lilies which waved slowly in the offshore breeze. On the wide hatches of the vessel dancers rehearsed by torchlight to the commands of a tall, thin master who carried a long staff tipped with the brass head of an ape. Now and again he would rush forward and viciously prod one of the dancers as he called out moves.

Miguel stood behind George and Cade, looking over their heads. He was not watching the dancers, but had his eye on a man on a ladder, which was stuck in the mud, who was painting something across the broad stern of the barge. He was only part way through his work but that left undone had been sketched out in chalk. The whole read BARQUE 121, then, along a horizontal LIGNE COMPLET.

A musketeer officer who had been watching the dancers, broad-brimmed, plumed hat held over his chest, hand held up to shield his moustaches from the breeze, suddenly turned and looked across to where Miguel, George and Cade were standing.

The hand dropped to the hilt of his rapier. Slamming the hat on his head, he ran along the gangplank, drawing his blade.

'They don't like us snooping, perhaps?' Cade said fearfully, backing away into the darkness.

'Wait here,' Miguel ordered, drawing his sword and running to the end of the gangway.

As soon as steel clashed, the musicians stopped playing and the dancers ran to the side to see what was going on, ignoring the master's angry command to return and continue the rehearsal.

The fight went back and forth along the gangway. Everyone could appreciate two excellent swordsmen were pitted against each other. Soon the dancers began to shout encouragement and applaud so the master shrugged, gave up and watched also as the duel became more and more furious and acrobatic.

Suddenly, at a point where the blades were moving so fast they had become a blurred tangle of silver, both assailants stopped fighting, saluted, then held their weapons aside and hugged each other.

'Why have they stopped? Go on! Go on!' George cried, his eyes sparkling. 'Let's see who's best!'

'He is!' Miguel shouted, holding up his opponent's arm. 'Aren't you?'

'*Non! Jamais!*' came the reply. '*Tu es toujours le meilleur!*'

And they embraced again on the gangway, clapping each other on the back, then strolled arm in arm towards the quay, chatting warmly as they went.

They were so entranced by the joy of their reunion that when they reached the end of the gangway where George and Cade were waiting, no halt was made for introductions, no gap appeared in the happy stream of conversation, just a glance along the harbour towards the lights of Les Écorcheurs was given, and a mutual agreement registered that this was the place for them.

'Your Double Bologna Variation is still too loose,' the musketeer was saying as they moved off along the quay. 'Haven't you been doing that finger exercise I taught you with a ten pound ball and string? It was so easy to get inside your guard.'

'What a wonderful sight you are, Carache! Dyeing the hair, I notice, or is it a wig?' Miguel said, taking a handful and giving it a tug. 'Well, you've got it nailed on, obviously. And twenty vultures could roost side by side on that moustache, which is twice the size since last I saw you. Your boots were always too big in the thigh but now they'd kennel a pair of badgerhounds. A madrigal choir could sing in your trousers. You've got more froth at your throat than a brewer's vat. You smell like a Romanian brothel at rose harvest. What's going on?'

'It's sad to note how you haven't changed at all, Miguel,' came the reply. 'Isn't that the same old leather jacket you had twenty-five years ago? And didn't I give it to you? Oh, what a pleasure to behold your ugly face. One glance was enough. That could only have been you standing there, chin stuck out, waiting to be punched.'

And more in this vein, oblivious to George and Cade, and the whole world outside their old friendship, these comrades wandered back along the harbour wall towards Les Écorcheurs.

Behind them, George trailed in a stirred but disconsolate mood, indignant at being ignored and forgotten. He had never seen Miguel fight like that before. It had been a marvellous, beautiful spectacle and he wanted to say so, to congratulate him, to be at his side, to bask in his friendship. Now another aspect of those feelings emerged. The further Miguel and his friend went away, arms around each other, laughing, delighted to be together again, the stronger and darker the competitive urge became.

George looked back.

With the tide coming in again over the mudbanks, the sign-painter was hurrying to finish his work because the enormous vessel was beginning to shift as water buoyed its hull.

On the barge, the dancers were still rehearsing, adjusting to the movement beneath as they leapt in the torchlight, the musicians playing, dancing-master rapping the foot of his staff on the creaking timbers of barque 121 as she moved off the bottom.

The applause these people had given Miguel and the musketeer at the end of their superb display of fencing skills was suddenly the sweetest, purest, most desirable reward anyone could wish for.

★

Everyone at the inn knew the musketeer and it did not take long for him to win George over. His affability was as developed as his swordmanship and he was used to the strange ups and downs in the moods of athletic young men. As the wine flowed and tongues were loosened, Carache tried to palliate the youth's jealous anguish, for kindness was a quality which increased in pace with the musketeer's consumption of wine.

'Pah! Fighting for show isn't real war. It's play,' he murmured, holding one drooping tip of his moustache as he drank from a basin. 'When the time comes to be serious most of that fancy stuff is put to one side, isn't it, Miguel? The cleavers and axes come out.'

'I can't believe that,' George said sharply.

'Oh, can't you? Why is that?'

'All war is an expression of individual conflict. To excel in it is to excel in oneself.'

'Aha! I hear a teaching I recognize.' Carache smiled and looked across the table at Miguel. 'So, like your clothes, old friend, your philosophy has not changed either. Which surprises me for such an active, delving mind, but there we are.'

'You must be the best swordsman in France!' George

said passionately. 'I've never seen anything like what you did. I'm still in a whirl with it. Don't belittle your achievements for my sake, please!'

'My son, I am a long way from being the best,' Carache said with a sigh. 'If you want the best, look to your tutor here. He was playing with me, really.'

George shook his head violently, protesting he'd never seen men so evenly matched.

'That was his doing. He likes to create that impression until the critical moment, then watch out.' Carache paused, swirling the last of his wine round the basin, looking hard at Miguel with a knowing, good-natured smile. 'For all his goodness and wisdom, he strikes with the speed of a serpent, don't you, comrade?' When no answer was forthcoming he went on with a touch of mischief. 'Well, if your infernal modesty won't let you agree so I can convince this boy, there are dead men I can name who would. George, you have been very fortunate. Listen to him, not me. He is a master of life. Even if I'd found him begging in a ditch today, I'd have still made that claim for him. We have endured, suffered and survived together some terrible times and places. He has saved my life, and I his. In that I suppose we are equal, but he made something of what we saw and experienced in his mind. I didn't. I remain as ignorant as the day I was born!'

'No matter what you say, you are a master of the sword, sir!' George exclaimed, raising his cup. 'I salute you!'

Carache raised his basin with two hands above his head and let a dribble of wine pour onto George's brow, then kissed it away.

'By the blood and the wine, my boy, I accept the honour you do me,' he said, tossing the lees down his throat and rapping the table for more, 'but you must have realized by now what lies at the root of my charm: I've learned nothing from life, so I pose no threat to anyone. As for achievements and the high opinion in which I'm held, ask my colonel why he posted me to guard a bargeload of ballet dancers.'

CHAPTER SEVENTEEN

—◆—

WHEN GEORGE WOKE up next morning queasy and heavy-headed he went downstairs to find milk and bread to steady himself. As he passed through the inn's main public room on the way to the kitchen he found Miguel and Shakespeare writing silently at opposite ends of a long sunlit table, occasionally lifting their heads and glancing at each other to see who was working the fastest.

Knowing better than to offer a greeting, George waved vaguely and carried on in search of the breakfast he needed. In the kitchen he found Carache sitting amongst the skivvies, telling a rambling tale about a candle-maker's wife he knew in Paris. To judge by his red-eyed look he had not been to bed. This impression was aggravated by the length of time he was taking to drawl through the story.

George obtained a cup of milk and some hot flat bread and went towards the door leading to the public room, but Carache stuck out his boot and waved a warning finger.

'Mustn't go in there,' he slurred darkly. 'They've thrown me out already. They're both writing their wills.' Then he guffawed sonorously and bade George sit down at the table with him. 'Come and be bored with these poor creatures. Let them enjoy looking at you. How long have I been living here now, girls?'

The skivvies smiled and went about their work but George heard the cook mutter from the oven, 'Too long, by half.'

'Oh, they've got used to me,' Carache said with resignation. 'I can't fool anyone any more, can I, my nymphs? They've seen through all my disguises, heard my tales, never believed them, a single one, not for a minute, have you? But you're fresh off the boat, George. Eat your breakfast and show them the whiteness of your teeth and the delicacy of your manners, my boy.'

George complied, much as he would have preferred a quiet corner of the public room to himself. As Carache searched around in his memory for the point where he had left off in his story about the candle-maker's wife, Cade entered and sat down to join them.

'Are they still hard at it in there?' Carache asked, jerking his thumb towards the door.

Cade confirmed that this was so.

'What are they writing that's so important?'

'I asked that question,' Cade replied. 'Miguel said it was a recent experience they'd had in common. As no research is needed, they've decided Miguel should be allowed to try his hand at some writing – suggestions Master Shakespeare might consider using, if he thinks fit.'

'What the devil are you talking about?' Carache demanded with a touch of exasperation, plucking at the broken ends of his waxed moustache. 'I can't see Miguel taking the lead off that fellow in anything.'

'You'd have to be on the inside to understand,' Cade

said condescendingly. 'Miguel usually does the spade work, while Master Shakespeare makes the actual play.'

'And what is this play about?' Carache wanted to know.

'You must walk before you can run, sir,' Cade said, spreading goose fat on a crust cut from a large loaf. 'First you must ask: what was the starting point? That they have refused to tell me, though I have my opinions – which I'll keep to myself.'

Carache got up and went to the door, edging it open.

'Come and look,' he whispered.

Cade joined him, peering over his shoulder.

'They're both writing at the same speed, aren't they?' Carache said.

Cade agreed this was so.

'One licks his quill, pulls his hair, rubs his nose, shuffles his feet, groans, frowns, just like the man at the other end of the table, doesn't he?'

'Now you've pointed it out I see it's the case,' Cade breathed. 'My God, they've both just scratched their left ear lobes at exactly the same moment!'

'Take another look at Miguel. His expression. His posture. Is that a man merely passing on suggestions?'

Cade immediately confessed a greater engine seemed to be driving the erstwhile researcher and plot finder along.

Nodding slyly, Carache turned to grin at Cade, gently touching the schoolteacher's pale cheek with a finger. 'Oh, yes. I think something else is happening, something *you* don't understand,' Carache chuckled triumphantly, closing the door. 'You forget, I know Miguel from long ago. Miguel the poet! My dear, what you've been looking at is two men writing a play in competition with one another.'

Cade gasped and returned to the table.

'You hear that, George?' he said. 'Now there'll be trouble.'

'Who cares what they write?' came the reply as the youth's eyes flitted from skivvy to skivvy looking them up and down. 'It's all lies anyway.'

Carache went quiet, his eyes cast down, an occasional unhappy grunt disturbing his big chest beneath the layers of sash, jerkin and shirt. Then he began scratching the flagged floor with the end of his scabbard.

'Poor Miguel,' he sighed eventually. 'It's sad to see him living in this man Shakespeare's shadow. In the old days he was always writing, but he never did anything with it. Trying to stuff too much into every line was his downfall, everything he'd read, everything he'd felt, everything he'd thought, and it was always poetry, poetry, poetry. Now he's having a go at plays. After all these years he still hasn't given up.'

'In my discussions with Mr Shakespeare, records of which I'm hoping to make into a little book some time,' Cade ventured, 'I've often asked him why he writes. His reply is always the same. He says the act of writing is his homage to life.'

'But that's Miguel talking!' Carache cried, 'I can hear him saying it!'

Shakespeare appeared at the door, still pale from the effects of his *mal de mer*.

'Would you mind keeping the noise down?' he said frostily. 'We're trying to get some work done in there.'

Carache got to his feet and bowed very low, sweeping the flags with the brim of his hat.

'I'm glad to have a chance to properly present myself,' he said. 'You were in bed last night recuperating from the wildness of the sea when we arrived, and this morning I was given the toe of my old friend's boot before I could say a word.'

Shakespeare said he hoped the gentleman would not take the request for quiet amiss, but there was much to do before the party departed for Paris.

Carache then formally introduced himself and added, 'Rest assured, your honour, I am not one to impede the path of genius in any way. I will rise now and go to my duties, taking along my companions here for a breath of fresh air, leaving you to the writing of yet another masterpiece. May Apollo guide your pen, and bless you for looking so kindly on the aspirations of my dear old friend within!'

★

George and Cade walked back along the harbour to where barque 121 was afloat again. The hatches were open, and George was astonished to see a host of wretched, filthy prisoners in chains being disgorged along the gangway to shiver in the cold spring wind under the eyes of armed guards, allowed to take the air while the hold was cleaned out.

'My work calls,' Carache said. 'A noble business, for a soldier, as you can see.'

'Who are these unfortunates?' Cade asked, his eyes wide. 'Were they there last night?'

'And for a week of nights,' Carache replied grimly, 'with the dancers thumping overhead. But that's the least of their pains and tribulations. They're special prisoners from the colonies and plantations who've been brought over for the King's justice.'

'They don't look capable of standing upright, never mind committing crimes,' George remarked, his eyes going round the silent, huddled crowd under the pikes of the guards. 'What kind of thing have they done to be dragged so far?'

'I don't know how much Miguel has taught you,' Carache said, 'so I won't reveal too much in case it does you damage. Let it suffice to say these crimes are so extreme and unnatural the Church, the scientists and university men are interested.'

George stared at the prisoners with new eyes, his pulse quickening. Some of them were women, their eyes gleaming wild and mad beneath shaggy mats of hair.

'Give me an example of the kind of thing they've done,' George asked.

'I daren't,' Carache replied. 'It's time for me to get things moving. Go back to the inn, now. Forget these people. God has.'

George shivered, his imagination aroused by a strange, pleasurable fear of these unspeakable offences. He was about to press Carache to tell him more when he felt his elbow being gripped.

'We should go,' he heard Cade say, 'there's nothing for you here.' When George turned to look at him the man's pallor was that of parchment.

★

Without mentioning the prisoners, Miguel announced they would be travelling up the Seine to Paris with the ballet company aboard barque 121.

By the time they went down to the quay there were two small shallow-draughted galleys in the harbour with hawsers connected to the barge. Once the gangway was removed, the oars were plied and barque 121 was pulled out to enter the river navigation. As the low, heavy hulk of the craft swung into the current and the rowers increased their rate in the galleys, singing could be heard from the hold.

'Did you know there were people down there?' George asked Miguel with feigned innocence.

'I assumed there were from the stench,' Miguel murmured, keeping his eyes on the bank where a company of mounted soldiers walked their horses in pace with the barge's slow progress.

'Your friend Carache says they're criminals who've done things so bad they can't be imagined.'

'Then he doesn't know what he's talking about. If an act can be imagined, not only can it be performed, it inevitably has been.'

George was quashed, looking to Cade for support but the little man shifted himself away, not wishing to take part in the conversation.

'How can they find anything to sing about?'

'Because they've impressed you so much, I should think,' Miguel snapped. 'Go and talk to the dancers.'

'What have I got to say to people like that?'

'Try out your charm on them.'

'Why don't you just say you've got something on your mind?' George retorted. 'And if there're things you can't bring yourself to talk about, why not admit it?'

Miguel got up abruptly and went to sit on the other side of the barge.

In his mind were beasts, spirits, witches. Equally preoccupied, Shakespeare rocked backwards and forwards, sat with legs over the blunt bows, eyes on the murky water below, remembering.

Sailing before the storm in the Channel the previous morning, heading towards the mouth of the Seine, five miles from land the *Jupiter* had run into a wide mass of weed. All the rubbish and detritus of the French and English ports seemed to have been scoured out by the sea and deposited on this soft, stinking island.

*

Thousands of gulls and terns wheeled over the rotting vegetation. Shoals of fish grazed at its edges and beneath. Occasionally a seal or porpoise would surface covered with slime, then dive back to feed.

The master had not been able to spot the weed in the *Jupiter*'s path because of sea mist and the ship had sailed straight into it and become stuck. For three hours the crew and passengers had to work at freeing the vessel from the clinging filth, clearing a way through to open water.

While in a small dinghy going ahead of the ship and helping members of the crew push the dense weed aside with boat-hooks, Miguel and Cade were first to see what was holding the weed together. Like the hub of a wheel, a huge tangle of blackened timber lay half immersed, roped round a massive stake to which a half-eaten carcase of indeterminate origin was chained.

The whole island stank of corruption and death. The seabirds fluttered and fought around the torn cadaver, picking off crabs and leeches. As soon as Cade saw what was at the centre of the jam, he crumbled, lying in the bottom of the dinghy and crying.

Having found many strange things in the sea over the years, the sailors were not aghast at the discovery. They had a sanguine interest in anything that came from the French side of the water, where people were a lot odder than themselves, and they soon worked out who the victim was, calling to their mates to come to the side and see the curiosity.

Drawing the dinghy closer, the sailors scrambled over timbers for a closer look, Miguel with them.

Shakespeare had dragged himself to the side of the *Jupiter* for air, afflicted by the stench which doubled the effect of his seasickness. Leaning on George, he watched the ship nose closer to the place where Miguel and the sailors were prodding around the stake and what was chained to it.

As the sailors clambered around, testing the chains, poking the carcase, they shouted what they guessed was the origin of this fearsome uncleanness in the blue sea.

Three weeks ago, in the city of Rouen which stands on the Seine with six great bends between it and the sea, a woman had been condemned to death for witchcraft after cursing the cattle of a neighbour. When the fire was lit a great rainstorm had broken out and no matter how hard they tried, the executioners couldn't keep the fire from going out. The woman, who was a young widow called Agnes Rimault, continually cried out this was proof of her innocence. The enraged mob, refusing to be cheated of their entertainment, had pulled up the stake with Agnes chained to it and all the faggots for the fire, tied them in a great bundle, carried them down to the quayside, and thrown the lot into the swollen Seine.

From there Agnes had been carried through the six great bends to the sea. Then the tide had taken her out while scum, slime, weed and filth gathered round her. At some point on this journey she had given up the ghost.

Miguel reached over to touch the hair that still gleamed in its festoons of mud and weed.

'Do we ever get away from the audience?' he said half to himself, looking at the foetid, heaving crust of the island, the screaming birds, the plunging porpoises, then back to the head and its inhabitants of worm, slug and limpet. 'They followed you all the way out here.'

Before returning to the dinghy and the business of clearing a way through the weed, Miguel disgusted everyone on the ship by the close examination he gave the horrible remains. The *Jupiter*'s master asked Shakespeare whether his friend happened to be an anatomist, physician or coroner because he seemed to have such a deep interest.

When Miguel came back to the ship, no one would go near him until the ship was well clear of the weed and strong breezes had blown the reek of death and corruption away.

'I was ashamed of you,' George said to Miguel in

Shakespeare's hearing. 'Why did you have to paddle about in all that?'

'The birds, the fish, the seals do, for food,' Miguel replied evenly, his eye on the horizon. 'And sometimes the mind needs food, eh, Will?'

Shakespeare shuddered, wanting to remove himself, to go and sit in a corner out of earshot, but his new self insisted that he remain and listen.

'I wanted to see what they'd tied round her neck,' Miguel said, showing them all a piece of rag. 'You'll remember, George, when criminals are executed, there's always a label, a final insult, a justification in case the angel of the innocent is watching. Here, Will, use it to keep the sun off your head.'

Shakespeare snatched the rag off and stared at it. Stitched across in letters of black yarn was SYCORAX. He immediately knew the word, its origins and meanings, sensing the wild, indignant, invisible woman who'd only escaped the flames to be cast into the river like night-soil and now clawed to get out of the filth of death to be reborn on the page.

The courage of his new imagination terrified him. Clinging to Miguel's arm he said, 'I wonder if she knew the mystery they'd tied round her neck?'

But Miguel was already busy, scribbling and crossing out, breaking the word down on paper. 'Mm . . . I can get "Many Pray Christ" out of it – Syc – ora. The X is pre-Christian symbolism, possibly Egyptian, meaning four cardinal points of the compass, that word *cardinal* starts me thinking . . .'

'Make what you like of it,' Shakespeare had groaned

feverishly, his brow gleaming with sweat again. 'To me she's the unburnable witch I've lived with all my life!'

★

In a corner of the hold of barque 121 the Hollehtoh brothers finished the song from the Okavango swamps they'd been singing to cheer up their fellow prisoners and listened to the thunder of the dancers' feet as they ran to take rehearsal places on the hatches, summoned by Monsieur Depilato, dancing-master and choreographer of the ballet *Diana and the Ephesians* due to have its première at the Louvre when King Henri the Fourth could snatch a few hours to attend during his preparations for a new war.

It was Monsieur Depilato's big chance. After a lifetime of teaching and playing second fiddle to other choreographers at court, he had been astonished when Queen Marie sent word the King wished to see a new work before he went to battle – something to celebrate in the liveliest manner love and the joys of peace. She had chosen him to create it.

The subject she proposed was the story from the Acts of the Apostles in which Demetrius, the silversmith at the temple of the goddess Diana in Ephesus (which held a huge statue fallen from the skies), led a riot against Saint Paul's preaching of the gospel.

'When you think of it,' the senior Night Rider said, adjusting his iron collar, 'all George can learn from this is how not only every political act pivots upon an individual conception, but every phase of History does also.'

The other brothers cogitated, then one grumbled that Cecil was being over-elaborate this time.

'He's forgotten how simple and natural getting what you want can be,' he added, pushing away a foam-flecked white settler from the French Caribbean who was running up and down on his chain on all fours like a desperate dog.

'Why do we have to come down here with these people?' the senior brother said. 'Is it one of Cecil's punishments? Or a *reminder*?'

The other Night Riders whistled through their teeth at the thought.

'We know he is cruel to his enemies,' the senior brother continued carefully, 'but we are his friends. Perhaps he's trying to tell us something? You know how subtle he likes to think he is, and somewhere, deep down, I think he believes a hunchback has to be clever to prove himself the master of a Nature which has cheated him of any beauty.'

This took a much longer time for the brothers to turn over in their minds, during which they shifted higher up the curved hull to avoid the flood of urine pouring towards the sump as prisoners got rid of the brackish water they'd been given for breakfast.

When no further refinement or development of the insight into Cecil's strange personality was forthcoming, the senior brother asked for close attention.

'Ever since we stepped into this barge, I have been wondering: why? Why? Of all the things we've had to do for him, this is the worst. So, there must be a special reason, and I think I may have worked it out.'

The other brothers leant forward expectantly, shutting out the din of the other prisoners, their hands cupped to their ears.

The senior brother took a deep breath and said, 'You know I would never raise your hopes unreasonably. But, could it be possible, just possible, the hunch is trying to tell us that if we are successful and Henri is killed, Marie de Médicis takes over, King James falls in love with George and makes him *de facto* ruler of Britain, the SVQ controls all the royal houses of Europe, the Age of the Five Queens is ushered in to last for a thousand years, then the time might have come to let us go home?'

A silence enfolded the three brothers who were listening. After twenty years away from their native land they could not believe this.

'Why should you think such a wonderful thing?' one asked. 'It can only be a dream.'

The senior brother took all their hands in his. 'You remember the man who came to paint the code on the barge at Honfleur?' he asked.

'We do!' they answered.

'You know I am ever-watchful for signs,' the senior brother continued. 'When we were on the quayside taking the air, I saw him leave the ladder, climb down here with one of his brushes, and I thought to myself: A message in Cecilian mode could be forthcoming. Come over here and look.'

Climbing over prisoners he led his brothers to a place where a lantern glowed dimly.

Crudely painted upon the timbers in yellow and black paint was a giraffe.

'That is his promise, I'm sure,' the senior brother declared. 'If all goes well and western civilization is transformed according to plan, we will get our liberty.'

The cry of gladness from the hold was so loud, so ringing, so jubilant, so unexpected from such a pit of pain and human misery, the dancers lost their time and had to go back to the beginning of their sequence.

CHAPTER EIGHTEEN

AT ROUEN THE barge was moored overnight and church and university men came aboard to study the prisoners, having ridden from Paris to be first and get the pick of the bunch. Carache had to remain behind and supervise while Miguel, Shakespeare, Cade and George went into the town. When they returned there was a coach parked alongside the barge and Carache was conducting the last of the academics onto the quay.

'Where have they been living all their lives?' he said to Miguel as the last of them left, clutching sheaves of paper containing the results of his investigations. 'That fool is excited because he reckons to have met a genuine devil-worshipper at last – down in the hold! Some poor madman living on an active volcano in the Antilles who decided it must be God and threw all his children into the crater as sacrifices.'

'Whose fancy vehicle is that?' Miguel asked, indicating the coach with a coronet painted on the side of the door.

'Oh, a couple. I said I'd keep an eye on it for them. They're having dinner in the town,' Carache told him. 'They arrived some time ago.'

'Did you get a good look at the woman?'

'He keeps her well wrapped up. But I caught a glimpse of a very bright pair of eyes.'

'Levelled at you, no doubt,' Miguel muttered, 'you incorrigible old cockerel. They're the people we're here to meet.'

A tall man came along the quay with a slight figure close on his arm beneath a heel-length cloak. They went to the other side of the coach and got in.

'Did they give the password when they arrived?' Miguel demanded.

'Not to me,' Carache replied. 'When the coach came I was busy sorting out a wrangle amongst the priests and professors. I went over as soon as I could and apologized for keeping them waiting but they ignored me and went off without a word.'

'Didn't you realize who they were?' Miguel snapped in exasperation.

Carache shrugged apologetically. 'Perhaps those bright eyes drove everything else out of my mind,' he said with a grin.

'What about the coachman?'

'There was no coachman,' Carache replied. 'His grace had the reins and he'd been giving the horses plenty of whip. When I went up to the window I said as much, and remarked that the road to Rouen is a rough one but he just looked straight through me.'

'He should have given you the password! He could be anybody!'

'That is exactly who I am,' a lilting voice said, then the man came round the back of the coach, alone. 'Who is the collector of passwords here? There are so many of you.' He laughed, an odd, high, careless whinny.

This was the Prince Condé, once an effete, spineless fellow whose sole claim to respect was his royal blood. When King Henri fell in love with the exquisite fifteen-year-old Charlotte de Montmorency eighteen months ago he ordered this prince to marry her and live at Court in order to secure her as his mistress.

But Henri the Goat had created Condé the Lion. As soon as the wedding was over the Prince told Henri there would be no access to the girl. When the King erupted into frustrated rage, Condé fled with Charlotte to Brussels, the capital of the Spanish Netherlands, for protection, whereupon Henri demanded their arrest and return. When this was refused, Henri started making preparations for a war with many Trojan echoes.

He looked upon himself as Menelaus but he was, in truth, Paris, the Helen-thief who'd been thwarted.

So, in the fragile person of his child-wife, Prince Condé held the door open for the new Iliad and Odyssey where Helen could be the hero. By bringing Charlotte back into France he risked everything but, as Cecil had explained at a meeting in London, everything was at stake. With Charlotte as bait, a gorgeous brilliant fly to a ravenous trout, the last hornocratic king would be caught and slain and the future fulfilled.

On the quayside the prince gave the password Prospero with a brave, resolute smile, then looked toward the coach window as the shutters creaked open.

Charlotte looked out at the six men standing on the quayside, all of whom were gazing at her. Her husband's adoring look was something she was beginning to understand. The musketeer's bold, direct stare she had encountered many times; the knowing but sad eyes of the burly

Moorish-looking man with the gold earring and spots (ink) on his brow, she had met amongst older, heart-travelled poets; the sly sideways examination of the balding, dotted (ink), dimple-chinned fop she immediately recognized as that of a practised actor; then there was the small, shrinking man – his agitated fear of instinct confused her, but she knew him for a schoolteacher; which left the last pair of eyes, clear eyes beaming with the unequivocal delight of the young male who has spotted his natural mate.

★

Henri the Fourth, king of France, was known to have kept a running total of sixty-four mistresses during his life, not counting casual encounters.

A faunish man of lean, hard, supple body darkly brown like well-used leather, overflowing with laughing banter one minute, wild despair the next, he had twinkling eyes that could suddenly slide into a void of longing, and a big, hooked nose which he kept raised to the air like a hound scenting hot, fearful quarry. A slovenly dresser, a swearer and oath-maker – 'By the flaming shit of falling angels!' 'Go grease your arse with the rope-sweat of Judas!' are a couple attributed to him – he was, by instinct, a nomad. Somewhere in his ancestry there must have been a Moorish warrior who had been stranded in the Pyrenees after a raid. This would help account for the man's profoundly polygamic passion and his preference for life in the saddle.

On this first day of his life's final fortnight Henri is fifty-seven years of age. He has been king of the French for twelve years; the only one ever to come from the warm south. His animal vigour and tireless spirit are marvelled at by those who serve him. As his ministers and servants have fallen away into retirement or the tomb over the years, exhausted and amazed by his relentless energy, and his worn-out discarded mistresses faded into convents, arranged marriages or suicidal spirals, Henri has ridden on regardless, holding together his kingdom and its interbred brood of envious, squabbling nobles by sheer force of his onward motion.

Those Frenchmen who did not object to Henri's cavalier attitude to religion (he changed faith from Protestant to Catholic with the same practised ease he leapt from one saddle or mistress to another) loved him as an apostle of that Dionysian cult of appetite which has always been the underlying faith of those with Gallic blood. He was someone the unthinking could admire and look up to, driven by their desires, proud of their passions, having that out-of-doors, demandingly hungry spirit of country folk and, like them, he had no use for the empty, the heartless or the purely ornamental.

And even those who disapproved of Henri and his antics found it difficult to dislike him. When Cecil had to put in motion the might of the SVQ against this most powerful of enemies, he was full of regret. There was an allure about the man, a strength, a wholesomeness which had never altered from the days he had fought and – so it was claimed by detractors and supporters alike – made love to wolves and bears in the Pyrenees.

Having the crown had not changed him at all. Instead of being overawed by Paris and the north, and adjusting his style to fit the patterns of the monarchy's contorted, unnatural past, he had brought the restlessness of the wind from the peaks, the scent of sage from the river banks, the cries of untamed hawks, and the vigour of instinct with him. Although the great royal palaces were his and that was where state business was done, if ever he was forced to be physically within, he was metaphysically without.

At a time when government and kingship were being ushered into lush, overdone interiors, heavy with perfume and intellectual intimacies, this knight of the road in his weather-beaten garb and dented sword refused to enter the boudoir of the state and took his people, and the women who were his people, needing his fire, his energy and seed, into the woods to share a bivouac made of green boughs.

Henri le Vert Gallant, they called him. The brave, evergreen lover who never shed his leaves.

Cecil met Henri during his long diplomatic career and had been very taken with him, feeling a strong, brotherly link. The hunchback knew all about lust as power but his craving had been disciplined by knowledge and intelligent appraisal of the long-term future. Elizabeth had convinced him territorial war and religious strife were caused by his sex operating above the source of power rather than below. But when he talked to the French king he found him strangely deaf to the argument. Henri had listened to the Englishman's logic, then blown away the web of warnings with laughter.

For this reason, Cecil found him unsophisticated and had not been able to give a hopeful report to the five queens, which he would rather have done, had it been possible. After all, Henri and the hunchback shared many ideas and feelings. As satyrs, both worshipped women, but Henri had not progressed to Cecil's state of enlightenment. He could not identify the needy, childlike wisdom within his passion, or understand how it could be the better, more submissive part of himself, the channel by which the female could constantly re-create the vigour of changeful birth in the daily life of the new state.

To Henri, lust was simply the way he was made, his sin, his pride; but he would never argue it as a way forward.

But, because her submission was essential to him, the Bourbon could never accept woman as his superior in politics, even though she was god of his bed. He could not see the chains that bound him, nor the whip that drove him. His sexual servitude was too much of a mystery, and far too powerful, to be of any use.

Queen Elizabeth recruited Henri's queen, Marie de Médicis, into the SVQ, soon after her disastrous marriage to Henri in 1600. She was now part of the conspiracy to destroy her husband.

The thinking in the SVQ was a man so compelled by carnal imperatives as Henri could never achieve enlightenment or balance, even through the medium of a favourite planted by the SVQ. His need was too great, too all-consuming, to admit intellectual influence of any kind via the flesh. Within the arena of the body, no logic fought. The French king could not understand the vacuum inside himself, and this Marie de Médicis grimly confirmed. Although only a banker's niece whose dowry had been Henri's written-off debts to the Florentine usurer, she had been scorched by her husband's cruel licentiousness to such a degree she offered her first-born Louis to the SVQ so he would never become like his father. She undertook to nurse the youth towards a sensitive, delicate manhood after Henri's death, and train him up in SVQ ideals. Because Louis was now thirteen and on the edge of puberty, it was essential his father be removed before sexual manhood arrived with the risk another monstrous libertine would be let loose to prolong France's agony.

Cecil's defence of Henri had been the fellow unknowingly worshipped a feminine ideal to the point of mania but seemed incapable of bringing it to any reasoned awareness. For some reason he could not translate his relentless sexual craving into political terms.

In 1598 Cecil had travelled to Blois for a private meeting after the signing of the Treaty of Vervin expressly to persuade Henri to accept the new thinking and change his ways before it was too late, but had met with no success. The French king assumed Elizabeth's first minister to be arguing as he did simply because a woman had sent him – and Henri never *listened* to women.

Assassins driven by religious principle had been queuing to kill Henri ever since he came to the throne, and the whole enterprise was openly discussed, just as getting rid of Elizabeth had been in the 1580s and 1590s when the Catholic powers were after her blood, but so far Henri's luck had held. He took few measures to protect his person and often wandered abroad in the streets without disguise or bodyguards, even though the king before him had been stabbed to death by a religious fanatic. This demonstrated his contempt for those church-men who had made plotting his death almost an academic study. On both sides of the sectarian divide, books and treatises had been written on how to do it. He'd offended the Catholics by being sympathetic to Protestants and the Protestants by becoming a Catholic.

A consensus had arisen that for anyone to murder him was justified and necessary, taking Seneca's line that God enjoys nothing more than seeing the blood of a tyrant spilled. The tyranny they alleged was of instinct raping revealed truth. So far, those who had been thus encouraged to make attempts on Henri's life had failed and ended up in the grave themselves, or what was left of them after his ferocious vengeance.

But the methods of the Papacy, the Jesuits, and all the different forms of Protestant puritan were ramshackle compared to the hard-headed, highly motivated power of the SVQ. The members condemned Henri not because he had offended God but because he blocked progress towards the new age. Cecil, who loved the man in a fraternal way, had done his best to save him, pleading for more time to persuade and cajole. However, by the end of Elizabeth's reign she had had enough of her counterpart. In fourteen years she had seen no improvement in him. After her death she knew he would get worse as his physical powers failed. The French state would become even more an extension of his body than it had been, increasingly victim of his anxieties about impotence and death.

Before she died it had been agreed with the four queens that should Henri still be king, and unreformed, by the time George went to be Frenchified, the moment would have come to remove him from the throne.

By 1610 Marie de Médicis had done her work for the SVQ and more. Not only was Louis heavily dependent upon her but he had all the makings of the classic weak, subjective homosexual who, once his mother was dead, and his need for strength and friendship aroused, would be vulnerable to a favourite – thus further consolidating and guaranteeing the SVQ's front from the Mediterranean right up to the Rhine in the east, the Netherlands in the north, leaving only Britain and Ireland to be won over through George's influence on James.

This great union of Europe's four most powerful nations would be the heartland from which the conversion of the German and Italian states, the Scandinavian kingdoms, Russia and the Slav nations, would be achieved. Patchy progress had already been made in many petty courts and prince-bishoprics, but the federation had to be complete and in concert on policy and all principles of action before embarking upon the crusade against the supreme Lucifer, the misogynistic enemy above all enemies, its cloven feet still firmly on European soil in Greece and the Balkans – Islam.

*

King Henri is in Paris at the Louvre palace, that grim old fortress guarding the Seine. Women with fortunes on their backs in silks and jewels wander the state rooms and corridors hoping to catch his eye. They have been sent by marshalls and ministers desperate to avert this mad war by throwing the beauties of France at him, hoping one will stick and make him forget little Charlotte.

But the goat-king, the loving animal that will usually eat anything, has his head down, his horns presented in defence of his heart.

There is only one female in the world he wants, a

child nearly a quarter of his age who blisters his soul with youth and unutterable loveliness.

The Spanish ambassador is admitted to the royal presence. Henri glares at him as if he were a snake which has slithered over his foot. Ministers cringe at the ferocity of that look. It is hot, demented, beyond reason or conciliation. They are dealing with a man in the toils of insane lust. In private they have told the Spanish ambassador as much.

But the man has his duty to do.

'Sire, I am here on behalf of my master, the King of Spain, to ask why Your Majesty has brought into being such great armies, and whether they are to be directed against him?' the ambassador says after the formal courtesies are over.

Henri sucks air up his long, hooked nose. The nostrils flatten against the bony arch. The full Bourbon lower lip is insultingly thrust forward as he replies, 'If I had ever treated the King of Spain as badly as he has treated me then I would have cause to ask such a question.'

The ambassador is nonplussed by this evasiveness, unsure what to do. He asks for any specific case whereby the King of Spain has behaved badly towards the King of France.

'He has turned the Prince of Condé against me,' Henri declares in a loud, angry voice, 'and abducted his wife.'

There is a hiatus as the Spanish ambassador confers with his aides. He has to find a way of dealing with this see-saw of lies and evasiveness on the one hand and directness on the other, yet not enrage Henri any further if possible.

'Sire, how could my master turn a prince against you who threw himself on his mercy any more than Your Majesty would do if a foreign prince came and asked a similar favour?'

Answering evasiveness with evasiveness was not the right approach. Henri's face darkens. His eyes begin to bulge and redden. His ministers have begged him not to lose his temper but the breach in his patience is widening.

'I have had reports that opiates have been used on the Princess to reduce her resistance,' he growls, 'also she has appeared at feasts with archdukes in Brussels tied to a chair.'

'Sire, I must protest at this calumny,' the ambassador says calmly. 'The Princess has been given all honour and respect.'

Henri falls silent. His limbs stiffen. The thought of Charlotte running away from him is a murderous one. All of spring, all of summer, all of life seems to have gone with her. If he speaks now he will weep and rage and call out her name. The sham of kingship will fall away, leaving him naked, his goat-sceptre standing from his loins like a spear thrust into his vitals.

'Will Your Majesty say something?' the ambassador enquires, making an extra bow in case the time had come for the full force of Henri's wrath to fall upon him. 'Or may I ask once more whether it is against my master the King of Spain you have massed such powerful armies?'

Henri shifts on his throne. Into his eyes comes the wild glee of satyriasis, ancient and terrible. He feels the saddle between his thighs, the sword heavy and sticky with blood in his hand. The perfumed smoke of love's artillery fills his head and he speaks, 'On my neck and shoulder I put armour to avoid getting hurt,' he says with a curving, faunish smile, 'and I shall grasp my weapon and strike those who anger me!'

The Spanish ambassador knows all is lost. He would have preferred the onslaught of Henri's rage to this obtuseness. He holds his hands in the air in a gesture that is impolite, impolitic and impertinent, but it comes from the heart. There is going to be a war between France and Spain over a girl! It cannot even be discussed because it is this old man's unmentionable sin, one he refuses to confront except on the battlefield.

As the ambassador looks into Henri's reddened, slanted eyes he realizes the man is hoping for a musket ball to strike him dead and cut short his pain.

'What am I to tell my master, the King of Spain?' he asks sorrowfully.

'Anything you please,' comes the abrupt reply, and the audience is over.

*

'What are you reading, wife?' Sir Thomas says from the other side of the fire, fur robe gathered to keep out the cool draughts of a damp Leicestershire May.

'Love poems,' Mary replies, without looking up from the brass and ebony bound book on her knee.

'Ah, love,' Sir Thomas wheezes, wetting his lips. 'Oh, what a business.'

'Would you like me to read one aloud?'

'How kind,' Sir Thomas says, 'but no thank you.'

Sir Thomas stares into the fire again, asking himself why he has refused this offer of gentle entertainment.

Mary has a warm, musical voice. The poems are good –
he knows this because his own copy was delivered with
other volumes from his London bookseller a week ago
and he's already dipped into the verses in the privacy of
his chamber – and anything is better than the merciless
silence of country life.

Things have been so bad with him since the party left
for France and the manor went quiet that today, in order
to occupy his mind, he has been driven to working out how
many hours he has been alive – which came to 592,991;
then how many hours he had *not* been alive between the
time of the original creation of life in 4004 BC (by Biblical
calculation) and his birth, which amounted to 48,591,720
hours; and then how many hours he would not be alive
after his death. This final sum he could not do, and it had
depressed him. The end of the world had been calculated
by his old friend Doctor Forman to take place on the
final instant of the year 2001, but that holocaust would
not mean the destruction of Time. Time would march
on because the coming hours (and the past hours) are not
subject to any power of existence but their own. Sir
Thomas would not be alive after his death for an inordi-
nate amount of hours, and life away from London stuck
here in Goadby Marwood was a herald of this infinite
desolation.

Mary turns a page of the sonnets. Sir Thomas watches
her, hawk-like. He sees the sparkle of a tear, the movement of her breast. Signs of life in the desert!

'You're upset,' he murmurs. 'How poignant to be
able to weep with the poet. If only I could join you.'

It is mid-afternoon on a rainy day. Late the previous

night Mary had been in bed asleep when she was suddenly awakened by powerful sensations of the heart as George fell hopelessly in love with Charlotte in Rouen.

So strong and mysterious was this feeling, so sweet, so absolute, she had got out of bed and gone to the door of Sir Thomas' room, which was at the other end of the house, and stood outside for a while, with her hand on the latch. Then she had woken up, felt ridiculous and hurried back to her room, opened the shutters and lain all night listening to the rain.

'Will Shakespeare wrote them,' Mary tells Sir Thomas, noticing how he receives this information with a smile.

'If I'm not mistaken, that is the very book he tried to knock Miguel's brains out with,' he observes, chuckling. 'How you must miss them all. Never a dull moment. I'm sorry not to be as lively, but when they return in triumph, and George comes into his own, you'll have a life worth living again.'

Mary gives the old man an appreciative glance. She has found congenial qualities in the ex-diplomat in spite of his advanced years and being foisted upon her. He is not inclined to condemn, or be sensitive of his status. Also, she can talk to him about concerns of the heart.

'No matter how great he becomes, these years away from me will always be a loss,' she confesses, closing the book of sonnets.

Sir Thomas is quiet for a while. He leans down, picks up a piece of wood and tosses it to the back of the fire. Sparks fly up the chimney and smoke billows into the room for a few moments, making him cough.

'It can be quite trying living with a young man of that age, as well as a delight,' he says. 'They can be very selfish, vain and stupid. It may be you have been saved from suffering.'

Not many gaps remain in their confidences. Mary takes this as an offer to close one of those still open. She pauses out of respect, looks across at the huddled figure and wonders whether he wants to go further, or should she leave the enigma where it is.

'I was often hurt,' Sir Thomas declares, looking into the fire as it settles. 'I always seemed to take the blame for whatever went wrong. But we are as God made us, I used to argue.' He sinks his long, thinly bearded chin into the fur collar, then eyes Mary sharply. 'That is no less true of your son than it is of me, or any man, or woman. I cannot see how anyone can be blamed for what love does to them.'

'We have guidance,' Mary remarks, holding the book to her like a breastplate.

'From whom, may I ask?' Sir Thomas asks, his eyes even sharper.

Mary falters, sensing his indignation and soreness. She is on the point of mentioning the Church. Sir Thomas sees how the warmth and luminescence has gone from her. The warm tear has been retracted. He knows her well enough to guess her train of thought.

He could not resist attacking where she was so weak.

'What do priests know?' he asks smoothly. 'Anything?'

Mary stands up, carries the book to the table, puts it down, walks a little, sighs, returns, picks the book up again and goes towards the door.

Cecil had warned Sir Thomas not to get too close,

not to interfere, and not to ask too much of this woman.
She is Sir Thomas's third wife, he is her third husband.
At the time of the marriage contract there were areas of
each other already fenced off, sensitive, personal, already
declared unexplorable but many of these had been opened
up during their mutual loneliness.

Mary has drawn Sir Thomas into her world, past and
present. When he first married her he had not much real
interest in living, having been a public servant for too
long and finding retirement and the coolness of their
initial relationship boring. Now he feels the urge to
challenge her. To challenge everything that flows from
her existence, her ambitions, her powers and weaknesses.

'Those poems were never written by Shakespeare,' he
says. 'The man's a sly, conniving, superficial gypsy.'

Mary is so astonished the book drops from her hands
onto the floor.

'What can you mean?' she asks.

Sir Thomas gets out of his chair and picks the book
up, then sits at the table with it open in front of him.
'I've had a glance at these sonnets,' he says, tapping the
page, 'and the Jew's fingermarks are everywhere. Wandering blood, you see. No barriers. Wherever I travelled
– Muscovy, Constantinople, Stockholm, Baghdad,
Algiers, everywhere! – I came across the kind of man
who would write these. Miguel is your heart's choice,
lady. He has depths Shakespeare would drown in.'

Mary cannot speak. The strangest gladness has gripped
her. Without knowing it she has always found something
the wrong way round in the relationship between her
two lovers. Sir Thomas's revelation, coming at a time

when George's far-off young love has filled her with freshness and clarity of purpose, makes sense.

'Not that I like Miguel better than the other fellow,' Sir Thomas adds. 'The Jew's too serious and proud for me. He knows too much and he hides the most part of what he knows, including the secret of the Void, which is his hiding place.'

'I can't follow what you're saying,' Mary said, with a laugh. 'It's not like you to talk in riddles.'

'In the old days I never spoke any other way. That's why I prefer the actor!' Sir Thomas continued waggishly. 'I'm easier with his type and have often let them rule my life. But you mustn't let such fellows get away with too much.'

'You've made me much happier than I thought you would,' Mary says, 'except for this constant harping on the Void, in which I refuse to believe.'

'I'm pleased to have made you happy, which is something I rarely achieve. As for the Void, well, it may only be your Lord in his night-cloak.'

Sir Thomas hears the rain dash against the window and leaves the table, heading back to the cheerful warmth of the fire, still speaking as he goes, 'What I don't understand is how Shakespeare can have such a hold over Miguel when he's got half the man's wits. I say the Jew wrote those poems. By what means were they printed under Shakespeare's name? Does the Jew put no value on himself? Are not sufferings precious? They determine the self. Can you explain it?'

'Does it matter who writes them as long as they are written?'

Sir Thomas is lowering himself into his chair, a careful process because he is tormented by haemorrhoids. With arms braced, joints quivering, mind prepared for the impact of pain, he looks across at her.

'If you've never thought that before,' he says, easing himself onto the cushion, 'I'm very glad I brought the subject up.'

★

The four queens have observed the mounting elaboration of Robert Cecil's methods with concern. Sympathetically aware of the empathic Ricardian hunch-belly, the demon child on the male shoulder, recognizing his goblinesque lechery, acknowledging his dionysian devotion to the Female void he must fill, they treat him as the arch-runt, the last of the all-male litter butting and shoving at the sow of History, that mother studded with a million teats.

Once the change comes about, Cecil will have sucked all he can and will drop off. Death by starvation of the spirit will follow because the adventure will be over. Incompleteness is what the Lord Treasurer really worships. It was this maidenly quality he always adored in Elizabeth and what beams out to him from every picture, statue and tapestry of her he puts in the great E-shaped palace which has now risen to roof height.

These days the hunch aches against his backbone, as he walks around his new palace and its gardens, overseeing the planting of vines – a gift from Marie de Médicis – or the installation of furniture which includes an S-shaped bed with a reverse V-shaped canopy and two Q-shaped chamber pots, one for each bend in the bed.

Today he has invited the four queens to an unveiling

in the Long Gallery. They sit at a table in front of the shrouded statue sipping a *vina da meditatzione*, a gift from the ambassador of the Kingdom of the Two Sicilies.

'Is it too early for news of George?' Catherine asks.

Cecil recounts the information brought in sonnet code by a pigeon from Paris only that morning.

'They're in Paris. As yet our boy is not aware he's the one who must strike the blow,' he adds, 'but he'll suspect by now that manhood can only be conferred upon an initiate by the shedding of blood, and he'll work out how it's all for his own good, I'm sure. Otherwise, he's not for us, is he, *mesdames*?'

'And Charlotte?' Jane wanted to know.

Cecil smiled, ringing his glass with a fingernail.

'One look was enough, his mother says. She felt it.'

Cecil then put down his glass and disappeared under the sheet which lay over the statue.

'No prizes for guessing what's under there,' Mary Stuart said as the fabric shook. Looking up and down the Long Gallery at the queue of images of her old rival she continued caustically. 'He never seems to tire of her like I did.'

'Oh, be quiet, you and your sour grapes!' Ann croaked. 'It's only because every man who gave you his heart ended up with a knife in it!'

Further altercation was cut short when Cecil emerged from under the sheet, eyes shining like a child ready to spring a surprise.

'I have a minute to say a few words of thanks,' he said, straightening his black velvet doublet which was zigzagged in silver. 'Two craftsmen have combined to make this masterpiece – Hans Kloof of Cologne, the world's best horologiographer, and our own man, that great teller of Time, William Shakespeare, whose play *The Winter's Tale* not only inspired the nation to believe She never died and would return, but also provided the original idea. Now, if we sit and wait for the clocks to strike, you will see a wonder.'

His eye ran along the Long Gallery and he held a finger to his lips. As soon as all the clocks began to chime the fifth hour of the afternoon, seventeenth of the day, he pulled the sheet away to reveal a life-size model of Elizabeth studded with jewels, latticed and barred with gold and silver, eyelids already fluttering, prim mouth widening into an ivory smile, enamel and crystal eyes flickering from side to side as she stepped down off her pedestal, announced in ringing tones that the hour had come, then lurched off down the Long Gallery singing, 'Sigh no more, ladies'.

CHAPTER NINETEEN

MIGUEL HAD SELECTED magic, where all things are possible and nothing is what it seems, to be the fountainhead of the play he was now writing. Overwhelmed by the grandeur and imaginative richness of the Lord Treasurer's conspiracy – the preparation, the knowledge of character, the attention to detail, the sheer machinery had finally forced him to break into the sphere of the necromancer and the world of spirits.

The swirling cloud of supernatural force in which the new play was forming reminded him of a duststorm of mica he had ridden through in Anatolia many years ago. The cloud of tiny particles had formed glimmering shapes in the air which appeared solid. Once entered, the cloud assumed further forms, never the same, always in motion, seeming to deprive the earth of its solidity and make it a transcendental place.

Now, sitting in a light fog outside a tavern on the right bank of the Seine opposite the Île de la Cité, Miguel watched the great church of Notre Dame appearing and disappearing as the wind blew fog from the river to surround the pale towers.

All's in place, he told himself. I have a few days to

rest, think, write a little, walk around, prepare for the chaos after the event, and the escape.

When George was told he must join the cast of *Diana of the Ephesians*, the youth had gone like a lamb. Wherever Charlotte was, George would go. She was to dance the nymph who had the goddess' pet *Tragelaph*, the mythical goat-stag, on a leash, while George was to play the beast itself, wearing a head armed with two sixteen-point horns, each point a loaded pistol.

With this battery of thirty-two shots, all triggered simultaneously from inside the Tragelaph, George would have the firepower of a squad of infantry. At short distance he would not be able to miss Henri.

As he watched the moving surface of the Seine, the weed-island floated back into Miguel's mind. He tried to think about something else. There was no stage play for him there. He'd been seduced by the horror, the stench, the corruption: all the stuff of plays, but no theme. But for there to be corruption there must have been something natural to corrupt – a paradise, perhaps?

'Adam and Eve and Pinchmetight went down to the river to bathe/Adam and Eve were drowned, who d'you think was saved?' Shakespeare said, coming up behind Miguel and giving his arm a tweak.

'I asked you not to follow me again.'

Shakespeare sat down beside him. 'Beware of sloth, but not of dreams,' he said cheerily. 'I've made progress. Want to hear it?'

'You'd best keep it to yourself or I might be tempted,' Miguel replied. 'Always on the look-out for something to lift.'

'Have you got anything more on paper? Or are you floundering around?'

'I'm floundering around.'

'Actually, I lied. I'm not writing anything either.' Shakespeare paused and cocked his head to see if the admission had any effect. When Miguel's expression remained unchanged, Shakespeare slapped his knee and exclaimed, 'The thing is writing itself. I go to sleep. I dream in verse. All I do in the morning is put it on paper.'

But Miguel's attention was elsewhere. A rowing boat had set out onto the stream from an overhanging house at the northern end of the island.

'Perhaps, for old times' sake, I should let you into my secret,' Shakespeare chattered on. 'First, find a historical handhold. Keep your eyes open and your ear to the ground. I think you might have been a bit slapdash lately. Are you missing Mary? The other work getting you down? Unable to concentrate? Why don't you put the play aside for a while? You can catch up later.'

The rowing boat was being turned by the current. One of the three people in it was yelling at the others in the confusion.

'They can't row, and they don't know the river,' a voice said behind Miguel and Shakespeare.

They looked round and saw a sturdy, oldish man with bushy white hair easing himself into a chair between them.

'If they go on like that I'll have to meet them somewhere downstream,' the man said. 'They should have told me not one of them can handle a boat.'

'They're friends of yours?' Miguel asked.

'Oh, no. Only servants,' came the reply. 'And what a

set of rascals they are!' The stranger laughed affectionately, watching the boat nearly capsize as the people changed places. 'But what would I do without them? They provide me with endless amusement.'

'You're not afraid they'll drown?'

'They couldn't manage that. Not one of them has enough real substance to sink. If they fall out of the boat they'll just float along with all the other rubbish in the river.'

Miguel smiled. The urbanity of the stranger was the perfect antidote to Shakespeare. He offered to buy the man a drink, which was accepted.

'Keeping useless servants is a very good way of avoiding too much self-criticism,' the stranger said genially. 'I can look after myself far better than they can, but without them I would not *be* myself, if you follow.'

The boat was now in mid-stream directly opposite. Miguel could see one of the three was a tall, rangy woman with waist-length red hair widely streaked with grey. Another was an apish figure with arms so long he couldn't manage the oar, and the third was a slip of a lad with a pointed, ethereal face.

'You have to pull together, you pair of cretins!' the woman shouted. 'Can't you work that out for yourselves? I'd rather share a boat with a herd of calving cows than you two! Give me that!' she yelled at the ape youth, slapping him round the head.

'If you don't mind me asking,' Miguel said. 'What function does she have in your household?'

The stranger smiled fondly as the woman seized the single oar the two youths had been passing between them and thrust it through a rowlock on the stern.

'You see, she's the one who's finally worked out why there's only one. The other two would never have done that. She has more intelligence than both of them put together. Also, she's a terrible shrew and hater of the male sex, which is a great advantage.'

'Having someone like that as a servant must give you headaches,' Shakespeare remarked, watching the woman as she swung the oar wildly from side to side, 'and she looks strong.'

'She is! She can knock me down with a single blow! Which is another advantage. You see, friends, we men must be constantly demeaned so we can study *in fear* what we must do for our place in the world. My wonderful Sighile has my permission to rail at me any time, and occasionally administer a beating when I need it.'

The boat was nearing the stone steps leading up to the tavern terrace, the woman working furiously at the oar while the two odd youths cowered beneath her arm.

'I have the two idiot males so she can keep her tongue razor-sharp and I can have the occasional respite,' the stranger said. 'Observe the power of the woman. How her eyes flash! How her body bends and shakes with inner fury. Don't you think she's beautiful? What man could turn away from her?'

Out of the corner of his eye Miguel saw Shakespeare sneaking a folded paper and pencil out of his pocket and begin writing in full view of the stranger. At this display of gross bad manners, something snapped. He suddenly wanted to frighten the stranger off.

'You speak of her very warmly,' Miguel said forcefully. 'She must be your . . .' he left a gap which could be insulting, then continued '. . . call it what you will.'

'What will Will call it? Paramour, of course!' the
stranger replied, laughing. 'Write that down, scribe! Of
course she is. She's my whore, my wife, my everything.
She has to be. How can a man enjoy being attacked by a
woman who doesn't know him intimately? It would be
quite pointless. She must have all his weaknesses at her
fingertips. We must talk.'

He got up and ran down the steps to hold the boat
and give Sighile his hand as she stepped out. As she did
so he took the oar from her and threw it at the two
youths, then put his foot on the bow and pushed the boat
back into the current.

'Learn how to do it, you two, and don't come back
until you have!' he called. 'Take it in turns.'

The youths immediately began to howl with fear but
the stranger turned his back on them and they were swept
downstream, fighting to get the oar back into the rowlock. As they went, Sighile shook her fist and bellowed,
'There's more use in limp celery than the pair of you.
What would have happened if I'd not been quick on the
uptake? We'd all have been drowned, so we would!'

The stranger then took her white, freckled hand and
led her to the top of the steps and made the introductions.

'My darling, these are the gentlemen the Hollehtoh
brothers have told us so much about,' he said. 'They are
working for the cause, but you should be forewarned:
everything we say will be recorded.'

*

Padraigh Rooney was the stranger's name. He had been
living in France for some years, having come in the first
place as retainer of Hugh O'Neill, the Earl of Tyrone,

who fled his native land after the plantation of Ulster. Soon tiring of the Earl's feckless ways, Padraigh had left his service and sought employment in Paris where his convincing tongue and enquiring mind might have a value.

Within two years he had been given the chair of Theology at the Sorbonne, a university currently in the doldrums because all the intellectual activity inside Roman Catholicism was going on in Rome and Madrid. French religious thought was a broken vessel lying around the feet of Henri the Unfaithful.

But Padraigh's mind had not been going down a speculative drain during these dog days of the faculty. After meeting with Sighile, he had formulated ideas which chimed with those of the SVQ and they had sought him out.

'If you hadn't had so much on your mind, you'd remember me from Rouen,' he told Miguel and Shakespeare as they dined inside the tavern. 'I came aboard the barge with all the other academics, but I was in my cap and robes and you had your hands full with Prince Condé and Charlotte, that beautiful little pearl. You know she's a complete dunce, I assume? Bear that in mind. You can't expect too much from her. She just *is*. But, to business now.'

A waiter came to the table and said two drenched youths were at the door insisting their parents were inside.

'Will you look after that for me, mavourneen?' Padraigh sighed. 'I have to get everything sorted out with Will and Miguel here. We haven't got long. Make them wait in the street till we've finished.'

Sighile tossed her head indignantly, muttered about

women always having to do the dirty work, and stalked off.

'We thought they'd take longer to get here,' Padraigh told Miguel and Shakespeare with an apologetic shrug. 'I don't want to discuss anything with them around. They don't know how to keep their mouths shut. Now, while she's out, so as not to upset her because they were lovers, I have to tell you Lieutenant Carache is dead.'

Miguel put his face in his hands.

'I respect your grief for your old comrade, but I must press on,' Padraigh said, stirring his soup. 'They made it look like suicide, but what musketeer would hang himself? Blow his brains out, yes, fall on his rapier, perhaps, but not the noose, and not with an Easter candle up his rectum.'

'Poor Carache. I'll have to kill whoever did it,' Miguel stated solemnly. 'It's my duty. He didn't want to help us until I asked him to.'

'Lord Cecil says you mustn't think about revenge, he'll look after the Howards, who were behind it. They have someone over here,' Padraigh warned. 'As for your friend doing you a favour, that was never the case. King Henri took Carache's wife five years ago, used her, then tossed her aside. It broke the woman's heart. One day she was a kind of queen, the next, a shell. Carache offered to take her back but she wouldn't have anything to do with him. Instead, she loitered around the Court, followed Henri on foot everywhere he went, then died on the roadside somewhere.'

'Cecil's sure it was the Howards?' Miguel asked.

'I can tell you that much. There're so many of them, what's the difference? And the Jesuit Molinists and Bauists and Knights of Calatrava have probably got a hand in it, but what does it matter? None of them are in Cecil's class. Those people from the colonies you travelled up with had more to offer than our opposition. Did any of them tell you about voodoo and Baron Samedi? Now, there's a force I wouldn't like to come up against without having the right weapons to hand.'

Miguel was astonished to see Shakespeare scribbling on his white linen napkin.

'What's the matter with you?' he cried in a passion. 'A man is dead and all you can do is write it down!'

Shakespeare looked up, his brow furrowed. 'What man?' he muttered, then went back to what he was writing.

Sighile returned to the table followed by the two youths.

'You can just stand there and wait till I've finished my dinner!' she snarled, sitting down. 'My life isn't easy, you'll appreciate. I have to do everything he can't be bothered with and that includes his own children.'

'How two such gifted and intelligent people as ourselves brought these two boobies into the world escapes me,' Padraigh said, eying the youths with disfavour as they dripped and shivered, staring hungrily at the bowls of soup. 'Here, you can split that between you.'

As bread their father tossed to them was torn in half and wolfed down, they were told to stand by the wall and wait until the meal was finished.

'Apart from the plot, and a grand plot it is,' Sighile said later on as she deftly dismembered a chicken, 'would anything else bring you to this old piss-pot of a city? Paris is all washed up. Even when the deed is done it will take years for the French to come round to the proper way of thinking. As soon as it's all over we're putting the boys into an orphanage and moving on to somewhere more lively.'

★

Henri had been forced to meet his detested queen. By law they must exchange witnessed signatures for the articles of regency which will apply while he is out of the country fighting the war.

After all is signed Marie de Médicis begs to speak to him privately. Unwillingly he agrees, but asks her to keep it short because he has much to do. When the ministers have been dismissed and they are alone, Marie goes down on creaking knees and begs forgiveness for being a bad wife.

'Until now I have not understood you,' she says. 'It has taken a child to show me how wrong I've been. At first, when she approached me woman to woman, I was suspicious . . .'

'This is one of your crude intrigues,' Henri snorts.

'For all your philandering,' Marie sighs, 'how little you know of women. Will you listen or shall I go?'

Henri knows there is an entire regiment of artillery outside, waiting for inspection. He will take them to pieces, break open their charges, stare down the muzzles of their cannon, weigh shot, canister and ball in his hands, check horse and harness, needing to know his troops can batter down the walls of Brussels to get at Charlotte.

'Be quick,' he says tersely. 'No more games, madam.'

'The child is afraid of you.'

'She would be better advised to be afraid of *you*!'

'Not any more. You must have beauty or life is meaningless. That much I realize. At first it was humiliating, now . . .' She smiles, beckoning him to give his hand and help her rise, which he does. 'You don't know how to behave to a girl so young, so delicate and fine. You've terrified the poor little hind with your ranting and roaring.'

Henri's beard quivers. He closes his eyes. A rough, unfamiliar sound comes from somewhere deep inside his chest. It is the first time his wife has ever heard him laugh.

'Now you will show me letters she has written you,' he says eventually, 'failing that there will be talk of secret meetings.'

'I have no letters. There have been no secret meetings. The truth may sound less straightforward but then it's generally more difficult to believe, I find.'

Henri looks at her with undisguised dislike, saying, 'I will walk up and down the room five times. If you haven't told all the lies you need by then, I'll leave.'

He begins to walk. Marie speaks swiftly and steadily, watching his feet.

'She has been brought to Paris by a young English lord who, like many of his countrymen, is disgusted by the conduct of his own king, who practises sodomy. This youth prefers to take his example from you, and his admiration is great. A man, Shakespeare, accompanies him, and a Jew who is his bursar. This Shakespeare writes plays which do very well in London. You might even have heard of him.'

Henri waves the suggestion aside. He does not spend

any time keeping up with what's happening in the theatre anywhere these days.

Marie flows on, noticing Henri is now walking more slowly. She has got his interest.

'These English people are travelling for the young man's education. They met Charlotte in Brussels and she asked them to smuggle her back to Paris to be with you. As you rightly guessed, Prince Condé took her away against her will. But she is frightened of the violence with which you pursue her, and the thought of this war with thousands dying because of her is heinous to the poor girl. What she needs is proof you can be gentle, then she will be yours.'

Henri has stopped walking. From where he stands the artillery regiment is visible through the window, drawn up with their great seige cannon and mortars. Before nightfall they will rumble north through the streets of Paris.

Brussels might fall to the guns, but will they win the heart of the girl? he asks himself.

He sits down.

'What a fool you take me for,' he murmurs. 'How were you persuaded to put this farago of nonsense to me? Have you no fear of what I might do?'

'At first I did,' Marie says, 'then I asked myself: what will he want to believe? That I desire his happiness? That she desires his happiness? We are both his women, as God in his all-seeing wisdom recognizes.'

Henri nods, straightens up, strokes his greying beard. Through his police, his government officers, his ambassadors, he has striven for this moment: a chance to be with his love without an army at his back, without her seeking to run even further away.

'If she is here then there's nothing to stop me tearing Paris apart to find her!' he says. 'And as for you, madam, I can have you racked till your great hams split and you tell me her whereabouts!'

His head sinks onto his chest and he groans at the emptiness of his threats. Glancing up he sees the triumph in Marie's eyes.

'No doubt the Princess Condé has been very precise about what I must do to be *gentle*,' he says with a smile. 'Give me my instructions.'

CHAPTER TWENTY

———◆———

GEORGE HAD NEVER felt so helpless. With Prince Condé attending every rehearsal at the amphitheatre in the forest at Fontainbleau, and escorting Charlotte to and from the riverside camp of the dance company, there was never any opportunity to approach her. All he could do was present himself to the best advantage by combing his hair, keeping tidy, walking well and dancing better than anyone else.

But he could only glance at Charlotte when her husband wasn't looking. Prince Condé had let it be known anyone staring at his wife would immediately answer for it.

The only person George could talk to about Charlotte was Cade, and his knowledge of love was a spring never unblocked. Miguel and Shakespeare were in Paris, forty miles away. Connah was with them. As far as George knew, Carache had returned to barracks in the capital once the colonial prisoners were delivered, leaving George and Cade to travel to Fontainbleau with the ballet company.

Cecil's anticipation had been uncanny. With the advice of Mary, the mother, the four queens and Marie de Médicis as a fifth, he had hit upon exactly the female who would disentangle George from any childhood bonds, free him from adolescence, incest, hero-worship and all other emotional dependencies, by deep enslavement of the heart – from which he would be liberated at the chosen time, created in the form of the perfectly balanced political lover.

Thus far, the plan was working. Charlotte on a stool in the woods beside her husband, dark eyes wide and limpid, lips apart, watching the dancers, drove George to near-madness. Lying under the saturated canvas of the tent at night he imagined her asleep in her husband's arms and rage gushed into his blood. What was an old man doing with such a jewel? The young are for each other. When would she look at him? When would she smile at him? When would she recognize his existence?

'Can't you sleep?' Cade asked.

'Shut up!' George snarled.

'You're making a lot of noise,' Cade protested. 'You're keeping me awake.'

'Then go and sleep outside.'

Cade apologized and shrank further down into his damp blankets. To be spoken to this way rankled with him, but he knew better than to attempt any rebuke. He would bide his time and carry on doing what he had to do. As an outsider, he had never really enjoyed Miguel's confidence; and his early adulation of Shakespeare had thinned under the tension they lived under.

All George would talk about was Charlotte, though Cade suspected he knew more about the reason they were in Fontainbleau with the dancers. Apart from incoherent erotic exclamations and somnambulistic onanism

David Pownall

(behaviour Cade was familiar with from his days as headmaster of a boys' boarding school), George had twice mentioned in his sleep the need for wadding in the ears to cut down the noise of thirty-two pistols fired simultaneously in a confined space. Because the Tragelaph they were using was only a rehearsal dummy, Cade had not yet worked out the technical significance of this.

When he had sent what information he had to the Howards via the English ambassador's pigeons the reply had been a chilling one for a man who'd undergone Cade's unique trial of death-in-life in Billesdon churchyard.

Dig deeper, was the message he got back.

*

Although the Howards had power and access to the King – Henry Howard, the man-loving Earl of Northampton, was Lord Privy Seal; Charles Howard, Earl of Nottingham, Lord High Admiral; Thomas Howard, Earl of Suffolk, Lord Chamberlain – as a family they were rooted in the shattered old male Catholicism which had staggered out of the Wars of the Roses swearing *never again*, then lain quiet while the Reformation raged.

Once the ruinous and bloody reign of Mary Tudor, their Catholic saviour, was over, the Howards had turned their backs on the idea of women in power for ever, but then had to face another one.

After sweating out the rule of Elizabeth, they moved quickly to welcome James and give unreserved support to Robert Carr, the favourite he'd brought down from Scotland, with all that relationship entailed.

In spite of Cecil's antipathy to them, the Howards

224

had felt safe. When they heard James airing his contempt for women – 'no other thing else but *irritamenta libidinis*' the monarch had declared – it had never occurred to the Howards how this might be sensibly opposed by people harking back to Elizabeth. She was dead. Life had moved on, in fact moved backwards to the days before the first experiment in female rule – their own Catholic catastrophe, Mary Tudor, daughter of the fateful union between Henry the Eighth and Catherine of Aragon.

It was a phase in English national politics best forgotten, except in the lesson it taught never to have a woman on the throne because she will only be ruled by her man, and her own heart will make that choice. In spite of the Howards' influence, Mary Tudor had been extreme and insane in her choice: Philip the Second of Spain, England's worst enemy.

It was something as entrenched, irremovable and simple as themselves that had stirred the dimness of the Howards. With great power and wealth in their hands, and their religion under royal protection in spite of Catholic plots earlier in James's reign, they could not believe Gloriana's power had not been interred in the tomb with her.

But the building of Hatfield, that declaration of regret for the passing of a famous time, could not be ignored. As the great red E went up and visitors, including the Howards and their clients, wandered through the rooms mocking yet marvelling at the hunchback Lord Treasurer's absurd devotion to his dead mistress, it began to dawn on them this was more than a manifestation of misshapen, mistaken, rather horrible love. Instead it could be a warning of opposition to James, a ruler already notorious for corruption, vice, weakness and superstition, as well as being an apostle of the Divine Right of Male Kings.

But the SVQ was close in its secrets. Even with the frenzied gossip, backbiting and espionage of the times, the sacred cause was not betrayed.

Cade had been recruited when *The Winter's Tale* had been delivered to Cecil in Whitehall on the way to France. A sharp-eyed Howard client whose son had been at the Billesdon school spotted him at Bankside and followed, having heard he was wanted for blasphemy.

That evening Cade was arrested by sheriff's officers and taken to the Bishop of London's prison where he let loose such a torrent of information about Jews, plays, beatings, boys, sheds and Cecil – whom he thought of as merely a patron of the theatre – that Thomas Howard, the Lord Chamberlain, had been notified.

Under the threat of being punished under the statute *De Heretico Camburendo* for his offence – which the encounter with the remains of Agnes on the weed-island had later served to reinforce – Cade had agreed to be a spy for the Howards. When a copy of Shakespeare's new play was filched and closely searched for symbolic messages and cryptic meanings by Ben Jonson acting for the Lord Chamberlain and the Master of the Revels, a shadowy connection between Hatfield and Queen Hermione's resurrection had emerged.

Since then, every incident, every contact, every move made by the party in France had been carefully watched, but to little useful effect so far because Cade's new masters could never conceive the vastness of the SVQ design.

What they did suspect, however, was a subterfuge whereby young George Villiers, Elizabeth's *page intime*, at the time of her death, was about to retract his testimony to the Privy Council concerning her last words and cast doubt on the legitimacy of King James's succession in favour of Henri the Goat, whom she had mentioned favourably during her reign because he was tolerant of all faiths, as she had tried to be.

This the Howards were determined to stop at all costs. A dream had become visible on their horizon, an ambition they had cherished for fifty years since the débâcle of Bloody Mary. The monarch, a *man*, was showing signs of a drift back to Roman Catholicism, the faith his martyred mother had baptised him into. This man already had a queen, Anne of Denmark, who had turned Catholic from conscience.

The reason James might change his faith could only be guessed at, as could the strength of his intention. But it was commonly speculated amongst the Howards that Catholicism, being the older, more knowing form of Christianity, had better access to absolution, plus subtler, more flexible methods of dealing with the sins of the mighty. The Pope could offer more comfort to a man of James's uncontrollable appetite than the silken but icy reproofs and veiled disgust of Puritanism.

★

Having fallen in love at first sight, and so completely and spontaneously, what little rational mind George possessed was knocked aside. When in Paris, Miguel had explained how the assassination was to work and what part George was to play in it. The lovesick youth had asked no questions but shown immediate enthusiasm for shooting Henri, who was a rival for Charlotte's love.

Once again Miguel had been awestruck at the depth of Cecil's planning.

George pleaded to be allowed to murder Prince Condé as well.

After rehearsals one evening, George, who'd had another day of frustration with Charlotte so near yet so far, was lying on his bed in the tent beside Cade. Some distance off, the dancers were singing around a bonfire. George didn't know where Charlotte went each night, but at the end of each day's work she walked away in the opposite direction to everyone else. Cade's opinion was she must be staying in the palace, but George thought otherwise.

'A fairy grotto is my guess,' he said, watching the black midges crowd into the seams of the canvas. 'Have you ever been in love?'

Cade admitted he had never had the need to possess another, only to be possessed by God, who had ignored him. 'But I have been ill with urges and emotions,' he added, 'so I have some idea what you're going through.'

'You can't have any idea at all,' George sighed. 'It's not about possession, but sharing your heart.'

'You know nothing about her,' Cade said. 'None of us have even heard her speak. She does her little dance with you on the leash, which you can't even see from inside that head they've got you in, then she sits down. How can you fall so deeply in love with someone you've only looked at?'

'That's where you're wrong,' George moaned. 'You don't feel the way she tugs that leash. I'm on the other end. I'm sure she's trying to tell me something.'

'If only Master Shakespeare could be here to help

you,' Cade sympathized. 'All these torments are present in exact reverse in *A Midsummer Night's Dream* when Titania falls in love with Bottom wearing the donkey's head.'

'Is anything real for you? Does anything ever happen which you haven't already read in a book?' George shouted. 'What I feel, this love of mine, is as real as the rain. Don't talk to me about scenes in plays!'

★

George woke the next morning feeling exhausted. Dreams had followed one after the other; violent dreams of loss, failure and inadequacy, always with Charlotte watching.

When he opened his eyes and returned to the true world, it struck him how much stronger he was in reality than in the dream. Here, he could do something to win Charlotte. Throw all caution, that enemy of love, aside.

Tell her!

Once the decision was made he felt much happier. But it had to be done immediately! Dressing quietly to avoid waking Cade, he ran through the lines of tents and along the path to the amphitheatre. From there he intended to go in the direction taken each day by Prince Condé and Charlotte after rehearsal.

As he ran he composed a declaration of love in French, harking back to a poem Miguel had taught him. Since being in France he had, so far, only used the language for commonplace everyday needs, eating, drinking, going, coming, but now those words began to glow in his mind, words he had not yet tasted.

It was the first hour of dawn, that magical time of

new light; a sun which has never arisen before, birdsong unheard until now, fresh webs and dew never crossed by human feet.

As George ran he drank in the pure air, wondering why he had waited so long to do this simple thing of telling Charlotte.

Soon he was in the forest. Ahead of him on the path five frightened deer leapt away, then he saw others springing into patches of light as he disturbed their feeding. When he reached the slope leading to the amphitheatre, which had been constructed on top of a swell in the forest floor, he saw what he knew must be a stag keeping pace with him on the other side of undergrowth, antlers held high.

George had done enough hunting to know the ways of deer. He had never seen a wild one behave in this manner before, staying so close to man.

A short distance before arriving at the amphitheatre, he stopped and watched as the four black men he had encountered on the night he ran away from Cade's Academy broke from the bushes and trotted through the entrance carrying a stag's head on a litter.

They seemed not to have noticed him. When he slipped through the entrance behind them and looked down, he saw Miguel and Shakespeare standing beside a blanket hung over a pole.

The Hollehtoh brothers put the litter down, then opened three small boxes and began fiddling inside the head, passing items to each other while Miguel and Shakespeare looked on. George realized this was the actual Tragelaph mechanism he was to wear, and its thirty-two pistols were being loaded.

He went back out of the entrance and ran round the perimeter wall. These doings were of no interest compared to his morning mission of love. He could catch up with everything later. Finding and telling Charlotte the news of his heart concerned him most.

*

Miguel blows a horn a few times to give the idea a hunting party is in the forest. The senior brother stuffs his ears with wadding and squeezes into the Tragelaph. Shakespeare takes ten paces, make a line on the boards with his heel, then backs the senior brother up to that mark.

'This is the recommended distance,' he says, 'now we'll get the angle of sight.'

Some pushing and twisting takes place. The senior brother now has the antlers lowered as if to charge a blanket draped over a wooden frame.

He shouts he cannot hold this position too long because of the weight of the device on his neck. He makes the point that thirty-two pistols, even small ones, tip the scales at well over seventy pounds.

'And George has a slender neck!' he adds. 'I think he'll need some kind of special harness.'

More discussion. It appears the Night Riders have already had considerable trouble with the only craftsman in Paris who is both gunsmith and theatrical prop maker. They do not wish to take the Tragelaph all the way back to the city for new work to be done on it, besides, Cecil decreed the man who made it had to die once delivery had been taken.

The senior brother is beginning to stagger and weave

about. The weight of the contraption is too much for him. He asks for help to remove it before he falls.

The Hollehtoh brothers see their leader lurching towards the box of gunpowder, about to step on loose balls left on the stage when the pistols were being loaded. The muzzle of the stag's head now sags to the ground as the senior brother's neck muscles finally give way under the strain.

Further along the forest path, with the rooftop of the palace of Fontainbleau in sight, George hears the thirty-two pistols go off, then the explosion.

Birds rise from the trees. Rabbits scamper. Squirrels pelt pop-eyed with fear along branches.

George runs on without breaking his stride. A thought struggles through to tell him the Tragelaph works, then this business of kings and death retreats into obscurity again, pushed back by Charlotte's little finger.

Having found no fairy grotto, he decides Cade is right. His love is somewhere ahead in that unreal palace, a house no one can *live* in, it is so full of rooms none of them have function or meaning.

He will break down the door of every one, daring with his unarmed body all guns, blades, bombs, engineered plots, machinations and peril-filled contrivances to find her and make his stupendous announcement.

★

Fontainbleau is empty. Not a guard, not a kitchen-boy, not a queen or a courtier. The palace stands with doors wide open, curtains blowing at the windows. Everyone has dropped what they were doing and gone. George finds pots on fires, baths full of water with towels laid out.

Swallows with the dust of Africa still on their wings have entered the silent spaces and fly about looking for places to build their nests.

At this time yesterday – the Ides of May – the palace had been poised to begin another day in its great round of royal life. The routine had started, the denizens awakened, the business commenced. Then news had come from Paris that King Henri had been stabbed to death in the street.

Before rushing out of the palace to take the northwest road to the capital, no one had thought to tell the dancers camped down by the river what had happened.

And brothers moving by secret ways with strange horned weapons had not heard because shunning all contact with the multitude had been deemed wise.

There had been a dance, a dance of death as Cecil had planned, a *pas de deux*, but its venue had been a crowded thoroughfare with waggons blocking the way as Henri took a short cut in his coach, hurrying to get out of the city towards Paradise. Someone had known he would go that way once his state business was finished in Paris. For a man impatient to go to where his love was hiding, it had been the obvious route.

A troubled, lonely man who had walked all the way from Angoulême; a poor man with his own knife from his own table had been told where to stand if he wanted to earn God's love and destroy the Antichrist.

George searched the palace from top to bottom for Charlotte and found no sign of her or any other living soul. Then he ran back to the amphitheatre to see if she had slipped past him and was already rehearsing with the others.

When he arrived he found Miguel, Shakespeare and the brothers gone.

The only life in the amphitheatre was a flock of geese which had alighted on the stage looking for food. They hissed and honked as they vyed with each other, open winged.

Shaking his fist at them in despair, George then raced back to the camp. When he broke through the trees and into the open he saw cows grazing in the field beside the river where the camp had been. Cade and the dancers had gone.

He was alone.

*

Whereas Fontainbleau stood empty that morning, Hatfield was full. A host of masons, gilders, plumbers, painters, glaziers, gardeners and assorted labourers came through the gates to begin a new stage in the building work, noise of their talk buzzing in the air. Of late the Lord Treasurer's debts had slowed down the completion of his temple to the Virgin Queen but recently fresh funds from Europe had liberated him from these strictures.

From the windows of the remaining portion of the Old Palace the four queens watched as the workmen trudged up the drive with their bags of tools.

In the evening there would be a masked ball. King James was to be there with his close men friends, the creatures of his heart. The four women would find time and opportunity to study the monarch closely.

If the arrangements were made intelligently, perhaps the king would even have speech with his mother without knowing it. She had a particular desire to be the first one to tell him a fellow king had been killed in the public street by a blow of steel, then watch it sink into his cold, woman-hating heart.

With masked guests dancing to music, images of Elizabeth everywhere the eye could see, Mary of Scots wanted to have her moment: she would remove her mask, look into his eyes and whisper, 'Murdered like your unmourned mother, and so many glad of it!!' before gliding away into the night like a black spirit.

CHAPTER TWENTY-ONE

———◆———

GEORGE BEGAN WALKING along the river towards the Paris road.

After an hour of desolation he heard a bell tolling. Increasing his pace, he came to a village. People were gathered outside the church. As soon as they saw George the cry went up 'Stranger! Murderer!' and they ran towards him.

The pursuit was short-lived. When George reached the cover of a nearby wood, the people gave up what seemed to be no more than sport and returned towards the church where the bell continued to toll.

Many coaches and carriages were on the road. Every one of them moving at speed as if lives were threatened. The cracking of whips and shouts urging horses on came clearly over the fields.

Where was Charlotte in all this confusion? Where had his love gone? Brought into his life by forces he did not comprehend, she had never spoken a word to him or recognized his existence. Now she had fled like a dream, taking the sane world – or what he had come to take for sanity – with her.

Disorientated, he walked away from the village, keeping his distance from anyone he saw ahead. There were no farmers in the fields, no children playing, no cross-country travellers on foot, only the occasional runner bearing the news of the king's death to out of the way places, news George did not know.

As evening approached and the last runner came through the last door, George became the only one in this landscape ignorant of what had happened in the rue de Ferronerie in Paris on the Ides of May.

By then he was lost.

★

It had struck James it would be amusing if he brought only men friends to Cecil's masked ball. Knowing the hunchback's reputation for womanizing, he extended the prank by putting all his companions in female dress at the beginning of the day, making them hunt with him in the chase, then bringing the whole blood-splashed company to the ball in their hunting garb. They stank as they stood on the steps, torches in hand, singing. When the doors were opened they rampaged into the house, prancing like deer.

'I've brought you *does* to love you,' James said as Cecil greeted him.

'My ablutions are all in working order,' Cecil replied smoothly. 'Would your hinds like to wash their behinds?'

James scowled. He had been working on his opening gambit all the way over to Hatfield. The need for a second to follow it up hadn't occurred to him. By now his frolicking, rough lads should have taken over, their tales of the bleeding, beaten deer, the plunging up to the armpits in search of the palpitating heart, the quivering

237

liver eaten raw, turning this tame ball into a wilder carnival. But the soiled, bloody band had returned to the door and were clustered round him like bullocks newly gelded.

'Tired, we are,' James said, fixing the Lord Treasurer with a lapidescent glare. 'If good manners have any say here in your over-big house, a man should be sat down with a drink in his hand.'

There was a pause in which only the music of viol and lute sounded from deeper in the house. Cecil raised his shoulder so the hunch lifted the back of his high collar.

'Forgive the smells and the dust and the newness of everything, sire,' he said, unruffled. 'As for the size of my house, everything I have is yours for the taking. Come, bring the gentlemen and be merry.'

Under the thousand eyes of Elizabeth, passing the four queens who stand in shadows, masked, the monarch lumbers goutily through to the ballroom with his deflated followers trailing in his wake, wondering why the hunch-back skipping ahead has such brave, impudent joy in him tonight.

★

Twenty-nine nuns in the house of the Poor Clares at Bericourt-le-Bosque had been on their way to Fontainbleau to petition their patron, Marie de Médicis, for additional funds to help fight an epidemic of smallpox amongst local farm workers when the Tragelaph had gone off. Prior to that, the sisters had heard the horn and assumed, as all were meant to, an early morning shooting party was out from the palace. Not wishing to face the banter of courtiers so close to the start of the day, they had taken refuge in the amphitheatre and found five wounded men, two white and three black, and fragments of a headless corpse. They had seen a seventh person, a fair-haired young man, who had come to the amphitheatre entrance, stared down at them and shaken his fist before vanishing into the forest, having mistaken them for a flock of geese.

When the Poor Clares sent two of their number to the palace for help, they returned with the news Fontainbleau was deserted. Nonetheless, the sisters proposed to take the gravely wounded men there rather than back to the convent, which was much further away. Miguel had begged them not to because it might cost him and his friends their lives and freedom.

The Poor Clares were in a quandary. These men were all foreigners, but their story of an accident with a pyrotechnical stage effect was credible. Many of the entertainers who came to the palace were from other countries. However, they could not understand why stage technicians should pay so heavily for what was only an accident.

Miguel explained how the troupe had originally come to France from England by invitation to create the firework display for the wedding of Prince Condé to Charlotte Montmorency. When the couple fled the country shortly afterwards, for reasons everyone knew, the troupe had been left stranded, and unpaid. They had lived hand to mouth for months and the work for the ballet was the first they had managed to get. However, they had been forced to lie about who they were because the king was arresting anyone who had a connection with

Prince Condé. With the money earned from *Diana and the Ephesians* the troupe would have travelled back to England, but this was now impossible because, once again, they were left unpaid.

The Poor Clares had heard about the great firework display at the nuptials, and they knew all the ins and outs of the Charlotte story. And these men were not only severely injured, poor and unable to help themselves, but also, indirectly, the victims of King Henri's sin of lust.

Making stretchers from their outer habits tied across tree boughs, the sisters carried the five men back through the forest to the convent, putting the wrapped-up fragments of the senior Hollehtoh brother on top of a large basket which held gifts of home-made mustard and jam they had been taking to Marie de Médicis.

When the senior brother was being prepared for burial in the tiny plot behind the convent that evening, many parts were found to be missing, including the head. The grief of the surviving brothers would have been softened to know this had lodged in a tree at the height a giraffe best likes to feed.

★

'My poor son is going through something terrible. I can feel it,' Mary said to Sir Thomas, holding her brow as they walked down the Long Gallery at Hatfield. 'I've never known anything as bad coming from him.'

Sir Thomas guided her to a seat by a window and sat her down, then took the other place himself.

'Is it love again?' he asked, mopping his brow with a starched white handkerchief.

'No, it is stronger, much stronger. How horrible!' She

held her head in her hands. 'I don't recognize this emotion!'

Their talk was interrupted by the King's companions in bloody gowns and wigs running down the Long Gallery pulling a carpet with James sitting on it, bellowing, 'Make way for Alexander the Great!'

'You see how that fool needs someone with a heart to guide him,' Mary said. 'If anyone is lost, it's him. I must find a quiet place where I can pray for my son to find the path.'

★

The other Mary had her moment. Late in the night when the torches were dying down and the guests slipping away, she found her son wandering drunkenly through an unfinished wing of the house, having kicked aside the barrier Cecil had erected.

He was with a youth who was holding him up, forced to listen as James droned through his deeds at the hunt. When Mary stepped out from behind scaffolding and told the youth she had important personal business with the King, James protested but was unable to keep the youth from leaving. Mary took the torch from him before he went.

'Madame, you take a risk with yourself,' James mumbled, sitting astride a carpenter's sawing-horse. 'How dare you interrupt my pleasure!'

She stepped closer to the figure swaying on the sawing-horse and held the torch closer to her face.

'Ugh!' James said, turning away.

'Who am I?' Mary asked.

Up till now drunkenness had buried his habitual fear

of assassination, but the unmistakable hatred in the old woman's eyes sharply brought it back.

'To me! To me!' he shouted, trying to bring his leg back over the sawing-horse and falling. 'Treachery here!'

There was no one to listen. The music was audible from below, a stately pavan.

'I'm not here to kill you, Jamie,' Mary said, crouching beside him. 'Have you no idea who I am?'

'State your business, and depart!' James whimpered, unable to meet her gaze. 'My friends will be looking for me. If you go now I'll let this insolence pass.'

'Who am I?' Mary said again.

James looked at her.

There was something in the eyes, a wildness, a fury, a suffering, a heat he remembered.

'Yes . . .' he faltered meekly. 'I have seen you, somewhere.'

'Oh, the Devil you have!' Mary snarled, seizing his beard. 'Then put a name to this woman you have seen SOMEWHERE.'

'Forgive me, but I cannot remember your name, madam,' James whimpered as his beard was held fast, with the torch perilously close.

'For one who claims to know so much about witches,' Mary hissed, 'you should be able to identify Hecate!'

James let out a low moan of terror and doubled up, his knees to his chin.

'Ah, now you're afeared at last,' Mary said. 'Lie there and listen, James Stuart. I have always watched over you. Hecate has been your guardian angel. Even with your storming and raging against our sisterhood, I have protected you. When others demanded your death, I said no.

He may be a fool. He may destroy our familiars in his courts, in his passions, but he loves us. I was right, wasn't I, little Jamie?'

There was a lost, terrified cry from the heap on the floor. With her hand in his beard, Mary shook his head for him.

'I thought so. Then all you have to do is keep loving me. You'll do that, won't you?'

This time James nodded of his own accord.

'I will do all you say!' he babbled.

'At some future time I will send someone, a beautiful messenger. He will be our go-between. Love and obey him in all things. If you defy him, we will destroy you and your eternal soul.'

'I will do anything you ask . . .' James groaned, 'anything at all.'

'A wise man would ask how to identify this messenger.'

'Madam, how stupid I am! Tell me how to know him, please!'

'You will know him by my sacred, overmothering mark: he will have a third nipple and from it he will be able to give you suck, ya great babby!'

James screamed in horror, shaking from head to toe. Mary nuzzled his ear, sticking her tongue inside.

'Feel me, son, feel me!' she whispered. 'There is a possibility you will wake up tomorrow and think this was all a dream. So I put a sign on you.' Here she scratched an X deeply on his brow with a nail the carpenter had left on the floor.

James screamed again. With her hand over his mouth, she went on, 'That long nail was one uncounted and unheard of till now: from the navel of Christ where once it was a cord. Do you want to keep it, or shall I take it home to Hades with me?'

'Don't want it!' James gibbered. 'For pity's sake, take it with you!'

Mary took her face away from his and leant back on her haunches, saying, 'Another of my proofs will come tomorrow: news the King of France is dead, killed in the street. That is our work. He disobeyed us. Don't make the same mistake, Jamie, or it will go very hard with you!'

Mary got to her feet. She could hear footsteps approaching through the empty rooms as people came in search of the missing king.

'I must go. Remember, Hecate will always be watching over you,' she whispered, touching him with her toe. 'Be glad of my interest, my wee bairn.'

Then she left him in the darkness.

★

The next day was the worst in James's life. Haunted by the horrible reality of the cross scratched on his forehead and the news of Henri's death, he sits in a toxic gloom refusing to see anyone. Every time he closes his eyes he sees again the accusing leer of Hecate, he struggles to remember where he had seen her before.

In spite of his campaign against witchcraft in the kingdoms under his fumbling rule, James has always had a secret doubt whether they have authentic existence or not. Sometimes the idea seems to be fatuous, at others very real. Now he knows the sisterhood to be no phantasmagoria. It exists like women exist. Women with resentment in their eyes, anger in their breasts. Women who smell of lavender in the darkness of half-finished rooms.

Since daybreak he has studied his copy of the new Bible he commissioned five years ago, reading all Saint Paul's misogynisms again for comfort, but none has been forthcoming.

He thinks to himself: Truly, the witch goes back to Eve and forward to where the serpent still waits, coiled round the future. God, his Son, the Holy Ghost, all the angels and archangels have not been able to defeat the witch of womanhood.

This heavy book with all its weight of holy tale and terror now reinforces the memory of that worn, cross-hatched countenance full of rebarbative spite, hair slashed grey with Time. He knows if he had held the good book between them as a shield, she would have gone round the side.

CHAPTER TWENTY-TWO

As THE POOR Clares went about the country districts giving help to the needy, they saw the fate of strangers and foreigners during the aftermath of beloved Henri's assassination. Because the killer had been soon caught, it was not vengeance against an individual that was unstoppered but hatred of national enemies.

Ravaillac, the assassin, had refused to name his accomplices, even under torture. Rumours flew up and down the highways of France – it was the Spanish, the English, the Protestants, the Jesuits, the Jews. But at first it was anyone whose face was unfamiliar. Countless strangers, exiles and wanderers perished in the mayhem. Then it became anyone who originated from outside the community and might still have connections, immigrants, those with the wrong kind of background.

So the Poor Clares considered it their duty to keep silent about the five badly wounded men being looked after in their tiny infirmary. When two of the sisters who were Italian and spoke French with a strong accent were attacked and beaten while on their rounds of mercy, the decision became as hard as rock. The nuns would never feed victims to the mob.

Meanwhile, George roamed in a great circle between the Seine and Marne rivers, keeping away from all habitation, living off what he found in the fields and woods. Eventually, still lost, his feet took him south.

★

On two of the infirmary beds at the convent of Bericourt-le-Bosque the pillows are higher because of manuscripts beneath. In both cases there are holes in those pages written before the débâcle at the amphitheatre, caused by flying pieces of the Tragelaph. The lives of Miguel and Shakespeare had been saved by having their plays close to their chests.

The Poor Clares love the theatre. Living near the palace of Fontainbleau, and having Marie de Médicis as their patron, they have always had access to the shows staged there. When the sisters discover they have not one but two playwrights in their midst, they are eager to supply them with everything they need to continue what they consider to be work as merciful as their own – in aid of those afflicted by boredom, amongst whom they often number themselves.

Marthe, a sister especially skilled in nursing and medicine, has another affliction which is linked to boredom. It has always troubled her and often crops up in confessions when she runs out of sins.

She is nosey.

When, on that day of disasters, the five men were brought to the infirmary and undressed, she was the only one who took the trouble to read the perforated manuscripts found on Miguel and Shakespeare. Although they were written in English, the sharp-eyed nun noted how similar the layout was on the page and how the opening lines were the same.

Now, while on her rounds in the middle of the night, having been bored by Nocturns in the chapel, she cannot resist peeking at what the two playwrights have written that very day.

Her interest has been excited because as the Vespers bell started ringing yesterday, both men put down their pens and announced in one voice, 'It is finished.'

By the light of her lamp Marthe slides the manuscript from under the circumcised Jew's pillow and looks at the last line of the last page. She then gently lifts Miguel's sleeping head and replaces the bundle of papers, holding the line in her mind while she crosses to Shakespeare, lifts his head very carefully, noting how little of the hair blown off by the explosion has grown again, takes out his work and checks the final page.

There it is.

Word for word, exactly the same.

Let your indulgence set me free.

She leaves the infirmary, returns to the chapel, kneels and humbly thanks the Almighty for relieving the tedium of these night hours. Her prayers ask and offer forgiveness because the deity is often guilty of boring her, a point her confessor never seems to understand.

★

In the morning Miguel and the three Hollehtoh brothers tell the Poor Clares it is time to leave. They must find George, swallowed up in the anarchy as he is. Their wounds have made it impossible to go out and search for him, but they believe he will have survived, being the sound, strong, independent English boy he is.

The Poor Clares have been keeping their ears to the ground for any news of a beautiful young man seen in the area. They all remember the glimpse of him at the amphitheatre when he shook his fist at them.

Only one clue has come to their ears: from fifty miles to the east in Le Forêt d'Othe woodcutters have seen a wild creature in human form sneaking out as the light fades to forage in the crops.

It sounds unlikely to be George but there is nothing else to go on.

But not everyone is going to find George.

Miguel says to Shakespeare, 'Obviously, I can teach you no more. You've equalled me. How you did it so absolutely, I don't know, but I can't reject the evidence of my own eyes. Now it's only a matter of time before you eclipse me.'

'I'll do that with the next play,' Shakespeare promises.

'I'm not going to wait around for that. So, I'm giving up poetry, I'm giving up the stage. The field is clear for you, Will. What I've written over these twenty years has always been for you. It could be argued that without you it would never have happened, so it was always yours in a way. Don't be ashamed.'

'I won't,' Shakespeare replies boldly. 'But I do have a confession to make.'

'Don't bother,' Miguel tells him. 'I've taken my decision. I'm moving onto other things. Gardening, perhaps, or planting a vineyard. You go home now and astonish the world, Will, and take my blessing with you.'

Shakespeare is suddenly terrified of being left alone
with this alien force in his head. He wants Miguel to stay,
for the old team to stay together. The story of Doctor
Forman and the transplanted genius is blurted out.

Miguel laughs and tells Shakespeare the first rule of
the dramatist is never to believe his own plots are possible,
then he'll work harder to prove himself wrong.

Shakespeare follows Miguel to the convent kitchen
and watches as his master's last play is fed into the fire.
He holds on to his own manuscript tightly but as each
page of Miguel's *Tempest* burns he feels the flame.

'Report everything that's happened here to Cecil,'
Miguel says, spreading the thick layer of paper ash to the
back of the fire. 'Tell him we'll find George and take him
to Blois, where they're expecting him. As for Mary . . .
I'll write . . . I'll write.'

That night Miguel and the three brothers glide out
into the darkness dressed as Poor Clares. On four horses,
one red, one black, one white and one grey, they ride the
roads and tracks, the white wings of their headdresses
flapping. When they reach Le Forêt d'Othe before dawn
the following day, they ride into the woodcutters' settle-
ment, rouse them from their beds and inform the dazed
men in voices of thunder that the wild creature they have
seen is the new Adam, keeper of the key to the Apoca-
lypse sacred to modern times, and how he will only come
when the black and white servants of the androgynous
Lord call him out of the wilderness.

The woodcutters are rough, superstitious men who
have always lived with spirits, dryads and sprites which
have genders as hard as wood. The Christ they revere is a
man, the Cross they see is made of timber cut with a

man's weapon. Having no wish to be involved with forces as mightily enigmatic as these, they spend the day at home sharpening their axes and digging their plots, leaving the four riders to flush the new Adam out of his hiding place.

When they see the strangers return with the wild creature, whose eyes are brilliant with joy at being found, who is as filthy, lousy and ragged as any desert saint, the woodcutters kneel by the roadside.

'Spare them a nod and a digital blessing,' Miguel whispers over his shoulder to George who is sharing his horse. 'They'll be talking about you round these parts for a thousand years.'

★

It is the middle of May, that best of months, two years later. Miguel is in the Syrian desert, outside the monastery of Telanissus, built around the pillar whereon sat Saint Simeon the Stylite of old. Miguel has finally tracked down the agent who killed Carache. It is Cade. After the long pursuit, Miguel's quarry has taken the vows of a monk, full of contrition. Miguel sits in the shade of a tamarisk tree by the main gate, wondering whether he should exact bloody revenge for his dear old friend or join Cade on the inside as a purer devotee of the Word, turning his back on this weird and worrying world.

The Hollehtoh brothers are in the wine business, working for French Huguenot refugee farmers who sold them passage to the Cape of Good Hope on the undertaking of five years indentured labour. It means the brothers must wait till 1619 to be free, but at least they are now back in Africa and only a thousand miles away from home. Closer is better than further, they say, weeding between the vines.

And George has been summoned home from Angers, where the final polish was being given, to attend the sickbed of Cecil.

Upon arriving at Portsmouth he is instructed to proceed to Bath where the Lord Treasurer is taking a watercure.

He finds the hunchback naked in a brick-lined tank of bubbling yellow water shrouded in sulphurous steam.

'The earth is sending up hot disturbance,' Cecil croaks. 'It happens periodically. The doctors say it's the best time to be here.'

He puts out a quivering claw and touches George's cheek.

'Are you ready?' he says.

George has no answer. He doesn't even understand the question. He would like to say, 'For what?' but in the sick man's eye is a warning not to.

'I'm sorry to see your lordship unwell,' he lilts, 'and hope you recover speedily.'

Cecil coughs in the yellow steam, sweat pouring down his narrow face. 'No time to waste, George,' he says. 'Oh, the heat! The heat!'

Violent bubbling comes up from the bottom of the bath. Cecil draws in his breath, wincing.

'Is there a bucket of cold anywhere?' he asks, starting to thrash around.

'No, my lord, but I'll go and get the servants to find some,' George replies sweetly.

'Do so, and hurry!' Cecil gasps.

George trips out. The attendants have gone off somewhere. He takes a promenade down to the main bath. A few patients are floating there.

'I say,' George calls out melodiously, 'you wouldn't know where I could get some cold water, would you?'

Laughter comes from the patients. An old man lying on his back with a white belly showing above the surface shouts that it's a strange place to ask for cold water.

George minces back to the room where Cecil is now flailing around, unable to clamber out of the tank.

'Try as I might, I couldn't find any cold water,' George says charmingly. 'Would you like to get out of there?'

Cecil is now hanging over the edge of the tank, his hunch exposed. The water erupts into furious swirls and surges, dragging him this way and that.

Raising his head, he cries, 'Hold my hands, boy! It's coming!'

The Lord Treasurer's grip is fierce. He screws his face up in agony and screams as the hunch splits bloodily open. A dazzling blue worm with a sucking mouth flies out and darts straight to George's breast, burrowing under his shirt. He backs away, beating at the worm. But it is long, long, long, slimy and flexible, uncoiling from the hunch like an umbilical cord. As it clamps its mouth on the middle of George's breast, he hears it hum like a feeding babe then an answering cluck from the gory, heaving crevasse over Cecil's backbone.

'Make him ready!' the hunchback cries.

George feels the worm suck, bite, twist, pull, chew at him. Pain flies to every part of his body. The glowing blue length lashes, loops, wraps itself around him like a squeezing snake. He sinks, faints.

When he comes to, Cecil has gone. Upon asking where the Lord Treasurer might be found, George is advised to take the London road, and hurry, hurry!

As he rides after Cecil, George keeps one hand under his shirt. There is something there, something new which must be explained.

But he is too late. By the time he catches up with Cecil at Marlborough, the favourite son of the Virgin Queen is dead.

★

In London Shakespeare is now at the apogee of his fame after the success of *The Tempest*. Recently George has been given a thorough examination by George Abbot, Archbishop of Canterbury and Cecil's successor as head of the SVQ.

Cecil himself lies in his tomb in the church at Hatfield with his wand of office between his thighs. The hunch is underneath, uncarved but understood. At each of the four corners of the alabaster monument is a bonny, bare-breasted female and the four queens are flattered he should have asked for them to be done in their prime.

'We must go and see your mother soon,' Shakespeare tells George as they wait for a boat to carry them from Lambeth Palace to Charing Cross. 'You need a good holiday at home.'

'Oh, she can wait,' George says. 'I want you to show me around.'

Shakespeare sighs. The towers of Westminster mock him from across the river. Brown water eddies below. The hours he has spent on his play about Henry the Eighth have convinced him Miguel's genius went with him. It was only as long as they were together the magic worked. Now he is in a cleft stick. George Abbot has instructed him to come up with a scenario, one to be followed when George meets James for the first time.

Every script he has written so far has been rejected. The Archbishop is wondering how Shakespeare makes a living at this kind of thing. To have written thirty-six plays and not be able to construct something as simple as this betokens unwillingness.

Shakespeare has had to admit defeat. The Archbishop has banished him from London in case his trustworthiness deteriorates even further. Also he has been forbidden to see Mary again. Only one place beckons.

He must go home to his wife.

'I've been meaning to tell you since you got back,' he tells George as they gingerly descend the slimy green steps to the wherry waiting below. 'Once this business with you is over, I'm retiring and going back to Stratford to revive the family glove-making business.'

'Whatever for?' George tinkles, his hand shrinking from the contact with the wherryman's horny paw. 'You've got everything a man could dream of here in London. If I had your money wild horses wouldn't drag me away.'

'You're too young to understand. Indeed, George, I hope you will never have the need to,' Shakespeare says, taking a seat.

'Understand what?' George pipes above the wind and the splash of oars as the wherryman misses his stroke because he's looking so hard at his young passenger. 'Sounds to me as if you're throwing everything away. Anyone can make gloves.'

'To be reborn one has to be on the stage where the first entrance was made,' comes the sorrowful reply. 'I've missed my true livelihood and must begin all over again in the way my father wanted me to.'

'Pooh! What do fathers know?' George replies, shaking his curls. The natural glow of his cheeks shows through patches in the thick powder he's wearing. Most of the paint has been licked from his mouth. Clouds part and a shaft of sunlight strikes down making him doubly gorgeous.

The wherryman groans, plunging his long black oars into the water, taking a half-moon course across the current in order to keep this Adonis in his craft as long as possible.

An old man, he has rowed this boat of his back and forth over the Thames for fifty years and seen many things. Before becoming self-employed he had worked on the royal barge and plied his oar for Elizabeth during her early years on the throne.

Looking at George with his mop of sun-reddened curls, the diamond light of unhampered freedom in his eyes, the wherryman feels young, thinking he's aboard with the Virgin Queen again.

Except for the beard.

★

After Shakespeare's suicide at Stratford hundreds of scenes for abandoned plays were found among his papers. Those people who stood to profit by his reputation remaining strong saw to it none of these fragments ever saw the light of day, even as objects of study. There were bits and pieces of plays about the Gunpowder Plot, even an attempt to put the Addled Parliament on stage, a sketch for a melodrama about the murder of Sir Thomas Overbury and the trial of Robert Carr, the fallen favourite, brought down by the SVQ to clear the way for George.

In the margin of one sketch headed by the Shakework stage direction: *The Forest. Enter GEORGE masked and horned, pursued by the KING and his MASTER OF VENERY and various attendant lords* the despairing author had written 'No good at history, comedy, tragedy, tragical-historical, historical-tragical, without the Wandering Jew I'm pastoral help.' (His best line, unless it was the undertakers'.)

According to Doctor Forman's account books, the transfer of genius had been for one play at a time (singularis) with a separate fee to be paid for each dose. This proviso can't have been pointed out to Shakespeare when he entered into the contract. By the time he had enough evidence to work it out, Forman was dead and no remedy could be made.

What made Shakespeare swallow the hemlock on his birthday in 1616 must have been his failure to write anything remotely akin to the quality of *The Tempest* once Miguel had gone, compounded with the humiliation of finding out that, for him, glove making was no more than a gesture.

There are 157 extant written reports of the meeting between James and George, which took place in the late summer upon the Feast of the Decapitation of John the Baptist, at Apethorpe House, the mansion of Sir Anthony Mildmay in Northamptonshire (within leisurely walking distance of Fotheringhay where James's mother, Hecate in his nightmares, had been executed by proxy twenty-seven years before).

All these reports were obtained from guests and staff a year or so after when George's star suddenly rose. Ambassadors feeling the balance of power shift in Europe because of this one young man wanted to know everything about him.

On the surface the occasion at Apethorpe was a house party, but it would be nearer the truth to call it an annual blood-pilgrimage. Every year since his haunting by Hecate at Hatfield James spent the late summer close to Fotheringhay, hunting round and round the old castle where his mother had, according to his belief, been butchered. His visit was a strange, sacrificial atonement, during which he spilled the blood of deer for hers, a ritual he had devized for himself as the true spiritual identity of Hecate dawned upon him.

This bloodshot, inflamed atmosphere was chosen by the SVQ for George's presentation. The means of introducing him to the King are variously reported. One claims George was put in a pie and served at dinner (echoes of *Titus Andronicus* Act V Scene III here – in desperation Shakespeare may have adapted themes from this early play); another that George was lowered on a painter's cradle to James's bedroom window where he performed a *passamezzo erotico* covered in gold paint.

But probably the one which contains the truth of what took place comes from Barry Fowler, a ewerer, who was appointed to stand by the King at table and help him wash his hands when he wanted to. James had no liking for water so Barry had nothing to do but observe. He tells us this record was written on the same night as the events described, part of his training for a career in Law:

> Upon espying two guests at dinner he had no knowledge of, His Majesty asked my master who they were. When it was told him one was Master Shakespeare, His Majesty grumbled that to be at the same table as a man who had calumniated so many kings put him off eating. My master at first took this in jest but soon found His Majesty to be in earnest for he threw down his knife and ordered the playwright be removed. This was a painful duty for Sir Anthony, but he obeyed, approaching Master Shakespeare to request he depart. When he saw my master coming towards him, Master Shakespeare rose to his feet with happy expectation, thinking he had been summoned to the presence of the monarch. So eager was he to be in place, he failed to hear what my master was whispering out of consideration, but went immediately and stood before His Majesty who looked upon him with great disfavour and said, 'Are you on your way out, Master Shytespeer, or have you come to rule the country?' Then, while everyone laughed at the playwright's discomfiture and disconcertment, the King got up from his place and went down to where Master Villiers was sitting, held his hand for a while and asked some questions about his parentage.

Whichever is the true account of James's first sighting of the man who was to rule him until his death ten years later, and then rule his son Charles, thus bringing England to a state of revolution that has been the model for all such conflicts, our information on the second phase of the SVQ's operation is not cloudy at all.

George denied the King what he wanted at Apethorpe. His Gallic blend of dignity and coquettishness was the admiration of all. Sarmiento, the Spanish ambassador noted how George 'picked up very quickly the knack of terrorizing the King of England with promises', but James was not besotted, only interested and, as it was his practice to shower sexual propositions about at random, hoping for one or two to stick, no particular significance can be attached to George's brush with him.

Cecil and Abbot had very carefully brought James to a pitch of disillusionment with love by the destruction of Robert Carr who had ended up in ruin and disgrace. Now in a dark emotionless desert, James was looking for light, but not *a* light.

Other youths attracted him after Apethorpe, but none of them said no. Then the time came for the second phase. Archbishop Abbot arranged for George to be presented again, his refusal on his head like a coronet of brave sincerity. This was achieved with the aid of Queen Anne, the alienated wife of James, who had recently filled the vacancy at Hatfield created by the death of Anne Boleyn at the age of 108.

Saint George's Day. The Queen's apartments.

Enter the King with Prince Charles.

Behind whatever arras there is, the Archbishop of Canterbury stands with George.

Enter the Queen. She asks Prince Charles for the loan of his rapier. When he asks what for? James says, 'To kill me with, of course. Lend it to her.'

Prince Charles hands over the weapon. The Queen takes it and points it at the King. He stands, legs apart, ready to take the thrust should it come. Joke or no, he doesn't care.

Anne's broad face is set in a simper.

'Now!' Archbishop Abbot whispers to George.

George steps out and kneels in front of the King.

The Queen reverses the rapier and puts the handle into her husband's hand and says, 'I humbly beseech Your Majesty, as a special favour to me, to knight this noble gentleman, whose name is George, for the honour of Saint George, whose feast it is today.'

James hesitates, rapier in hand. A thought wanders into his mind. Wouldn't he rather the Queen had taken her womanly revenge than this blatant pantomime?

He sighs. What has this youth done to deserve the honour, small as it is, except to say no, no, no, and mean it . . . until now?

James leans down. He looks George meanly in the eye and says, 'One day this sword will be a proper weapon. If you come by me you will have to grease and sharpen it!'

The rapier touches George's shoulder.

Anne has heard what her husband said to George. Also, she has come to know Mary, the lad's mother, through the four queens, and her heart is quaking with horror. How can any woman sacrifice the fruit of her body on this iniquitous altar?

It must be done or there will be no future, she tells herself. I am mother Abraham offering Isaac, but this sordid god will accept. When the knife is raised, no one will stay my hand. No ram will appear stuck in a bush by its horns. This is an act of cruel faith in the bargaining power of love.

Drawn and grim, Anne steps forward immediately the King has done the dubbing. She fiercely grips George's neck and holds him down with an executioner's hand.

Then, turning her eyes prayerfully upward to heaven, she says in an angry but intimate voice, 'And I ask that Sir George Villiers, as he now is, be appointed a Gentleman of the Bedchamber.'

Heads together, the surviving queens look down from the gallery above, knowing that from now on it is only a matter of time before George comes into his own.

From beneath their veils of mourning run tears which fall like English rain.

★

Goodbye to this boy, then, as he stands in the bishop's garden at Farnham, Hampshire, a few months later, having been told the time has come to say yes. His own freedom must become the freedom of power.

From below in the town comes the song of reapers who have washed their throats clean of field dust. All their songs are about love of one sort or another.

To George, the sound the reapers are making might just as well be from a wild sea at the bottom of a high, white cliff.

From Farnham George will go on to be more of a king than the King himself because the women behind him are working the world.

At Brooksby, where the boy had his beginning among the grassy humps of the disinherited poor, Mary feels for

Sir Thomas's hand in bed, anxiety twisting like a vine around her heart. She is prepared for success, the deepest of all pains.

The reapers are completely silent now.

Somewhere the poet writes a part.

The actor learns his lines.

The stage is swept.

George begins to wander up and down, his feet silent on the turf, the moonlight in the spangles of his hair.

To claim an empire he only has to climb a stair.

Clouds are coming from the west. The reapers feel the change in the weather and they start to worry about the morrow. This brings back their song, but now it is a sad, intermittent music, reducing to a few phrases with silence on either side.

★

In the King's chamber the lights are glowing and moths are flying in through the open window. He fears soft, fluttery things, and his great phobia is bats. All the servants are out of the room so he has to get up to close the window himself.

He sees a boy walking up and down with his hand inside his shirt, feeling over his heart.

'Is that a prayer you're making?' James calls down with a laugh. 'Do include me.'

George feels the third nipple harden.

Milk threatens.

It is time for him to go up.